CROW'S LANDING

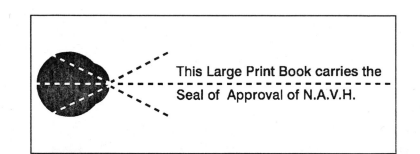

This Large Print Book carries the
Seal of Approval of N.A.V.H.

CROW'S LANDING

BRAD SMITH

THORNDIKE PRESS
A part of Gale, Cengage Learning

GALE
CENGAGE Learning·

Detroit • New York • San Francisco • New Haven, Conn • Waterville, Maine • London

GALE
CENGAGE Learning·

Copyright © 2012 by Brad Smith.
A Virgil Cain Mystery.
Thorndike Press, a part of Gale, Cengage Learning.

Thorndike Press® Large Print Crime Scene.
The text of this Large Print edition is unabridged.
Other aspects of the book may vary from the original edition.
Set in 16 pt. Plantin.

LIBRARY OF CONGRESS CATALOGING-IN-PUBLICATION DATA

Smith, B. J. (Brad J.)
  Crow's landing / by Brad Smith.
    pages ; cm. — (Thorndike Press large print crime scene) (A Virgil Cain mystery)
    ISBN 978-1-4104-5243-6 (hardcover) — ISBN 1-4104-5243-3 (hardcover) 1. Large type books. I. Title.
  PR9199.3.S55148C76 2012b
  813'.54—dc23   2012026801

Published in 2012 by arrangement with Scribner, a division of Simon & Schuster, Inc.

Printed in Mexico
1 2 3 4 5 6 7 16 15 14 13 12

CROW'S LANDING

ONE

The boat was moored out near the middle of the river, a few miles north of the town of Athens, at a point where the stream swept around a wide bend, the channel flowing southeastward for a half mile or so before swinging back to the south. They had anchored just before dark, having made a hundred and twenty miles that day.

Parson had been watching the sonar for the last hour and when they came to a drop-off that read sixty-one feet, he cut the engines and lowered the anchors, fore and aft. The sun was fading fast, slipping down into the pine forest to the west, and the light that remained filtered through the tree line, casting the surface of the water in orange and red hues. The banks on both sides of the river were largely deserted along that stretch. There were a couple of ramshackle cabins visible on the east shore, and a farmhouse on a hill set farther back. A herd of Holsteins grazed on the slope beside the house, the white on their hides also colored an odd hue of orange by the descending sun.

A man in an aluminum boat was trolling along the western bank, moving south with the current. The man wore a fedora and was smoking a pipe. He had one hand on the tiller and when Parson waved to him, he lifted the pipe briefly above his head in reply. He continued downriver, the outboard putt-putting quietly across the heavy night air, and soon disappeared around the bend.

Parson fired the barbecue and cooked steaks that they'd bought earlier that day while fueling up at a marina in Peekskill. The woman had been reading in the cabin all afternoon, some novel she'd picked up in Charleston when they'd stopped there for a day on their way north. The book was about a slave woman who'd escaped from her owner in the middle of the Civil War and made her way north to Boston. Parson knew what the book was about because she kept telling him about it, insisting that he should read it when she was finished. She told him that she thought it would resonate with him, even more than it had with her. She'd actually used the word *resonate*. Parson didn't much care about his history, how his ancestors had gotten from wherever they had been to where he was now. It didn't matter to him, and even if it did it wouldn't make any difference, not to somebody living in the present. In all probability his ancestors *had* been slaves, but what did that have to do with him? Besides, Parson didn't read much, and when he did, he didn't read fiction. What did he care about some story some writer made up?

She came up from the cabin while the steaks were sizzling, smoking a joint and carrying a bottle of Chardonnay she'd just opened. She handed the joint to Parson and poured wine for both of them before sitting down on the padded bench on the rear deck of the Chris-Craft. She wore a bikini top and a bloodred sarong, her blond hair tucked beneath a cotton baseball cap. She was deeply tanned, both from the trip and the two weeks earlier in the Bahamas.

She'd made a salad earlier and they ate that and the steaks, sitting at the pull-out table on the deck, finishing in near darkness. It was very quiet on the river; from time to time they would hear a gull, and once a pair of mallards flew directly overheard, quacking in that anxious manner that ducks seemed to possess. They finished the wine with the meal and afterward she took the dishes down to the galley to wash them.

They had been on the water since seven that morning and at ten o'clock she announced she was going to bed. Parson followed shortly after, first checking the bilge pump and the marker lights. He would have preferred to leave the lights off, but then they would run the risk of a tugboat or trawler ramming them in the dark. The sky was clouding over as he went below, huge puffy clouds pushing in from the west, floating in front of the rising moon like ships at sea.

When he woke, it was five minutes to two. The wind was up and the boat was riding the waves, the bow making soft slapping noises on the water. Parson wondered if that was what had awakened him. He lay there quietly for a time. Beside him, the woman was sound asleep, naked beneath the cotton sheets. Faint light showed through the window beside her. Parson could see the panther inked on her shoulder, and it looked as if the cat too was asleep, its head resting on her upper arm, its body tucked into the covers below.

After a while he rose, pulled on his pants, and went up top. The moon was still visible, but smudged now beneath gray cloud cover. Looking at the outline of the riverbank to the east, it seemed to Parson that they had drifted with the current. He checked the sonar; it still read sixty-one feet so it must have been his imagination. The anchor ropes were tight and secure.

He walked to the side of the boat to take a leak before going back below and that's when he heard the sound. It was very faint, a soft splash on the surface like someone skipping a stone, and he thought at first it might have been a fish jumping. Then the clouds shifted and the moon shone through for a few moments. There was a boat maybe two hundred yards away, coming silently toward him, as if adrift.

But it wasn't adrift. There were men in the boat, and the noise he'd heard was an oar hitting the water.

Parson made for the bench at the rear of the Chris-Craft, pulled the cushions from it, and opened the lid. Inside there was a false bottom of stained plywood. He pulled it out and tossed it aside. The stainless steel cylinder was underneath, wrapped in blankets to keep it from rolling around. Parson grabbed one of the handles and, heaving the heavy cylinder out of the hiding place, dragged it to the transom and threw it overboard.

He turned back and once again caught a glimpse of the approaching boat before the cloud cover returned, this time obscuring the moon completely. Parson walked quickly to the bow and dove into the cold water. He stayed beneath the surface as long as his breath would allow, came up for air, and went under again. When he was certain he couldn't be seen from the boat, he settled into a breast stroke and swam for shore.

He could hear voices behind him, floating across the water. Excited voices, shouting, cursing. Looking back, he saw lights on the Chris-Craft, and on the smaller boat now tied to the big vessel.

The last thing he heard was the woman calling his name.

Two

Seven years later —

On Friday afternoon, Virgil delivered a couple of yearling steers to the abattoir outside of Saugerties and on the way home he stopped at Slim's Roadhouse for a pitcher of beer and an order of chicken wings. It had been sweltering the past few days and the stockyard at the slaughterhouse was like an oven; the place was in a hollow where there was no breeze at all, just a couple dozen steers standing in the steaming lot, the manure almost liquid in the air, flies hovering by the thousands. Virgil had released his steers into the lot and headed for town.

He was at a table near the front windows, working on the beer while he waited for his order, when Mudcat McClusky came through the kitchen and into the bar carrying a large Styrofoam cooler, which he propped on the counter and opened to reveal a half dozen striped bass inside. The fish were still alive, flopping in the tepid water, gasping for breath. They were of a nice size for eating, five- and six-pounders, the colors bright, eyes clear. Mudcat said he caught them out in the Hudson, off Kimball's Point, a village just north of Athens. If there were two truths to be known about Mudcat, one was that he was as lazy as a pet coon and the other was that he was full of shit. Nobody in the bar believed that he'd caught the fish now on display in the Styrofoam cooler. He may have bought them from whoever did catch them (unlikely, as Mudcat was both cheap and chronically broke), or he may have stolen them out of somebody's boat, or he may even have just borrowed the fish for half an hour for the sole purpose of bringing them into the bar to brag. The latter scenario grew more plausible; when the cook from Slim's came out of the kitchen, sharpening a filleting knife, Mudcat quickly put the top on the cooler and headed out the front door.

It didn't matter to Virgil whether it was Mudcat or somebody else who caught the stripers. The fact remained that somebody had caught them and by the time Virgil finished his beer and his wings, he'd decided he would play hooky the next day and head out to try his own luck. He hadn't been out in his boat much since earlier in the spring, when the striped bass began their run, despite promising himself he would use it regularly. But by April the new calves were coming, and May was planting time and most of June was spent haying. Now it was nearly July and his wheat was just about ready for harvest, but according to Mudcat McClusky, the stripers were biting again off Kimball's Point. Virgil could use a day off.

He usually launched at Brownie's Marina, in a cove just north of the town. The place was a local hangout, he'd discovered. There was the boat dock, and the marina, which sold bait and angling gear and a few things like soda and chips and sandwiches. Adjacent to the marina parking lot was a roadhouse called Scallywags, the standard dockside venue, a beer and wings joint that sold better than average food and had two pool tables in the back. Virgil usually stopped in at Scallywags for a cold draft or two after he'd been out on the boat. He got to know some of the locals, including Mudcat McClusky, and occasionally he played some eight ball with them.

The "Brownie" who owned the marina was a fat slug named Gordon Brown. Virgil learned that he'd been a cop in Albany for thirty years, a sergeant for the last ten, before cashing in his pension and buying the marina. Virgil knew Brownie as well as he wanted to. The man was a barely functioning drunk and a gossip who appeared friendly on the surface until it became obvious that he didn't have a good word to say about anybody who wasn't within earshot. Virgil had never been a fan of cops in general — the luscious Claire Marchand notwithstanding — and he had no trouble disliking Brownie at first sight.

The next morning he was up before the sun. He'd overwatered the stock the night before, and he threw the horses some feed and had a quick look at the cattle in the back pasture before heading out. He reached the marina at dawn. It was warm already; the temperature had been routinely hitting the midnineties every day and today would be no exception. There was a cash box by the launch for anyone docking a boat before the tackle shop itself opened. It operated on the honor system and Virgil used it whenever the shop was closed, and even when the shop was open. It was quicker to slip a fin in the box, and it saved him from feigning small talk with Brownie, or Mudcat, who sometimes ran the shop when Brownie was gone for the day or was too hungover to open.

Virgil launched the cedar strip and tied it off to the dock while he parked the truck and trailer in the large paved lot between the marina and Scallywags. By the time he fired the old Johnson up and chugged away from the dock, heading for the channel, there were three other boats in the lot, lined up and waiting to launch.

Virgil idled out past the pier, watching an elderly Vietnamese man casting off the rocks with a silver spinner, reeling in slowly. When the man nodded to Virgil, he nodded back and then, past the pier, pulled down the peak of his Mud Hens cap, opened up the outboard and aimed the bow of the boat into the current, the front of the cedar strip rearing up in the water for a hundred yards or so before planing out. The wind was slight, but it was out of the east and Virgil angled straight into it, thinking that the fishing was likely to be poor. Anybody who fished knew that the fish didn't bite much when the wind was from the east. It was one of those things that people knew to be true, even if nobody seemed to know why.

To Virgil, it didn't matter all that much if the fish were biting or not. He'd be more than happy to take home a couple of stripers for his supper, but if he didn't there was good beef in the freezer and potatoes in the root cellar. He'd eat well that night either way. He liked being on the river, alone in the sixty-year-old boat. As a rule he drifted with the current, rather than trolling, because he enjoyed the quiet of that, the only sound the soft slap of the waves against the cedar hull of the boat.

The last time he'd had the boat out on the river, Claire Marchand had been with him. The stripers were finished with their spring run, and they were really just out for a cruise, although they did stop and cast for pike in a weed bed for half an hour. But mostly they'd just idled down the river toward Rondout Creek, where they had docked for a couple of hours and had lunch in Kingston before heading back north. It was a warm May afternoon. Virgil had finished planting just a couple of days earlier, and they talked about that. After a while the conversation shifted to a case Claire had been working on, a kidnapping of a ten-year-old girl from a schoolyard in Troy, which had, untypically, turned out well when the girl's stepfather was arrested and the girl recovered unharmed. After the talk of the farm, and of Claire's job, was finished, Claire broached the subject of Virgil himself. Specifically she wanted to know why Virgil couldn't give more of himself up, why he was so unavailable on certain emotional levels. Virgil thought about it for a while and then replied that he couldn't answer that question, and if he could, then probably Claire wouldn't have needed to ask it.

The rest of the trip had been pretty quiet. Virgil felt as if he'd disappointed her somehow but wasn't at all sure what to do about it. They didn't see each other much over the next couple of weeks and then Claire flew to London for some security conference, and then on to France to visit some long-lost relatives. She was still there. She had called a couple of nights earlier to say that she was having a fine time, learning about her roots. Virgil had a feeling that her newly discovered kinfolk were not emotionally unavailable.

Virgil was alone again, and he didn't mind it, as much as he genuinely enjoyed time spent with Claire. Still, he was more comfortable than most people with solitude, he suspected. For one thing, a man was less likely to find trouble when he was on his own. Since he was a kid, he had possessed a propensity for getting into trouble, some of it of his own accord and some of it purely by accident. Just last year, for instance, he'd been arrested for murder, escaped jail, fell under suspicion for a second murder, and was finally shot in the earlobe by the woman responsible for both. If that couldn't be categorized as a propensity for getting into trouble, Virgil didn't know what could.

But a man couldn't find trouble out on the Hudson River, all alone with his thoughts and his fishing pole and a half dozen cold beers in an ancient Pepsi cooler. After all, what could possibly happen this far from everything?

By noon, Virgil had given up on the stripers and was anchored in the main channel straight out from Kimball's Point, using a walleye rig baited with minnows. He had no luck with the walleye but he did catch a half dozen good-size perch, as well as a sheepshead that had to weigh fifteen pounds or more. He kept the perch for his supper and released the sheepshead. It was shortly after one o'clock when he reeled in his line and stepped to the bow to pull up the anchor.

But the anchor didn't come. It was stuck fast to something on the bottom, trapped in some rocks, he assumed. He jerked the rope quickly back and forth, hoping the action might dislodge the anchor, and pulled on it again. When it didn't yield, he started the boat and maneuvered it around for a better angle. Still it wouldn't budge.

Virgil sat down on the bench seat, the rope in his hands. The anchor was new, a galvanized triple hook that had cost him twenty-eight bucks. He bought it from Brownie his first time at the marina, before he realized he wanted nothing to do with the ex-cop. He didn't feel like cutting the line and leaving the anchor on the bottom.

So he took the rope in hand again and pulled, this time propping his heels against the transom and putting his back into it. And the anchor moved. Not much more than an inch or so, but it moved. Which probably meant that whatever it was caught on would be coming up with the anchor. It took Virgil ten minutes, alternately pulling and resting, then pulling again, the rope burning the spar varnish from the top edge of the transom, to bring it to the surface, and when he did he was finally able to see what he had hooked. But seeing it and knowing what it was were two different things.

It took an effort to pull the thing over the gunwale and into the boat, where he carefully rolled it onto the slats of the floor. It was a cylinder, seaweed covered and green, about four feet long and maybe sixteen inches in diameter. It had steel loops welded to it, one on each side, like handles, and was completely sealed; there was no cap, no valve, nothing that would allow access to the contents. Virgil scrubbed away some of the grime with his hand and saw that the metal was gray underneath and, as it wasn't rusted, he assumed it was made of either aluminum or, more likely — given the weight of the thing — stainless steel. The cylinder weighed probably a hundred and fifty pounds.

When Virgil got back to the launch at the marina, he had no intention of telling anyone about what he'd found attached to his anchor. Those intentions didn't matter one way or the other, though, with Mudcat McClusky standing on the pier, waiting for him to dock. Mudcat spent most days hanging around the tackle shop, playing gofer to Brownie, and every time a fisherman came in off the river, he hurried down to the launch to see what they'd caught. By the time Virgil had the cedar strip winched onto the trailer behind his pickup truck, Mudcat had spread the word and there were half a dozen people standing around, looking at the cylinder. Nobody had a ready opinion as to what exactly the thing was, except for Mudcat, who was an expert on nearly everything, although this expertise was somewhat tempered by the fact that he was basically an imbecile.

"Gas cylinder," he said, his foot up on the tongue of the trailer, his tone somewhat proprietary, due to the fact he'd been the first to spot the thing in Virgil's boat. "Nitrogen is my guess."

Wally Dunlop, who was standing nearby, shook his head at the pronouncement, looking at Mudcat as he always looked at him, with a mixture of pity and contempt. Virgil got out of the truck and walked back to the trailer; he really didn't care to be the center of attention, or to get involved with Mudcat's speculations, but he needed to tie the boat down.

"There's no valve," he said. "It's not a gas cylinder."

"It's got no valve, you fucking dummy," echoed Wally to Mudcat. "How you gonna get the gas out?"

"Who you calling a dummy?" Mudcat demanded.

The discussion continued on the dock as Virgil secured the cedar strip and drove the truck and trailer to the back of the lot and parked it. Walking past the boat, he glanced first at the cylinder and then toward the gang of curious onlookers by the launch.

He went back and removed the padlock and safety chain from the trailer hitch and used it to secure the cylinder to a steel cleat on the boat.

He headed into Scallywags for some lunch, and most of the bunch that had assembled on the dock followed. Mudcat walked back to the tackle shop; as Virgil crossed the lot toward the roadhouse, he could see him inside, talking animatedly to Brownie, presumably spilling all he knew about the mysterious cylinder. Which was nothing, but that wouldn't stop Mudcat from telling it.

Inside the roadhouse, Virgil had a draft beer and ordered a burger with fries, which he ate at the bar. The talk centered around the cylinder. Mudcat soon wandered in, not wanting to miss out on the discussion.

"What're you going to do with it?" Wally asked.

"Cut it open, I guess," Virgil said. "Must be something in there. Thing weighs a ton."

"What if it's radioactive?"

Virgil smiled. "Maybe it's kryptonite. I could sell it to Lex Luthor."

"He's not a real person," Mudcat scoffed. He shook his head. "Thing's probably empty anyway."

"Like your head?" Wally suggested.

"Fuck you," Mudcat said, his standard reply whenever he found himself out of his depth, which was quite frequently.

After a while, the conversation regarding what was in the cylinder faded, mainly due to the fact that nobody had the slightest notion what it might be. After Virgil finished his lunch, Wally challenged him to a game of eight ball and he accepted. They shot three games for a buck apiece, splitting the first two with Wally winning the rubber. Virgil tossed the dollar on the felt and went to the bar to pay his bill.

"Who the hell is that?" he heard Wally say.

Virgil turned to see Wally staring out the plate glass window to the parking lot, where a man in a brown suit was in the process of hooking Virgil's trailer and boat to the back of a dark blue SUV.

By the time Virgil went down the steps and crossed the parking lot, the hitch was already in place. The man doing the hitching was maybe fifty, overweight, and the combination of the oppressive heat and the act of lifting the trailer tongue from Virgil's truck and transferring it to the SUV had left him panting for breath. He had dark hair, plastered to his forehead, and pale, pockmarked skin. He wore a shirt and tie with his brown suit, the tie loosened, the white shirt stained with something, possibly coffee. Virgil would wager his best breed cow that the man was a cop.

"What are you doing?" Virgil asked.

The man reached into his jacket pocket and produced a gold detective's shield. "Albany police. I'm confiscating this boat."

"For what?"

"Involvement in illegal activities."

"That's a load of shit," Virgil said. "You got a warrant?"

"You think you're on TV?" the man demanded. He pulled a black handgun from inside his jacket and held the barrel a foot from Virgil's nose. "Here's your fucking warrant, big mouth."

Virgil stepped back. "Take it easy. You don't have to take my boat."

"You don't tell me what to do," the man said. "You're lucky I don't lock you up. This is racketeering, trafficking, conspiracy. Smart thing for you to do right now is shut your fucking mouth. We'll be in touch."

He walked around and opened the door to the SUV, the gun still in his hand.

"What about my boat?" Virgil asked.

"I said we'll be in touch." The man got into the car and drove off. Wally, who had tagged along when Virgil left the roadhouse, stepped forward as Virgil watched his boat disappear down the highway.

"He didn't ask nothin'. He didn't even ask your name." He paused a moment. "Something not right here."

"No shit," Virgil said.

THREE

Dusty didn't even bother with an alarm anymore. By six o'clock the neighborhood of Arbor Hill was so noisy — with garbage trucks in the street, the city buses running, impatient carpoolers honking their horns, and neighbors arguing about who came home late last night or who didn't come home at all — that it was impossible to sleep late.

Usually she remained in bed until six thirty or so, taking that time to plan her day — do a mental shopping list, decide which bills needed paying now and which could be put off until payday, think about what Travis needed for clothes, shoes, or anything else.

Getting up, she would knock on his door as she made her way to the bathroom and give it another rap as she went down the narrow hallway to the kitchen, where she would start the coffee and make lunches for both herself and Travis while she waited for it to brew.

This morning she was distracted by the presence outside of a camera crew from the CITY NOW news channel. Looking down from her third-story window, Dusty could see a blond reporter standing in front of the walk-up down the block, her back to the building, as she faced a man with a heavy camera propped on his shoulder. After a moment, it occurred to Dusty that it would be a live broadcast and she turned on her TV to hear what the woman was saying. Apparently there had been a drug bust somewhere in the building during the night; two men had been arrested and taken away hours ago and CITY NOW was showing its viewers where the bust *went down,* as the woman phrased it. Dusty flicked the set off as the pretty blonde was attempting in vain to pronounce the word *methamphetamine.*

She poured coffee and walked down the hallway.

"Travis!" she said. "Move it, dude."

He wandered into the kitchen a few minutes later, dragging his backpack in one hand. Dusty poured cereal for him and had two slices of toast with honey for herself. She really didn't care for breakfast, but since starting work for Murphy Construction she'd dropped a couple of pounds. Her jeans fit a little looser, she knew. But then she always had trouble keeping on weight. Even in the joint, with physical activity at a minimum, she hadn't gained a pound. Maybe being pissed off was a calorie burner.

They were out the door at a quarter past seven, at which time the TV crew and reporter, apparently having exhausted all the ways to take moving pictures of an inert building, were packing up.

Dusty's truck was parked on the side street behind the apartment building. They walked around the corner, Travis with his knapsack on his back and Dusty carrying her nail gun and carpenter's apron in one hand, her lunch in the other. Her truck was an old F150, with over 300,000 showing on the odometer, a half-ton she'd bought a couple of years ago from a roofer she met on a job and had dated a few times. He had been enamored enough of her to sell her the pickup for a thousand bucks. The relationship didn't last more than a month; the truck, on the other hand, had staying power. Besides brakes and regular oil changes, she'd had no maintenance problems with it, although sometimes it wouldn't turn over and she had to pop the hood and cross the solenoid with a screwdriver she kept wedged between the battery and the inner fender for that purpose.

This morning was one of those times. Getting out of the truck after the key failed to start it, she told Travis to slide over behind the wheel and pump the gas pedal a couple of times once she had it turning over. For Dusty, the truck not starting was a pain in the ass, but for a six-year-old, running the gas pedal was a minor adventure. She glanced at him through the windshield as she opened the hood. He was quite serious in his task, tongue clenched between his teeth, his dark brown eyes fixed on the accelerator, ready for his moment to swing into action. The instant that Dusty crossed the solenoid, he pumped the pedal and the engine started right off. He smiled at her as she got back into the truck, as he always did, a look of shared accomplishment.

They drove north on Clinton, the early traffic still light. On the street the shopkeepers were putting their trash out and the homeless were a step behind them, looking for whatever treasures they might find in the refuse. Travis watched out the window while idly playing with an Iron Man action figure in his lap. Dusty had to wonder at the scene on the street, how it appeared through his eyes.

"Iron Man can fly," he said after a while.

"I know." Dusty turned left on Lark Avenue, hitting the gas to make it through a yellow light.

"He's got jet propellers."

"He does." They were nearing the day camp now and Dusty was looking for a place to park.

"Superman can fly all by himself," Travis said.

"That's why he's Superman."

Travis nodded and looked up through the windshield, toward the sky above the buildings, as if he might catch a glimpse of the Man of Steel soaring past at that very moment.

"Yup. That's why he's Superman."

The subdivision was on the northern edge of the town of Rensselaer and, after dropping Travis off, Dusty headed back south and took the Dunn Memorial Bridge across the Hudson River. Aside from the usual jam-up at the ramp for 787, traffic was still reasonable for the hour, and she arrived on site well before eight. It was a new project; Monday had been her first day there, and there were nearly a hundred houses to go up, along with some commercial space for minimarts and dry cleaners and whatever else might find a home in a spanking new development. Dusty parked in the mud lot across the road, beside the work trailer that sat beneath the huge Murphy Construction sign overlooking the subdivision. The job foreman was in the trailer, drinking coffee, sitting at a table that must have been twelve feet long, its surface covered with blue-prints, tools, hard hats, gloves, and a lot of discarded takeout coffee cups. Dusty stepped inside the doorway.

"Anything I need to know?"

It seemed as if it took him a moment to place her. There were a lot of workers on the project — plumbers, electricians, brick-layers.

"You're framing the town houses in the cul-de-sac?"

"Yeah."

"You're good to go. Put your hard hat on."

She picked up a copy of the prints and spent the morning laying out the interior walls of the town houses. They were fram-ing with wood, two-by-fours and two-by-sixes. A lot of the builders were using steel studs now but David Murphy was a tradi-tional type. He'd grown up in the trade — his father was a carpenter who had built barns on the prairie before moving east dur-ing the Second World War — and he stayed with the tried and true, even though it was more expensive to use wood. Dusty preferred it, too.

Shortly before noon she was nailing in lintels above the bedroom doors when Nick Santiago came on the site, noisily, puffing on his cigar, his leather coat out of place amid the dust and dirt. He pulled some blueprints from an oversize leather case and spread them out over Dusty's own set, which she had laid out on a makeshift worktable, a half sheet of plywood across two sawhorses. It was all an act on Santiago's part, as he never looked at the prints afterward. They were probably the same prints Dusty was using anyway. He removed his fedora and slapped it on the table as well, then took a couple of puffs on his stogie as he stood, spread-legged, his thumbs in his belt, casting a critical eye at the work being done. Dusty gave him a look of amused dismissal, knowing him to be a major league poser. The temperature would reach ninety by ten o'clock and Santiago shows up in a leather coat and fedora. What was he, a Bedouin?

"Looking good, people," Santiago said.

There were a couple of tradesmen in the adjoining unit and presumably they, along with Dusty, were among the architect's "people." Like Dusty, they didn't pay him any mind. Santiago stood savoring the fat cigar for a moment longer, as if waiting for somebody to react to his presence. When nobody did, he started for the adjacent unit, and as he passed Dusty, working the nail gun, he gave her ass a squeeze.

"Good work, sexy," he said and kept walking.

Dusty stopped and watched him as he stepped through the studding and into the next town house, where he struck up a conversation with an electrician who was stripping wire beside a breaker panel. After a moment Dusty turned and walked over to the table, where Santiago had moments before displayed his blueprints like Frank Lloyd Wright revealing the plans for Falling Water. She fired a half dozen nails into the brim of the architect's hat and went back to work.

Santiago stuck around for half an hour or so, playing the part as he walked from one unit to the next, and then, apparently satisfied that the minions were doing justice to his master design, returned and rolled his prints into his case and got ready to leave. Dusty had just stopped for lunch, and was passing behind him as he reached for his hat.

"What the fuck is this?" he shouted. "You nailed my new fedora to the table!"

"Touch my ass again and I'll nail it to your head," Dusty told him and kept walking.

With the continuing heat wave, Dusty and some of the other workers ate lunch in the basement of the new project. It was cooler there, and quieter too, away from the noise of the excavators outside. Dusty sat on a piece of discarded rigid insulation and stretched her legs out, her back to the cool of the concrete wall. She was the only woman on the job site but she knew a lot of the other tradesmen, at least by sight, from other jobs and they had long ago stopped trying to shock her with their jokes and their language. Stan Meadows, a plumber, usually sat with her, and even he no longer teased her about her tattoos, or what he perceived to be her wild lifestyle. He had no idea that Dusty's life these days was as tame as a house cat's.

"What was Santiago ranting about?" he asked her when he sat down.

"Something about his hat," Dusty said. She was eating a tuna sandwich and leafing through a real estate flyer she'd taken out of a curbside display on the street outside the day camp.

Stan unzipped the cooler bag that served

as his lunch pail and produced a sodden submarine sandwich half the size of a football. Stan was in his late fifties, and maybe twenty-five pounds overweight, with thinning hair and a thick brown mustache that suggested, to Dusty anyway, a caterpillar that had somehow found itself on the plumber's face and decided to stay there. Dusty could feel Stan watching her as he bit into the messy sandwich.

"What?" she said at last.

"You're always looking at those real estate flyers," Stan said. "How you figure to buy a house? Shit, truck you're driving isn't worth two hundred bucks."

"Maybe I'll win the lottery," Dusty said. "And leave my truck alone. You drive a *mini-van,* Stanley."

"You even buy lottery tickets?"

"No. They're a tax on the stupid. You buy 'em?"

"Well, yeah."

Dusty smiled and took another bite of the sandwich. Stan missed the inference but that was typical of Stan. He was a man content in his own world and as such he had the skin of an alligator. He mounted another attack on the sub before pouring a cup of tea from his thermos. Chomping away at the bulbous mass, he smiled lasciviously at Dusty.

"You could always come live with me," he said. "You oughta see my house. It's a showplace. Heated pool, central air. Got a wet bar. *Two* fifty-inch TVs. My house could be in a magazine. You should see it."

Dusty shook her head. She couldn't find it in herself to be offended by Stan. He was too normal, too middle-class-nice to pull off being a letch, even when he tried.

"How do you keep it so nice?" Dusty asked. "You know — working every day."

"Well, between the wife and me —"

"Oh, you got a wife, Stanley?"

"Yeah." Stan smiled. "About time I traded her in on a younger model though."

Dusty rolled up the flyer, got to her feet, and stretched. "Then you're only going to have half a house. And half a pool. And *one* TV." She rapped him on his balding head with the flyer. "Better stick with what you got, buddy."

She finished all the framing on the unit that afternoon and by quitting time she was nailing furring strips above the exterior walls, using scrap pieces of two-by-fours. David Murphy came on site a half hour before it was time to quit, pulled into the lot across the road, and sat there for a time, talking on a cell phone. In spite of his wealth and his success, he still drove a truck, a Dodge crew cab, its fenders and rockers muddied from whatever other projects it had visited that day. When he got out, he was wearing his usual attire, a faded work shirt and jeans. Dusty knew he was in his seventies, but she suspected he could still swing a hammer all day if needed. He went into the trailer for a while and then came over to the units. She heard him joking with Stan the plumber. Maybe Stan was bragging about his magazine-worthy home. When Murphy walked over to where Dusty was packing up for the day, he took a quick look around at what she had done, not making a big show of inspecting her work, but inspecting it just the same.

"Hello," he said.

"Hey."

"How's it going?"

"Okay." She hesitated. "Nice working with wood again."

Murphy nodded. Dusty unplugged her nail gun and took her apron off. It was five past five, she knew — she had just checked her cell phone for the time — and she needed to pick Travis up.

"You still looking for extra work?" he asked.

"Yeah."

"I bought an old three-story brownstone, the corner of Madison and Canfield. Needs to be gutted."

"Over by the university?" Dusty asked.

"Yeah. I'm going to put in student apartments."

"I'll do it."

Murphy dug a key and a scrap of paper with the address on it from his shirt pocket and handed both over. "Be a Dumpster there by the weekend. Get someone to help you."

"I can do it," Dusty said. "Cash job?"

"You want cash?" Murphy waited a moment for her to reply, but she kept quiet. "Now you wouldn't try to cheat our good government out of their fair share of your income, would you?"

"I might."

She thought for an instant that he might smile, or object, but he did neither. "We can make it for cash," he said.

"Good," she said. She gathered her lunch box and her tools and started to walk away, then she stopped without looking back at him. "Thanks," she said.

"Dusty," Murphy called before she made it out the door. "What happened with you and Nick Santiago today?"

"Nothing much."

"He says you ruined a two-hundred-dollar hat."

"Oh, that."

Dusty turned back to Murphy, taking a moment to adjust the belt on the carpenter's apron in her hand. It seemed that he was waiting for something more by way of an explanation. But she didn't offer.

"Sometimes the world doesn't turn the way we'd like it to," he told her. "I don't want to tell you how long I've been around, makes me feel old, but the thing is — sometimes when things don't go the way you want, you still have to act civilized. Even if it eats at you." He waited a moment. "Okay?"

Dusty nodded. "Okay. I'll tell him."

"Tell who?"

"Santiago," Dusty said. "Next time he touches me, I'll tell him that it would be in his best interests to act civilized."

She walked out. She was putting her gear in the back of the truck when he caught up with her.

"Hold on," he said. "Are you saying he put his hand on you?"

Dusty opened the door to the Ford and stood there, thinking about what to say and how to say it. "This ain't recess in the schoolyard. I'm not here to tell tales."

Murphy watched as she got into the truck. "All right," he said. "But whatever he did, he won't do it again."

FOUR

Pulling away from the marina, Dick Hoffman lit a cigarette while keeping watch in his rearview mirror, thinking that the owner of the wooden boat might decide to follow him. By the time he reached the highway that led back into the city, he was satisfied that he wasn't being pursued. The guy was a hick, but even a hick wouldn't chase after a man who had just shoved a 9mm Glock in his face. Still, there had been something about the guy that had unnerved Hoffman. He was raw and plenty strong-looking and he came right at Hoffman in the parking lot, as if he might take hold of him, which is why Hoffman pulled his piece. The hick stepped back at that point, but he still didn't appear scared, not in the least. Pissed off was more like it, and he probably had reason to be, seeing his boat towed away. Well, fuck him. He had nobody but himself to blame. Hoffman didn't want the goddamn thing. If the hick hadn't chained the cylinder to it, he'd still have his little wooden boat.

He finished the first cigarette and lit a second off the butt. Until he got the call about the cylinder, Hoffman had been having a bad day. He'd gone zero for ten at the track the day before — hadn't even cashed a fucking place ticket — and went to Merton's for dinner, and stuck around long enough afterward to get about three-quarters drunk, and suffered the indignity of his credit card being refused when he attempted to pay his tab. He'd ended up writing a check that he knew was going to bounce, so that morning at ten o'clock he walked into his bank and demanded a meeting with the loans manager.

It didn't go well.

The manager was a new guy named Ollinger and he looked as if he had just stepped off the cover of some computer geek magazine. Skinny, with rimless glasses, hair carefully mussed with little streaks of blond in it. He regarded Dick Hoffman as if he was a panhandler.

"What can we do for you today?" he asked after they sat down, his eyes shifting to a computer screen in front of him.

"I want to see about a line of credit,"

Hoffman had said.

"It shows here that you already have a line of credit." Loans Manager Ollinger pursed his lips. "And it's been exhausted."

"Yeah, I'm aware of that," Hoffman said. "Why you think I'm sitting here? I need a new one."

"Well . . . it doesn't work like that," Ollinger said. "You can't just start a new one."

"Then extend the one I got."

"We just can't extend . . ." Ollinger sighed heavily and hit a few keys on his computer. "You can't use up the line and then solve things by making it bigger. You have an inordinate amount of debt here, Mr. Hoffman."

"*Detective* Hoffman. So what do you need — collateral?" Hoffman asked. "I got twenty-nine fucking years serving this city. I got an iron-clad pension waiting. If that isn't secure, then nothing in this world is."

"That's fine," Ollinger said. "But what we're looking at right now — well, we can't just keep advancing funds like it's . . . Monopoly money."

"Monopoly," Hoffman snapped. "You think this is funny?"

"No sir."

Hoffman felt his pulse begin to pound.

45

He felt shitty enough, with a hangover and no breakfast, just a cup of bad coffee from the minimart down the street from his house in Colonie. He forced himself to look away from the geek and out the window to the street below. Traffic was stopped; a dump truck attempting to make a right turn on a narrow side street hadn't made it. The traffic was tight up the truck's ass; the driver couldn't move forward because of a parked car and he couldn't reverse into the traffic behind him. It was a stalemate.

Hoffman turned back to Ollinger, who was still staring at the computer screen, looking a little nervous now. Seemed that kids nowadays spend their whole lives looking at computer screens. Maybe one day this kid will look up and discover that he's fifty-two and broke. Like Hoffman.

"I put my ass on the line for people like you," Hoffman told him. "For fucking little geeks sitting in their safe little office cubicles. You think you could do what I do? You think you'd last a day out there? No, you never think about it, do you? You never think about where people like you would be without people like me."

Loans Manager Ollinger finally took his eyes away from the screen. He shook his head apologetically and offered his palms

46

forward to emphasize that there was nothing he could do. "Why don't we go through your assets and see if there's any way —"

Hoffman got to his feet. "Fuck you. Your problem is you think you're in charge. Well, you're gonna find out different. You don't control shit."

Walking to his car, Hoffman thought back to the geek's expression when he left the office. No doubt the smug little prick ran around telling his coworkers all about Hoffman's meltdown the minute he left the building. No, he probably wrote it all out and sent it to everybody in an e-mail. Or put it out on Tweeter or whatever the fuck it was.

Hoffman headed for the station after leaving the bank. Sitting at a light on Madison Avenue, he saw Soup Campbell scurrying along the sidewalk, head down, his pace quick like a man on a mission. Waiting for the light, Soup glanced over to see Hoffman watching him, and right away he did an about-face and beetled into the alley. Hoffman made a U-turn in the intersection and followed. Soup was running now and Hoffman gunned the sedan up beside him and opened the car door, slamming Soup from behind and sending him face-first onto the pavement.

Hoffman got out and walked over to where Soup was writhing on the ground, his knees pulled up to his chest. Soup was skinny as a rail these days, with bad skin and a couple of missing teeth in front. Hoffman lifted him up and pinned him against the hood of the car.

"Dumb fuck. You don't run, I don't chase you."

"I ain't doing nothin'."

"You might as well wear a sign says you're holding," Hoffman said. "Running like a little punk. Let's see what you got."

Hoffman held Soup with one hand and rifled through his pockets with the other, turning out a half dozen little bags of crack and a small roll of twenties. Hoffman tossed the dope onto the hood and counted the cash. Two hundred and forty. Hoffman stuck it in his coat pocket.

"You dealing now, you little fucker?"

"No way. That my personal shit."

"You're not smart enough to deal drugs, Soup. You're barely smart enough to use them." He turned Soup around to face him. "Tell you what you're going to do. You're going to dump that shit in the storm sewer over there and then I'm going to let you walk. You're lucky I'm feeling generous to-day."

Soup glanced down at Hoffman's hands, looking for the cash. "Motherfucker, you just ripping me off."

Hoffman took a quick look behind him to see they weren't being watched and then turned and drove his fist into Soup's face. Soup went down on one knee and Hoffman pulled him back up. "What did you say?"

Soup put the back of his hand to his lip, which was split and starting to bleed. "Nothin'."

Hoffman stuck around long enough to watch Soup break open the bags and pour the cocaine into the sewer grate.

"There now," he said. "Don't you feel better? Now you're a useful member of society. Nobody says you have to be a fuckup all your life."

"Up your ass."

"That attitude could still use a little work," Hoffman had said before leaving Soup, bleeding and pissed off, in the alley.

Driving into the city now, the confiscated boat in tow behind him, Hoffman thought of how his day had progressed, from bad to good. Life was strange. When he reached the city limits he went to a Home Depot and used some of Soup's cash to buy bolt cutters. He could've gone downtown and picked up a set at the station but he wasn't sure just what his options were yet with regards to the cylinder. He had a growing suspicion, however, that downtown wasn't going to be a part of that picture.

From Home Depot he drove to his house out in Colonie and backed the boat into his garage. Unhooking the trailer from the SUV, he parked the truck outside in the driveway and then, went back inside the garage, closing the door. Using the bolt cutters, he cut the chain that was wrapped through the handles of the cylinder. The thing was a lot heavier than he anticipated and it wasn't easy getting it out of the boat. He had to stand it on end and tip it over the gunwale, and when he did, he couldn't control it and it tumbled over the side and crashed down onto the concrete. Hoffman jumped back to avoid a broken foot. The cylinder clanged noisily against the cement; luckily the handles prevented it from rolling away and smashing into the door. Hoffman cut a length of rope from the anchor line inside the boat and hooked it through one of the handles of the cylinder and dragged it to the storage locker at the back of his garage, then stood the thing on end and maneuvered it inside and locked the door.

He drove back to the station downtown and parked the SUV in the lot outside. He signed the vehicle in and went inside, sat at his desk, and went through the motions of filling out some reports until five o'clock, and then got into his own car and left.

He met Mickey Wright in Dunnett's on Western Avenue. Hoffman had called Mick earlier, on the drive north from the marina. Mick had his own table at Dunnett's, or at least it was a table that the regulars vacated for him whenever he showed up, which was pretty much every day for the last five years. The table was just inside the door leading to the back alley, the entrance that featured the handicapped ramp that had been installed, originally anyway, for Mickey Wright.

Mick was at the table when Hoffman walked in, his wheelchair angled so he could see the big-screen TV in the corner, although when Hoffman arrived Mick wasn't watching TV, he was reading a newspaper. In fact, he read the newspaper out loud to Hoffman as he sat down across from him.

"Under the conditions of the plea bargain, the twenty-two-year-old admitted to shooting the woman but claimed it was in self-defense as she had threatened him with a knife. Although the police failed to turn up the knife in question, he was sentenced to time served plus a day in jail." Mick tossed the paper aside and had a drink of beer before he said anything else. "A fucking joke. This whole country has become one big fucking punch line."

"Think I don't know it?" Hoffman said.

The waitress came over and Hoffman ordered a rye and seven, and another beer for Mick. After a while Mick would switch to Scotch but he wasn't there yet.

"So where is it?" Mick asked.

"Stashed."

"What is it?"

"Huh? You know what it is."

"I never saw it though. What does it look like?"

"I don't know. It's about four feet long." Hoffman held his hands up, fingers spread. "This big around. Got two handles, like loops, welded to it. And heavy. Unbelievably fucking heavy. Strained my guts getting it out of the goddamn boat."

"What boat?"

"Long story. The dummy who found it, I had to seize his boat."

"It's got a lid of some kind?"

"Nothing. Welded shut, tight as a nun's snatch."

The waitress brought the drinks and Mick checked out her legs while she put them down. She was wearing a short red skirt and a white dress shirt, with the sleeves rolled up and the top couple buttons undone to show some cleavage even though she didn't have much to show.

"You think she's wearing panties?" Mick asked, watching her walk away. "Bobby Simmons says sometimes she doesn't wear panties when she works."

"How would Bobby Simmons know?"

"Good question. She wouldn't let him anywhere near her little cooch."

Hoffman took a drink of rye. He wanted to get back to the subject at hand. He never remembered Mick as a guy who talked about sex much, not before the shooting that put him in the chair. Now he did it all the time. Hoffman suspected it was because talking about it was all he could do nowadays.

"So does that sound like it?"

"Maybe," Mick said. "I told you — I never saw the thing. It was pitch dark that night, that's how Parson gave us the slip. He tossed the thing and followed it overboard. Shit, night like that, dark as coal, how you going to see a nigger in the water?"

Mick finished one beer and started on the other.

"And this was where?" Hoffman asked. "Because apparently this hick fisherman is

53

saying he hooked it out from Kimball's Point. Just above Athens."

"It was near Coxsackie," Mick said. "Deep water."

"Then how did it get to Kimball's Point?"

"The current. Been seven years, right? Give it enough time and the thing would've ended up in Yonkers."

"It's too heavy. Maybe this is the wrong cylinder."

"You figure the Hudson River's full of them?" Mick asked. "Moving water is a powerful thing. You ever see those tsunami pictures? Besides, you'll know soon enough, once you cut it open."

"And what's supposed to be in there?"

"According to the snitch, a hundred pounds of pure coke. Straight from Colombia."

"Snitches lie all the time."

"Yeah, they do. But whatever it was, it was enough for Parson to haul it all the way from the islands and when things got hot, to dive into some deep fucking waters and swim for shore in the middle of the night. So I'm thinking it wasn't piña colada mix he was transporting."

"Who was the snitch?"

"Some semirespectable businessman-slash-dealer, a real tough guy who folded like a tent in the wind when we found pictures of naked little boys on his home computer. He had all the details. The dope went from Colombia to the Bahamas and up the intercoastal. On a boat called *Down Along Coast.* McGarry was running the department at the time and he wanted the bust. He could've informed the feds and they could've busted Parson anyway between here and Florida. But McGarry kept it quiet, let them sail right up the river."

"Why did you hit him that night?"

"He'd sailed into the Hudson that morning and he was going to be in Albany the next day. We didn't know where he was going to dock. We couldn't risk losing him. That night was our chance. And then we blew it."

"How?"

"Parson got shit lucky, that's how. Two in the morning and we're just a few hundred yards away, running silent, oars and paddles. And all of a sudden he comes out on the deck. Maybe he heard a fish jump, who knows? But he makes us. Another five minutes and he was toast."

"So him and the cylinder go overboard?"

"Yup."

"What about the woman?"

"She stayed with the boat. Maybe she

55

couldn't swim."

Hoffman finished his drink and signaled for another. "She went to jail though. What for?"

"The boat was in her name. We found a few ounces of coke on board, some grass too. Recreational. She took the fall for that. She wouldn't give Parson up, wouldn't admit to even knowing him. Everybody was pissed about losing the big score so they came down hard on the woman, made it trafficking and made it stick. She got a raw deal, tell you the truth. Did two, three years, if I recall."

Mick picked up his beer and glanced at the TV as he drank. A red-haired man with the rubbery features of a cartoon character was standing in front of a screen that showed the temperature for the coming days. Apparently the heat wave would continue.

"We sent divers down, but they couldn't find it," Mick said. "That water out there is deep and murky. We were fucked the minute Parson tossed the thing. McGarry should have let the feds take him down. But then there'd be no newspaper headlines for McGarry."

The waitress brought the round. Mick told

her to put it on his tab and Hoffman didn't argue.

"So Parson gets away and now he's retired?"

"Yeah, he's retired," Mick said. "And the moon is made of cheese. What are you going to do with it?"

"How do you know I'm not going to turn it in?"

"Because you would have done it already. Instead you called me."

Hoffman fell silent and sipped at his drink. If he had known Mick was going to pay for the round, he'd have ordered a double.

"You know there's a story that the thing is booby-trapped, right?" Mick asked.

Hoffman set his glass down. "No. Where'd that come from?"

"The snitch," Mick said. "Said that Parson wired it up in the islands. To discourage anybody from fucking with it."

Hoffman considered the unlikely nature of this for a moment. "Sounds like bullshit to me."

"Me too," Mick said. "Have to be pretty sophisticated stuff. But it wouldn't cost a dime to invent the story." He took a long drink of beer. "But who knows?"

Hoffman reached for his cigarettes and

hesitated, had a look around to see if it was allowed. There was a guy at the bar pulling on a nonfilter while he pumped coins into the poker machine so Hoffman lit up. He inhaled deeply and let it out.

"What should I do, Mick? We're talking, what, a couple million dollars here."

Mick turned away. Hoffman knew that there was a time when he wouldn't have had the nerve to suggest to Mick Wright that he do anything but turn the cylinder over to the drug squad. But the Mick who was a gung-ho cop with two working legs was a different man from the Mick in the wheelchair. The shooting that put him there had happened one night, in an instant, but really it had never stopped happening.

"So you think she's wearing panties?" Mick asked, looking at the waitress, who was now behind the counter, talking to a young guy in a Yankees cap. "You know what I think? I think she just says shit like that to get guys like Bobby Simmons all worked up. Cuz she knows that none of them is ever gonna get close to her. She's just doing it to make them crazy. Maybe they give her bigger tips, thinking it's going to get them something."

Hoffman never so much as glanced over at the waitress, he just kept his eyes on

Mick. Waiting for Mick to look back his way.

"Fuck 'em," Mick finally said. "People will say you have to do what's right but I gave that department my fucking legs and now they tell me they're going to cut my disability benefits. I have to go to court to fight them for it. You going to tell me that's right? What good's it going to do to turn it in? There's no way to connect it to Parson or anybody else. So keep it. Sell it. It's the lottery."

"Who do I sell it to?" Hoffman asked.

"Chrissakes," Mick said. "Who do you think?"

FIVE

Virgil went home and did the chores that afternoon and afterward he sat on the porch and drank a beer while he tried to make sense of what had happened at the marina. It wasn't an easy thing to do, given that he'd been left completely in the dark by the cop who had taken his boat. And while it didn't take a genius to figure out that the cop had really been after the cylinder, the fact remained that he had taken the boat.

Virgil had picked up the old cedar strip the previous fall, at a run-down farm east of Rhinebeck. Virgil had been in the market for a hay baler and he'd found one advertised on the bulletin board at the local co-op. Virgil's baler — the one that had belonged to Tom Stempler for decades — was on its last legs, having been welded and straightened and repaired so many times that it was no longer practical to keep fixing it. The old-style balers were cheap nowadays; nearly everybody in the feed business had gone to the large round bales. They required less manual labor, and the bales could remain outside, which meant that it wasn't necessary to send anyone into a sweltering hay mow in the dog days of summer. Virgil was old-school though; he didn't mind the time in the hay mow, and besides, he couldn't afford one of the expensive round balers even if he wanted one.

The ad on the bulletin board offered, along with the baler, all kinds of other equipment, including a Ferguson tractor, a three-ton grain truck, and an "old Ford car." It was on a piece of coffee-stained foolscap, scrawled in pencil, in the handwriting of either a toddler or an unsteady senior citizen. The latter turned out to be true. The farm was on a dead-end road and the owner was as beaten down as the place itself, his years somewhere north of eighty, Virgil guessed, his face puffy, his hair lank and gray under a sweat-stained John Deere cap. The farmhouse was neglected, a stucco two-story now covered by aluminum siding, the siding falling away here and there to reveal the brown pebbly stone beneath. There was a fairly new Chrysler sedan parked beside the house.

The farmer was a talker, in the manner of

a guy who didn't get much company, and he introduced himself as Montgomery Woodbine. He admitted that he was now a farmer in name only; he'd been born in the house, he told Virgil, and he'd worked the land his entire life. Now he rented the acreage out to a local cash cropper and he was finally pushing sentimentality aside and going through the process of selling off his remaining equipment.

"I don't know what any of it is worth," he told Virgil. "These days I don't know what a hundred dollars is worth. Not much."

They were standing in the gravel driveway of the house. Virgil had called earlier to say he was coming and the old man had obviously been watching for him. He was out the front door, pulling on his denim jacket, before Virgil got out of his truck. He came down the steps cautiously, on rickety knees, and met Virgil in the drive.

The baler was a McCormick Model 45 and it was stored in a dusty and cobwebbed machine shed off to the side of a bank barn. It was at least forty years old, although it looked as if it hadn't been used for thirty of those years. Montgomery Woodbine opened the sliding doors at both ends of the dark shed so that Virgil could take a better look at the machine. It was in very good shape;

the tires had plenty of tread and even the drive chains looked almost new. All the U-joints and bearings were dry of grease from years of sitting, but they didn't appear worn at all.

"What's your price?" Virgil asked.

Woodbine removed his hat and gave his scalp an energetic scratching with the tips of his fingers. "You're a farmer yourself?"

"Yeah."

"Would you give two hundred dollars for it?"

Virgil said that he would. "But I think a scrap dealer might offer you more than that."

"A scrap dealer did. That's why I asked if you were a farmer. It's still a good baler. I'd rather not sell it to somebody who's just going to melt it down for the steel."

After they made the deal, Virgil took a walk around the shed and had a look at what was left. There was a threshing machine that really *was* suitable for a scrap dealer, or maybe a museum. The stake truck was rusted badly and nearly worthless. The old Ford mentioned in the ad was a three-window coupe from the early thirties, tucked away in the corner of the shed. One of the shed's ceiling joists had splintered and fallen and was resting on the roof of the car. The black paint was faded through to the metal in places, but the car appeared to be intact and complete. It had Ohio plates from 1959.

"What year is this?" Virgil asked.

"Nineteen thirty-two," Montgomery Woodbine said. "First year for the V-8."

"Right out of a gangster movie."

"Funny you should say that." The old man moved toward the car. "Lookit here." He wiped the heavy dust away from the paint to reveal a bullet hole in the panel a few inches behind the passenger-side window. "My father used to tell a story about this car. He said it came from around Steubenville, Ohio, and that Pretty Boy Floyd stole it and was driving it when the cops spotted him. They put this bullet hole here chasing him."

Virgil stepped forward to have a look. He stuck his forefinger in the bullet hole, and he nodded, not wanting to step on the old man's tale. "You figure that really happened?"

Woodbine laughed. "I know damn well it never. I put that hole there myself. I was target shooting at an elm tree outside here, missed the tree, and the bullet went through the plank wall and hit the car." The old man shook his head. "My father liked to pull your leg if you let him. There's people around here who still tell about the time he fought Jack Dempsey to a draw."

"Never happened?"

"No, sir." Woodbine rubbed more dust from the car. "I got a fella coming out from the city today to look at this. I'm told these things are popular nowadays. People paint 'em up and put new motors in them and hydraulic brakes and whatever. I told the fella on the phone I wanted ten thousand dollars, figured that might turn him sour on it, but he never backed off an inch."

Virgil bent forward to look inside the car. The upholstery was torn in places and it appeared that mice had made off with some of the stuffing. Otherwise the car was in remarkably good condition. "Well, if I had ten thousand dollars, I might just make you an offer. But with my luck, the cops might mistake me for Pretty Boy Floyd."

"Oh hell, he's been dead for years," Woodbine said seriously.

"I still don't have ten thousand dollars," Virgil said. "I mentioned I'm a farmer?"

The old man laughed like he knew exactly what Virgil was talking about, and Virgil turned away and that's when he spotted the cedar strip runabout, tucked in the other rear corner of the machine shed, under some disintegrating canvas tarp and about a half inch of dust and swallow droppings. It was a sixteen-foot Peterborough, built in the Ontario town of the name, which meant that someone probably had crossed Lake Ontario with it at some point. The boat had a hole the size of a man's head in the bow, and the ribs inside were rotted, although the cedar planking itself was intact. There was a twenty-horse Johnson outboard hanging loosely on the transom. Virgil walked over for a closer look.

"I bought that for my son," Woodbine said. "Him and a couple of his dunderhead pals ran it up on some rocks in Lake Katrine one night, knocked that hole in the bow. They said it was high winds that did it, but I always figured it was too many Miller High Lifes and too few brains. We towed it home the next day and it's been sitting here ever since."

Virgil did another turn around the boat. There was some writing beneath the grime on the transom and he wiped the dust away to read it.

POP'S CAMP
CROW'S LANDING, N.Y.

"What will you take for it?" Virgil asked.

"Why would you want it?"

Virgil shrugged. "My grandfather had pretty much the same boat. Had a cottage up in Quebec. I could use a winter project."

"Make me an offer."

"A hundred dollars?"

"I'll take fifty."

"You're a hard man to do business with, Montgomery Woodbine," Virgil said.

They went into the house, where the old man rummaged through a pine hutch and found the original bill of sale for the baler, and the service records for it — when it had been greased, what parts had been replaced, and all the rest. Virgil paid the man in cash and towed the baler away that day. Later in the week he returned, pumped up the tires on the trailer, and took the boat home.

He spent the winter restoring the cedar strip. Once his corn was harvested and the fall plowing was done, the workload relinquished somewhat heading into December. The cattle and calves still required feeding morning and night, and the ever-fluctuating herd of rescued horses needed the same. And there was always firewood to cut. Still, Virgil knew he would have some time on his hands in the winter, which was why he bought the boat.

It had been years since the garage beside

the house had seen a vehicle inside and Virgil had converted it into a workshop of sorts. He installed a woodstove in the corner and gathered all the tools from the four corners of the farm — chisels, saws, wood bits, drills, planes — as well as a Beaver table saw that had somehow ended up in the milk house at some point in the past. He bought cedar planking to fix the hole in the boat's hull from a man on the Irish Line who made birdhouses, and white oak for the ribs from a horse farmer who'd purchased a couple thousand board feet of the stuff for fencing before deciding to go with the electric ribbon now favored by equestrian types, or at least equestrian types with the money to afford it.

Virgil milled the oak down to half-inch strips on the table saw, rounding the edges with a router. He built a steamer out of a steel drum and a couple lengths of aluminum downspout and slid the new oaken ribs inside, stoking the woodstove until the lengths were as pliant as licorice. Then one by one he clamped them into place in the boat and fastened them with cinched copper nails. He repaired the hole in the hull with the new cedar.

When the repairs were done, he sanded and buffed and smoothed the cedar and applied four coats of spar varnish. He pulled the pistons from the old Johnson motor and installed new rings and rod bearings. He rebuilt the carburetor and polished the magneto and changed the plugs and when he put everything back together the motor started on the third pull.

He finished the restoration in late March and on the first warm day in April he towed it to the river, stopping at the place called Brownie's at Kimball's Point. Virgil launched the boat, fired the motor, and idled out into the bay. He spent some time adjusting the carb, then went for a run. The old engine purred along nicely, and the boat planed out, handling the waves beautifully. Virgil spent a couple of hours cruising, stopping here and there to wet a line. The boat leaked a little at first and he had to bail the bottom several times. But the cedar soon grew saturated, and it swelled just as it was designed to, and the leakage slowed and finally quit. Virgil got a couple of nice stripers that day. He'd been back several times since, most recently that very morning. He enjoyed the old boat, and now he was going to have to find out how to get it back.

The next morning he drove into the city in search of some answers. He could have stayed at home and waited for the cop who had confiscated it to be "in touch" as he promised, but Virgil was pretty sure he'd be waiting a long time for that to happen.

Apparently there were three or four precinct houses in the city. On Broadway a man in a pinstripe suit directed Virgil to the one on Arch Street. It was a grungy neighborhood in an old part of the city and the building, a four-story redbrick, fit right in with the surroundings. Virgil told the woman at the front desk what he was there for, then told the story again to a sergeant who came down a flight of creaky stairs at the back of the room. Finally, after waiting out front for forty minutes, he told it for a third time to a detective named Malero. Apparently Detective Malero had already heard it because he answered the accusation before Virgil got finished telling it.

"This department never seized a boat yesterday," he said. "Nobody in this department, in uniform or plainclothes, was even near Kimball's Point yesterday. We have no jurisdiction there." They were sitting in a large room, at Malero's desk, surrounded by similar desks. There were other cops, some in uniform and others not, in the room. They were talking among themselves, or working in front of computers. "The badge you saw, what makes you think it was Albany PD?"

"That's what it said. And that's what the guy said who was flashing it."

"But you never got the number?"

"No," Virgil said. "I didn't get the serial number of the gun he stuck in my face either."

Detective Malero raised his eyebrows at the sarcasm. "You should've gotten the badge number."

"I would've, if I'd known the guy was going to steal my boat."

"If somebody stole your boat, sir, I can guarantee you it wasn't a police officer," Malero said. "I took the time to check with the state police too. They never had a call out at Kimball's Point. Have you considered the possibility that it was somebody posing as an officer? Maybe one of your friends playing a joke on you?"

"He had a badge like yours, and he had a gun like yours. And as jokes go, it wasn't all that funny."

"I was just speculating."

"I appreciate the effort," Virgil said. "You guys drive navy blue SUVs?"

"We have different vehicles that we use."

"Any of them navy blue SUVs?"

Malero answered that by not answering.

71

Shaking his head to show his aggravation at having to deal with this, he took a pad from a drawer in his desk and searched through the clutter until he found a pen. He asked Virgil for his name and address, and he jotted them down.

"I'll need the boat's registration number," he said.

"It wasn't registered."

Malero looked up. "Why not?"

Virgil shrugged. "It's an old cedar strip I bought for fifty dollars last year. I restored it over the winter. I guess I never thought to register the thing."

Malero put the pen down. "Christ. We're talking about a fifty-dollar boat? You think a police officer from this department drove out to Hooterville or wherever you're from and stole your fifty-dollar boat?"

"I told you I restored it," Virgil said. He indicated the pad in front of the detective. "See — that's why you need to write stuff down. I restored it and rebuilt the motor. So it's not a fifty-dollar boat anymore." He hesitated. If he was going to tell the detective about the cylinder, now was the time.

"Okay," Malero said. "So it's not a fifty-dollar boat. But it's not registered, so I guess we can make the argument that the thing doesn't even exist. How do we go

72

about finding a boat that doesn't exist?"

In that instant, Virgil was no longer thinking about telling the cop about the cylinder. He got to his feet. "Oh, it exists. That's not the problem here. The problem here isn't even that neither one of us knows where it is. The problem is that only one of us gives a flying fuck."

He went through the station and out the front doors and onto the street. He'd parked a couple blocks away, in a municipal lot, and as he was walking toward it, he passed the compound where the department parked their vehicles. There were quite a few cruisers inside, both marked and unmarked, and several SUVs, mostly dark blue or black. Virgil wished he had thought to take the plate number of the truck that had towed his boat.

Walking past, he saw a guy in a suit, a cop by the look of him, talking to a man in jeans and a faded beige shirt. The second man had his back to Virgil; his gray hair reached past the collar of the shirt. There was something familiar about the guy but Virgil, unable to see his face, couldn't say what it was. As he walked past the compound and into the lot where his truck was parked, he glanced back. The man had finished his conversation and was now out on the sidewalk, approaching the lot where Virgil stood.

It was Buddy Townes.

Virgil waited until Buddy made his way to a dark green Cadillac, maybe fifteen years old, with the right rear quarter crunched in, the damaged taillight secured with a liberal application of duct tape. Buddy fished his cigarettes from a pocket before opening the driver's door. He was lighting a smoke when Virgil spoke.

"I heard you ran off to Florida."

It took Buddy a few moments to place him. When he did, he smiled. "Break out of any jails lately?"

"Nary a one."

Buddy pulled on the nonfilter and nodded his head, as if agreeing to a statement nobody had made. "You want to grab a beer?" he asked.

"It's ten o'clock in the morning," Virgil told him.

"Rye, then?"

They settled on coffee at a greasy spoon a couple of blocks from the police station. Buddy looked about the same as the last time Virgil had seen him, when Virgil had been on the run from a murder charge in Ulster County. Buddy was fifty-five going on seventy, his face lined and creviced from too many years of liquor and tobacco and

74

general self-abuse. He wore a gray mustache now, the ends dipping down past the corners of his mouth. His voice was, if anything, harsher than Virgil remembered, as if somebody had taken a wood rasp to his vocal chords.

"That Florida dream was a good one, in theory anyway," he told Virgil when they were settled at a table. "But there were certain things I hadn't counted on."

"Like what?"

"One — my amazing capacity for pissing away money," Buddy said. "And two — my equally amazing capacity for finding a high-maintenance and weak-moraled broad to help me do it."

"Sounds like a perfect exacta."

"It was a perfect something. Fun while it lasted, though."

Virgil dumped a little cream into his coffee. "Did Jane Comstock really give you a million dollars?"

"No," Buddy said. "I asked for that, and she gave me half. And then you and Claire Marchand ran her to ground anyway. She should have kept her money. But she's got plenty left, she ever gets out of jail."

"How did you end up here?" Virgil asked.

"Here in the city? Well, I don't live here, I'm just in and out. Back to doing some investigative work to pad my shitty little pension. Couple of criminal lawyers in town I work for. Nobody as much fun as Mickey Dupree, but these guys still have pulses."

Virgil smiled. "Mickey Dupree. Shit, I went to jail for killing the guy, and I just now realized I never even knew the man. That sound right to you?"

"No. But it sounds about the way things are." Buddy tested the hot coffee. He gestured out the window to the city outside. "No, I wouldn't live here in the city. I rent a place on the river, near Coeymans. Got used to living on the water down in the Keys. Winterized cottage, with a woodstove and a dock. A few bars nearby, within staggering distance. I fish every day I can. I got a little aluminum with a ten-horse on it."

"I had a boat once," Virgil said and he told Buddy about the incident at the marina.

"And metro is denying any knowledge of it?" Buddy asked when he was finished.

"They're suggesting it wasn't a real cop."

Buddy took a drink of coffee, thinking. "It's still a stolen boat. And you're a citizen making a complaint. They can't exactly ignore that."

"Apparently it's a jurisdiction thing."

"But the cop who took it claimed to be

76

Albany PD?"

"Yeah," Virgil said. "And he had the badge."

"They should be looking into that, if nothing else."

"Another thing against me," Virgil said. "The boat wasn't registered. I bought it from a farmer and fixed it up and I never thought to register the thing."

"Do it now."

"How?"

"Find out if the farmer had the numbers and do it after the fact," Buddy said. "It's still your boat. Just because somebody stole it doesn't change that. You filed a theft report. The cops can't ignore that."

"I guess not." Virgil finished his coffee.

"But that's not the bigger question here," Buddy said. "Obviously the guy wasn't interested in your boat. You got no idea what was in the cylinder?"

"None. The thing had no cap, no valve, nothing to access it. It was welded tight. And I'm pretty sure it was stainless steel, which means it would have lasted a lot of years down there."

"Sounds like something you would do with contaminated waste," Buddy said. "But why the fuck would anybody want to seize a cylinder full of waste?"

"And pretend to be a cop while he was doing it."

"Yeah," Buddy said in agreement. "I can ask around if you want. I don't know these boys like back in Ulster County, but I can ask."

"Sure. I couldn't care less about the cylinder, I just want my boat back."

"I don't blame you," Buddy said as he stood up. "But you got to be curious about that fucking cylinder, man."

"Yeah."

They left money for the coffee on the table and walked out onto the sidewalk. Buddy lit a cigarette before turning to Virgil.

"You realize that curiosity can be a dangerous thing."

"That's just for cats," Virgil said and he crossed the street, heading for his truck, and home.

Driving out of the city, Virgil went back over his conversation with the detective named Malero. While it was obvious that the cop had zero interest in the missing boat, Virgil's gut told him that the man wasn't actually covering anything up. Maybe it *was* somebody posing as a cop who took the boat. Or an ex-cop with an agenda. If either was the case, then maybe Buddy Townes would turn something up.

Whoever it was who had taken the cylinder, he'd shown up at the marina pretty damned quick. It couldn't have been more than an hour from the time Virgil docked the boat until the man in the SUV arrived. Someone had called him and Virgil was about ninety-nine percent certain who that someone was.

He pulled into the marina shortly before noon, parked by the tackle shop, and went inside. Mudcat McClusky was at the counter, selling bait minnows to a couple of fishermen, both elderly and of Asian descent. One man asked if they were catching perch off the pier. Normally a question like that would have Mudcat rambling at length, delivering all manner of detail regarding the fish being caught, whether what he said had any truth behind it or not.

"I ain't a fishing guide, nipper," he said to the man. "You're gonna have to figure that out for yourself."

Virgil held the door for the two men as they left, and he saw the anger in their eyes.

"Hey, Virgil," Mudcat chirped when they were gone.

"Where's Brownie?" Virgil asked.

"Went over to Home Hardware for deck screws. We're fixing those stairs down to the dock. I'm going to —"

"Who'd he call about the cylinder yesterday?"

"What do you mean?"

"Yesterday," Virgil said. "I came off the
river with that steel cylinder in my boat and
you came down to the dock and had a look
and then you came scurrying up here like
the little schoolgirl that you are, and told
Brownie about it. And then he walked over
to that phone there and made a call. Who
did he call?"

"Come on, Virgil," Mudcat said. "I never
done any such thing. I don't think I even
mentioned the cylinder to Brownie. None
of my business."

Virgil watched Mudcat's eyes, how they
shifted back and forth, looking for someplace safe to settle. "When's Brownie due
back?"

"Anytime now . . ." Mudcat began, but
then he changed his story. "No, actually, he
has business in town. He could be gone a
long time. I wouldn't wait on him."

"No, I think I'll wait," Virgil said. "And
I'll meet him in the parking lot, before you
get to him, and the first thing I'm going to
ask him is whether or not you told him
about the cylinder. And if he says yes —
then you and I are going to have a problem,

Mudcat. The boys over at Scallywags tell me that you've been beat up about a hundred times for being a lying, thieving little weasel. So I guess a hundred and one isn't going to bother you much."

Mudcat was chewing on his bottom lip as he listened to the threat. Apparently the prospect of a hundred and one was bothering him quite a bit. "You know, maybe I did mention the cylinder. In passing. But I don't remember any phone call." He was quick to elaborate. "I'm not saying there wasn't one. I mean, I was in and out. You know?"

"Yeah," Virgil said. "I know."

He went outside and sat down on the bench in front of the shop to wait for Brownie. It was an exercise in futility, he knew, but he had to go through the motions if for no other reason than to let Brownie know that he wasn't fooling anybody. But Virgil knew that Brownie would deny having anything to do with the matter.

Which is what he did, when he showed up fifteen minutes later.

"I never made a phone call," he told Virgil. "Who the fuck do you think you're talking to?"

"I was hoping you might tell me who it was you called," Virgil said. "But I'm thinking that's unlikely, if you're going to lie about making the call in the first place. Right?"

"Get the fuck out of here," Brownie said. He turned to walk away but then stopped and came back. "I'll tell you what I saw yesterday. I saw you coming off the river with a steel cylinder you picked up someplace and then Albany PD shows up and seizes it, along with your boat. Which makes me wonder just what the fuck you're involved in, pal. And now you got the nerve to get in my face?"

"So it was Albany PD?"

"What?"

"The cop. He was Albany PD?"

Brownie hesitated. "I got no idea."

"Yeah, you do. You couldn't see the badge from the bait shop, and the vehicle was unmarked. But you know because you called him."

"You can get the fuck out of here," Brownie said. "And don't come back. I'm taking away your docking privileges."

Virgil smiled. "You're taking away my docking privileges the day after your buddy took my boat? That's like taking a man's shoes after you cut off his feet. I'm beginning to think that you and Mudcat are sharing a brain, Brownie."

Virgil got into his truck and drove away,

leaving Brownie fuming and spitting ob-
scenities in the parking lot. By the time he
got back to the farm, Virgil had to accept
the fact that the day had been wasted; he
didn't know any more now than when he
got up that morning. Well, he had established that Mudcat and Brownie were a pair
of liars, and that there was something
sketchy about the sweaty little cop in the
SUV who had stolen his boat.

But those were things he already knew.

Six

The auction sale was Saturday morning, on the southern shore of Lake George, at a consignment place called Terrapin's. They'd been in business for ten years or so and they handled mainly estate items — high-end furniture, glassware, some artwork. They rarely had cars to offer, and Parson was banking on this working to his advantage.

He picked Zoe up at her apartment just before eight. The sale started at ten and it was an hour and a half to get there. Parson had no idea just when the vehicles would go under the gavel, so he wanted to be there on time. Zoe had worked the bar the night before, one of the places on Madison that catered to college kids, and when he arrived at her walk-up on Ontario Street he'd had to knock on the door to get her out of bed, and then wait in her cramped kitchen while she took a shower. There were dirty dishes on the table and in the sink, cigarette butts in coffee cups. A bottle of Jack with maybe half an ounce left, on the table. A pair of large black cowboy boots were in the middle of the floor, as if they'd been removed in a hurry, and a man's denim jacket on the back of a chair.

As he waited, a fat white cat wandered out from the bedroom and jumped into Parson's lap before he could swat it aside. He was wearing brown pants and a black golf shirt, and both were now covered with white fur. He spent the next five minutes listening to the noisy shower in the bathroom and plucking the hairs one by one from his clothes.

When Zoe finally came out, wearing jeans and a Lynyrd Skynyrd T-shirt, her hair still wet, Parson was standing impatiently by the door.

"How do you live like this?"

"Bitch, bitch," she said.

They took 87 north. Parson was driving the black Escalade, not wishing to call attention to himself as a dealer by arriving in one of his muscle cars. Zoe was quiet until she'd had her takeout coffee.

"So what are we doing?" she asked.

"They've got some vintage hot rods," Parson said. "One of them is a '70 'Cuda ragger with a Hemi," Parson said. "Sup-

85

posed to be numbers matching."

"All right," Zoe said. "How high do I go?"

Parson flipped open the console compartment and handed her an envelope full of thousand-dollar bills. "Thirty grand here. If I can queer the provenance, it'll go cheaper. If I can't, it'll go higher and we'll pass."

Zoe yawned. "All depends who's there, right?"

"Way it is."

"Maybe somebody smarter than you."

"Can't see that happening, Zoe."

"I know *you* can't."

"Make sure you get the title when you pay."

"Right. I've never done this before."

"You're cranky in the morning."

"You'd be cranky too on three hours' sleep."

"Nobody told you to stay up all night screwing, Zoe."

"I was *working.*"

"I saw the cowboy boots in the kitchen. You working on a ranch these days?"

Zoe reached into her coat for her cigarettes. "You weren't so critical back when they were your boots."

Parson laughed. It was true. He and Zoe had had some times together. They had even talked about moving in, having kids. But then she went bad on meth, and Parson had left her alone. When she came back into his life, a couple years later and clean, he'd been glad to reconnect but the sexual thing was gone. The dope had taken her down physically, and she never made it all the way back. Her cheeks were sunken and her eyes were dull, as if something had smudged her soul and she couldn't get it clean.

But she was a good partner when he needed one, like today. She was smart and knew how to keep her mouth shut. And she was always up for making a quick five hundred. Of course, knowing her, she'd probably spend it on the guy who owned the cowboy boots, the guy who was, presumably, still snoring away in her bed this morning.

"You're not going to smoke in my car," he told her now, watching her fish around in her purse for matches.

"Let me out then."

Parson shook his head in resignation. "Use your coffee cup for your ashes," he told her. "I don't want you getting my ashtray dirty."

Zoe lit up. "You are an anal motherfucker, Parson."

Terrapin's Auctions was housed in a converted barn on a paved road a few hundred yards from the shore of Lake

George. Parson could see the cars set to go on sale from a quarter mile away, lined up in the parking lot in front of the building. The vehicles were all from the same era — a Thunderbird, a GTO, an Impala, and the 'Cuda. The online literature advertising the sale stated that they were part of a collection of the man whose estate was on the block today, and that they were older restorations. They looked good from the road.

"The white one on the end," Parson said as they drove slowly by.

"I know what a Barracuda looks like," Zoe snapped.

He dropped her at a gas station a mile away and while she went inside to call a cab Parson drove back to the auction house and parked in the lot behind the barn, then walked over for a closer look at the cars. They'd been done up right, probably ten or fifteen years earlier, although somebody had decided to change the GTO from an automatic to a four-speed and, rather than find the proper console, they had cut an ugly hole in the existing one to accommodate the shifter. Still, it was only the 'Cuda that interested Parson. He had the production figures in a notebook he carried and he checked the numbers on the door plate against those on the inner fenders and those on the engine block. He pulled on coveralls from the back of the Escalade and crawled underneath to make certain that the transmission and differential were original as well. It was a good car. The odometer read 43,000 miles and Parson had no trouble believing it was accurate.

Zoe arrived while he was checking out the 'Cuda, and he saw her as she got out of the taxi and went directly inside to register to bid. Parson shed the coveralls and went to sit on a picnic table in the shade of some maple trees in an expanse of lawn beyond the auction parking lot, checking and replying to messages on his BlackBerry while he waited for the auctioneer to come out. Zoe never came back outside and Parson presumed that she was watching the sale.

It was almost noon when the crowd started streaming out of the barn and began to gather around the cars. Parson watched for Zoe and then he saw her, wandering along, admiring a small painting she'd obviously just bought.

The Barracuda was the big-ticket item and so the auctioneer would offer it last. The other cars were nice but not particularly rare, and they went fairly reasonably, the GTO with the butchered console topping the bunch at $16,200. When the auctioneer began to sing the praises of the 'Cuda, Parson got up from his place in the shade and began to walk. He reached the periphery of the circle surrounding the auctioneer as the man was stating that the car was "numbers matching."

"It's not," Parson said loudly.

The auctioneer turned on him. "I beg your pardon."

"That's not the original engine," Parson said. "That motor's out of a '68. It has nine to one compression heads, and a cast iron intake manifold. Tear it down and you'll find the crankshaft has four-inch main bearings. The Hemi they made in '70 was four and a half."

It was pure double talk but Parson was pretty sure it would fly. He stood looking at the auctioneer, not in a challenging manner, but rather as someone just wanting to set the record straight. This was the tricky part of the proceeding. Everything that Parson had said was bullshit and if there happened to be somebody present who could verify that the car actually was as advertised, Parson was out of luck. But that rarely proved to be the case. Even if somebody suspected that Parson was bluffing, people were usually reluctant to present themselves as experts when there was money at stake.

The auctioneer was not happy. He shifted his glare from Parson to a man in a pink fleece pullover, standing just outside the door to the barn. The man was obviously either handling the estate for the family or, more likely, a relative of the deceased. As Parson watched, the man looked skyward and shrugged his shoulders in an exaggerated gesture. That was it for the auctioneer. He was pissed at the development, not just for the lost revenue it would cost him, but also because his company had advertised a vehicle that, apparently, was not what they claimed. He made a little speech, the standard spiel about buyer beware, clearing the house of all liability, and said that they would continue.

When the bidding began, Parson offered a couple times for appearance's sake, then dropped out at fifteen thousand. Zoe bought the convertible for twenty-two five. Parson knew it would have reached at least three times that if he hadn't spoken up. The auctioneer knew it too.

Parson walked to the Escalade and drove off, stopping again at the gas station at the corner, while he waited for Zoe to pay for the car and obtain the title and bill of sale. She showed up fifteen minutes later, getting out of a cab, still carrying the painting. She handed Parson the remainder of the cash in the envelope and he put it in the console as they drove off. He would send somebody over that afternoon to trailer the car to his shop.

"You pay yourself?" he asked.

"Yeah," she said. "The dude in the pink sweater was badmouthing you."

"He should've pulled the car," Parson said, "the minute I opened my mouth."

"That's what the auction house told him," Zoe said. "Too late though."

"Fuck him."

"How rare is it?"

"Ragtop, with the Hemi and the automatic, they made nine that year."

"So what's it worth?"

Parson smiled. "It's worth whatever I can get for it."

Zoe lit up again, to Parson's dismay. "Tell me something," she said. "What are you going to do when the day comes that you can't get somebody like me to do your bidding? Pardon the pun."

"Come on, Zoe. Don't you treasure these moments together?"

"Answer the question."

Parson smiled at her. "You know the deal. I buy it, I have to show ID and then it's in my name. And if the same guy who questions the car buys it, it's suspicious. Especially when it happens over and over. This way, I ask the questions, drop out of the bidding, and then Zoe Smallwood buys it. Nobody suspects anything."

Zoe thought about that. "That's just a fancy way of saying you like to get other people to do your dirty work for you."

Parson smiled but said nothing. They were on a country road, heading west toward the thruway. There were orchards and vineyards along the way. Roadside stands offered fruits and vegetables, jams and preserves.

"What's the painting?" Parson asked.

Zoe showed him. It was an oil painting of a frame house at the end of a street, with rolling fields beyond. There was a front porch with a swing on it, and a black-and-white dog sprawled on the boards at the top of the steps, head resting forlornly on its front paws, as if waiting for someone to return.

"Why did you want that?" Parson asked.

"It reminds me of my grandmother's house," Zoe said. "I used to stay there summers when I was a kid."

"You're so sentimental, Zoe."

"Well, that makes one of us."

Parson shifted his eyes from the painting

back to the thruway. Zoe sat smoking and after a while she turned and put the painting on the floor in the backseat.

"So what about it?" Parson asked. "You ever going to have kids?"

Zoe didn't reply at first. She finished the cigarette and stubbed it out in the coffee cup. "I always figured on it."

"How old are you now?"

"Forty-one."

"Still young enough."

"I guess." She watched out the window, to an orchard across the way, the trees already heavy with apples.

"What about you?" she asked. "You're the one always wanted kids."

"Still do."

"What are you waiting for?"

Parson smiled. "The right brood mare."

"You're such a fucking asshole, Parson. You know that?"

SEVEN

Dusty spent Saturday at the brownstone at Madison and Canfield. Gutting the old building was a bigger job than she'd expected and by noon she was second-guessing herself, thinking that maybe she should have taken Murphy's advice and gotten some help. But then she'd be splitting the money.

She started on the third floor, removing the doors first, and then the casings from the doors and the windows, and finally the baseboard. The trim was of red oak, and unlike most houses from the era, it had not been covered with a dozen coats of paint over the years. Dusty assumed that Murphy would want to retain the woodwork, so she carefully pulled the nails from everything and carted it all down to the basement, where she stacked it on some shelving there. If it turned out that Murphy didn't want to keep it, Dusty would buy it from him and sell it. There were plenty of antique dealers in the city who would jump at the period trim.

Back upstairs she removed a bay window overlooking the Dumpster on the ground below and began pulling down the lath and plaster from the ceilings and walls, tossing the debris into the container below. It took her the remainder of the day to gut the third floor. Once the plaster was gone, she had to remove the knob and tube wiring, some of which was still live, and the two-by-four framing itself. Afterward, she spent a half hour sweeping up. She'd worn coveralls and a ball cap and dust mask, and by five o'clock she was covered with plaster dust and just plain grime from head to toe. She left the coveralls and mask there and headed home, where she had left Travis with a babysitter from the building. Back in the apartment she stayed under the shower for a long time, washing away the cobwebs and dirt and rock wool insulation from her hair, her ears, even her nose. She'd put in eight hours, and would charge Murphy twenty-five an hour. She was exhausted but two hundred dollars was two hundred dollars.

She made mac and cheese for the two of them for dinner and then she fell asleep on the couch while Travis watched *Shrek* for the hundredth time. He woke her when the movie was over, and told her to go to bed before heading off himself. Role reversal.

She would have gone back to the job on Sunday but earlier in the week she had made an appointment to look at a house out in Cobleskill, a place she'd found in the real estate flyer she'd been reading at work, the same day that Stan the plumber had suggested she move in with him. She considered canceling but then was afraid the place would sell before she got another chance. She was basically fooling herself anyway, thinking she could swing the financing, but in her more optimistic moments she envisioned a situation where the current owner might hold the mortgage, with a minimal down payment. The chances of that happening were nearly nonexistent, but it didn't cost anything to dream.

She packed Travis into the truck, leaving early enough to give them time to swing by the old neighborhood to pick up some cheese at Cabretta's on Bleeker Street. Dusty had hung around the place when she was a kid, and Mrs. Cabretta, ancient even back then with long curly chin whiskers and a lingering smell of garlic about her, had liked Dusty, even though Dusty was a pretty accomplished shoplifter from the age of about five, and occasionally would help herself to the hard Italian licorice or the dark chocolate displayed by the cash register. Eventually she found out that Mrs. Cabretta was aware of her thieving all along, and as soon as Dusty knew that, she quit doing it. She even went to work at the store for a few months when she started high school, but that was right around the time she began to hang out at the park, getting high and jacking cars instead of licorice, and her career stocking shelves didn't last long. Now she made a habit of stopping in at least once a month to pick up a half a pound of cheddar, or pecorino, but mainly to say hello to Mrs. Cabretta, who had remained very protective of her, even when Dusty had gone to jail. Mrs. Cabretta had been convinced that whatever had happened was not Dusty's fault. This from the woman who had turned a blind eye to Dusty's sticky fingers way back when.

Today, however, the forgiving old lady wasn't there; a sullen girl of about seventeen or eighteen was working the counter. She had very dark hair and brown eyes and Dusty assumed she was one of the several grandchildren. Her foul mood was probably due to the fact that she was a teenager working on Sunday morning. But Mrs. Cabretta had to be seventy-five or even eighty by now. It was time she took the odd day off.

She bought the orange cheddar that Travis liked her to use for grilled cheese sandwiches and as they were walking back to her truck, she saw Shell near the entrance of Jefferson Park, standing by her peanut cart. Dusty checked the time on her cell and figured she could stop and say hello.

Shell's name was Michelle but nobody ever called her that, not that Dusty had heard anyway. She was ten or twelve years older than Dusty and she'd come to the city from Jamaica when she was a teenager. She was very large, maybe three hundred pounds, and her body was scarred and burned and broken from her days with the needle. Her past had robbed her of much of her beauty, both inside and out, but it hadn't stolen her brilliant smile and she showed it when she saw Dusty and Travis walking across the grass.

"Hey, girl," she said.

"Hi, Shell."

The big woman leaned down and offered her hand to Travis. "Hey, little man. I be calling you big man before long."

Travis hung back. Shell was an intimidating figure; her hair hung in long braids, adorned with glass beads and silver trinkets, and her breasts were huge, each one half the size of Travis, who held on to Dusty's leg before finally offering his hand to the large woman. They shook solemnly and Shell turned back to her cart, where she had on display everything from peanuts in the shell to cashews to pistachios. She had fresh-popped corn as well and she filled a bag for Travis.

"What you doing here on a Sunday morning, Dusty?" Shell asked as she drizzled some viscous yellow liquid over the popcorn. "Don't tell me you homesick for the park?"

"I miss this place like I miss acne," Dusty said. She held up the cheese in her hand. "Heading out for Cobleskill and stopped by Cabretta's for some cheese. Wanted to say hi, but there's some newbie working the counter. Guess the old lady's taking a day off."

The big woman handed the popcorn to Travis, who thanked her without being reminded by Dusty. Shell smiled at him while speaking to Dusty.

"She dead."

"What?"

"She died maybe two weeks ago," Shell said. "I shoulda called you, guess I never thought."

"What happened?"

Shell shrugged. "People get old, then they die. This news to you?"

"I guess not," Dusty said. She wished she had known. She would have made it to the visitation at least. She tried to remember the last time she had talked to the old woman. More than a month ago, she guessed. She had seemed the same as ever that day, asking the same questions she usually asked, not really pausing to hear the answers. She always made a fuss over Travis, even though she had a busload of her own grandchildren. Great-grandchildren too.

Dusty took a look around the decrepit park. It was pretty quiet. Sunday morning coming down, like the song says. There were a couple of teenagers playing one-on-one across the way, on a patch of cracked concrete that served as a court. Travis saw them and took a few steps toward the game, munching his popcorn as he watched. A few people were sitting on benches, clutching takeout coffees, others wandering aimlessly. A couple of older men were sleeping on the grass. Or at least they looked older.

"I don't know anybody down here anymore," Dusty said. "Where'd they all go?"

"Jail or the graveyard, I suppose," Shell said. "Ask me, one place bad as the other, but then you know all about that shit." She paused, watching Dusty watch Travis. "Some of 'em make it out to the burbs with their little shoe box houses. Like Jules. How she doing?"

"She's good," Dusty said. "Her husband's a bit of a caveman but he got her out of here, at least. He works steady."

"What about you? You still building them houses?"

"Still building them houses," Dusty said. Now she turned away from Travis, who had stopped on the grass a few feet away. "How you doing? You okay, Shell?"

"Yeah."

"Being good?"

Shell shook her head, as if she was bored with the subject already. "You asking me if I'm using? Yeah, I'm using methadone. On the government's dime. Tell me — that being good? That being better than a righteous junkie?"

"That's the idea, isn't it?" Dusty said.

"Guess it is. What about you — you being good?"

"Have to be, Shell. I got a parole officer." Dusty indicated Travis. "And I got this guy. I'm straight and narrow."

"Whatever get you up the mountain." Shell watched her a moment. "So maybe you don't need to be coming round here. Nothing but bad history."

"I can stop and say hi to you, Shell."

"Don't need to."

"But I do," Dusty told her. "Other than Julie, you're the only one came to see me in prison. You telling me I can't stop and say hello, Shell?"

The big woman shrugged. "I'm not telling you shit. You gonna do what you want anyway. Always have."

"Not always," Dusty said. She smiled sadly at Shell but let it go and turned to Travis. "Okay, dude, let's get a move on."

"What's on in Cobleskill?" Shell asked. "Going on a picnic with your cheese?"

"Nah," Dusty said. "Going to go look at one of those shoe box houses you were talking about."

Cobleskill was a forty-five-minute drive west of the city. The town was small, population six or seven thousand, and it was home to the state agricultural college, as well as a bedroom community for people who worked in the city but didn't want to live there. Dusty knew the area a little; one of her friends from the old neighborhood had gone to school there and Dusty had visited her occasionally on weekends, when things had been in party mode. She remembered a bar in town called Reggie's. She really didn't remember much about the town, but then her memory was a little foggy in general when it came to those days.

The house was in an older subdivision on the north side of town. The homes there were well kept, the lawns trimmed, the driveways paved or laid in interlocking brick. The real estate agent handling the listing was named Cheryl Smythe. Dusty had spoken to her on the phone a couple of days earlier and they had arranged to meet at the house at one o'clock. Dusty arrived in town a half hour early, and she and Travis drove around a little, checking out the schools and the shopping centers and the parks. They took a pass through the university grounds, largely deserted on a Sunday morning, before driving around the residential areas, looking for other places for sale. Dusty jotted down two numbers to call later. Travis was not enthusiastic about the trip.

"Not another one?" he said when they pulled up in front of the house with the sign on the yard featuring the smiling face of Cheryl Smythe. "Why do we have to do this every weekend?"

"Because it's fun," Dusty told him.

"Fun?" he said. "Have you ever had fun?"

"Come on," Dusty said. "Wouldn't you like to live here? Have a lawn? You could ride your bicycle to school."

"I don't have a bicycle."

"We would get you one."

Travis looked at the ranch-style house, and he glanced up and down the block. "How come they all look the same?"

Cheryl Smythe was waiting inside, looking a few years older and a few pounds heavier than the woman on the sign out front. Her smile was not quite as welcoming either, once she saw Dusty, in her jeans and Patti Smith T-shirt, with her tattoos and the crescent moon scar from Albion Correctional still prominent on her cheek. Dusty saw the judgmental look, and she saw the woman shift her eyes from Dusty to Travis, as if checking to see if he was likewise marked up. Like they were circus people or something.

Dusty was there to go through the house and she didn't give a shit what the woman thought of the way she looked. Cheryl Smythe's hair was coiffed and highlighted with blond streaks, and she had been Botoxed very recently; Dusty could see the tiny needle marks on the too-smooth skin between her eyebrows.

She did a pass through the house with the woman trailing, while Travis loitered in the living room. Cheryl Smythe managed to overcome her negative reaction to Dusty, probably realizing that there was at least the possibility of a sale.

"This place is in very good shape," she said. "It's had one owner since it was built and they are very meticulous."

"Needs windows," Dusty said.

"Down the road, yeah."

"Not far down the road," Dusty said. "The front sidewalk is heaved. Looks like tree roots pushing it up. The basement okay? No leaks?"

"Not that I know of."

"Not that you know of," Dusty repeated.

"It does need a few things," Cheryl Smythe conceded. She was getting a little agitated. "That's why it's going so cheap."

"Two hundred and thirty thousand is cheap?"

"Nowadays it is. Especially if you want something in a decent neighborhood." The agent paused a moment, then pushed on, as if she couldn't quite help herself. "I have to say — you don't look like the typical buyer for this area."

Dusty turned to the woman as Travis came into the room.

"Mom, can I go in the backyard?"

"Yeah. Stay in the yard though." Dusty waited until he'd gone. "So," she said, "you don't think I'd be interested in living someplace decent?"

"Now come on," Cheryl Smythe said. "That's not what I said at all. It's just that you look more . . . urban. Like you'd be more at home in the city."

"I thought home was where you hang your hat," Dusty said.

"I guess it is."

"Sometimes home is where you hang your head. Right, Cheryl?"

The agent had no answer for that. She did, however, look at her watch, suggesting she had other places to be.

"So, what will they take?" Dusty asked. "Two ten?"

"No," the agent said. "They might go as low as two and a quarter, but that would be the bottom." She went into her purse for a business card, which she laid on the kitchen counter. Evidence that she had shown the place. "You do realize, of course, that most banks now require thirty percent down."

"Yeah. I do realize that."

"Well, that's a substantial sum of money,"

the agent said. She was on her own firm ground again, and she grew condescending. "Even if you were to get it for two hundred and twenty-five thousand, you would still need . . . well, I'll just tell you what you'd need."

She pulled a calculator from her purse and began to punch in numbers.

"About sixty-eight grand," Dusty told her. "That's what I would need."

The agent shook her head at the interruption and kept punching. She seemed disappointed to learn that Dusty was right. "Well, sixty-eight, five," she corrected, needing that small victory.

Dusty nodded and looked out the window. Travis was swinging from the lower limb of a red maple tree, his shirt pulled up to reveal his skinny belly.

"And do you have that?" Cheryl Smythe asked.

Dusty turned. "No. Not on me."

EIGHT

Parson was under the '41 Cadillac ragtop, removing the starter. He'd been searching online for a week, trying to find an NOS starter for the car and finally he'd given up. He would have the old unit rebuilt.

"I can buy the car for twenty grand," he said as he worked. "The price is right if it's as good as it looks in the pictures. But then I have to ship it from Argentina. Those cabriolets are rare though."

He wheeled himself from under the car on the creeper, the starter in his hand. The floor was finished concrete, smooth as an ice rink, and heated to a constant sixty degrees year-round. The garage itself was cleaner than most homes, and bigger, covering more than three thousand square feet. It, too, was climate controlled, and featured two hoists and a machine shop for rebuilding engines and transmissions. Parson usually had at least three restorations ongoing, and often as many as six. Right now he had a '67 Shelby ready for paint — the paint bay was in a separate building — and the Barracuda he'd bought a few days earlier up on blocks, with the drive train removed, the transmission on the bench, and the Hemi on an engine stand. Under cover at the far end of the building he had a 1958 Corvette, a '67 Jag, and a '32 Ford three-window coupe that was all original, right down to the factory paint. In fact, the deuce coupe was the rarest of finds — even though it had a few scratches and blemishes, the fact was that any cosmetic work would actually diminish its worth.

In the front corner of the building was an office of sorts, although there were no walls, just a desk and a couple of chairs, a Mac computer on the desk, along with a half dozen issues of *Hemmings Motor News.* Cherry was sitting there now, reassembling a Browning .45 he'd been cleaning while Parson removed the starter. Cherry wore a snug black T-shirt advertising the gym that carried his name, his huge biceps straining the sleeves. The semiautomatic looked like a toy gun in his hands.

Parson put the starter on the stainless steel workbench that stretched across the end of the building and shrugged out of his coveralls. He still lifted three days a week and he was thick across the chest and shoulders, although not as big as Cherry, and he had to order his coveralls custom made.

"What's it worth done up?" Cherry asked. Meaning the cabriolet.

"Minimum seventy-five grand," Parson said. "I could hot-rod it and go crazy with the power train, but I'd keep it stock if it hasn't been messed with."

"Argentina," Cherry said. He put the barrel onto the Browning, then he smiled. "Any way you could route it through Colombia?"

"I've thought about it," Parson said. "Argentina's not exactly next door, but it might be close enough. There was a time when I could have made something work. Not sure about it these days."

Parson fitted a socket to a ratchet and began to remove the end plate from the starter. He wanted to have a look at the armature before taking it for the rebuild. The phone rang and he reached for the portable on the bench, tucked it under his chin while he worked. "Empire Restorations," he said into the receiver.

"I'm looking for Parson," a man's voice said.

"You got him."

"I need to talk to you."

"You're doing it," Parson said, working the ratchet. "Who is this?"

"Dick Hoffman."

Parson hesitated a moment, and then he frowned, glancing across the garage to Cherry. "Well, well . . . *que paso,* Detective? Been awhile. You still ass-fucking crack whores down in Jefferson Park?"

"You're a funny man," Hoffman said.

"Really? I wasn't trying to be. What can I do for you?" Parson laughed. "I mean, really — what could I possibly do for someone like you?"

"I have your property."

"You have my property?" Parson said. "No. I don't see how that could be. I think maybe you dialed the wrong number, Detective."

"Maybe I did," Hoffman said. "Maybe it was somebody else who tossed a cylinder full of cocaine into the river seven years ago."

Parson glanced toward Cherry again. He wondered at the likelihood that the call was being recorded. But for what? "I'm pretty sure I have no idea what you're talking about, Detective," he said.

"I've got your coke," Hoffman said. "The good news is — I haven't decided what I'm going to do with it yet."

Parson laid the ratchet down and walked over to the open door of the garage, where he looked at the rear of his house. Built in 1923, the place backed down to the river, a masterwork of fieldstone and brick, copper roofs and leaded windows. It had allegedly belonged to the city's top bootlegger of the Prohibition period. The man had made a fortune running rye and gin across the lake from Canada. Rumor had it that his rivals had forced him into retirement in 1928, although his body was never found.

The pool guy had arrived a half hour earlier and now he was kneeling on the flagstone patio, preparing to drain the pool. Parson had had enough of chemicals and algae. He was making the switch to salt water.

"Sounds to me like you're suggesting that I am involved in the illegal drug trade, Detective," Parson said into the phone. "And nothing could be further from the truth. I restore antique cars for a living." Now Parson turned and walked directly toward Cherry, raising his voice slightly. "I know nothing about cylinders of cocaine dumped in the river. Sounds like something out of a movie."

That got Cherry's attention and he set the Browning aside.

"There's nobody recording this," Hoffman said. "If that's what you're worried about. I think you're all caught up in the fact that I'm a police officer."

"I'm not worried about anything," Parson said. "I don't remember you being much of a cop anyway. As far as I'm concerned, this is a crank phone call. You might as well be asking me if I have Prince Albert in a can."

"What?"

"It's an old joke, Detective," Parson said.

Hoffman didn't say anything for a few moments, as if he was regrouping. "All right," he said. "Look at it this way, Parson. I'm a private citizen with a large amount of cocaine for sale. If you don't buy it, somebody else will."

"Good luck with it then."

Hoffman hesitated again and Parson smiled, sensing the man's frustration. "You're not interested? It's your dope."

"You're telling me you're trying to sell me something I already own?" Parson asked. "Where is your moral fiber, Detective?"

"Hey, we can play it that way," Hoffman said. "Let's say, hypothetically, that it does belong to you. Then I'll just hand it over." He paused for effect. "Of course, I suppose there would be a recovery fee. For retrieving the thing to begin with."

"What kind of fee?"

"I'm not a greedy man, Parson. Five hundred thousand."

Parson laughed. "Like I said, good luck with it. If you even have the thing."

"I'm looking at it right this minute."

Parson moved back to the workbench. "Why would it turn up now? How would it turn up now?"

"What do you care," Hoffman said. "Maybe some dumb fisherman from Kimball's Point found it. Maybe I was able to make a deal with him on it. But apparently I'm not going to be able to do the same with you."

"Guess not," Parson said. "You're on your own."

Hoffman's disappointment in the negotiation was tangible, even over the line. "All right then," he said. "Oh, one more thing. This story about the thing being booby-trapped. That's bullshit."

"Is it?"

"It's not feasible."

"Why not? All you need is some plastic explosive and a coded lock."

"Battery operated?"

"You see an extension cord running out of it? You really don't have to be very smart to be a cop nowadays, do you?"

"The batteries would be dead by now," Hoffman said, choosing to ignore the shot about his intelligence. "Seven years, the batteries would be dead."

"Would they?" Parson asked. "Batteries go dead from use, not from time. You ever see that little Energizer bunny, Detective?"

"I don't believe it."

"Then cut it open. You'll have sixty seconds to punch in the code. I can't wait to read about you in the paper tomorrow morning. Half-wit cop gets blown to pieces."

"Fuck you, Parson," Hoffman said and the line went dead.

Parson clicked the phone off and set it on the workbench. He turned to Cherry, sitting at the desk.

"Up jumped the devil," Cherry said.

"Yeah."

"You figure he's really got it?"

"He's got it," Parson said. "Or he knows who does. To make this up would require a lot more imagination than a moron like Hoffman could ever manage."

"Why is he calling you?" Cherry asked. "Does he think you're going to cop to it, the dumb fuck?"

"He's looking for a buyer."

"You're shitting me."

Parson picked up the ratchet. "Sounds like

Detective Hoffman is looking to expand his earning potential. Not exactly a surprise. He's so crooked he has to screw his shorts on in the morning."

"What's he looking for?"

"Five hundred large."

"Shit. He's living in a fantasy world."

"Yeah, he is." Parson removed the plate from the starter and slid the armature out. He looked at the windings without seeing them, his mind on Hoffman.

"How did it show up?" Cherry asked.

"Says a fisherman hooked on to the thing. Down by Kimball's Point."

Cherry finished assembling the .45 now and he slipped a full clip into the gun, racked the action. "You want me to drive out there?"

Parson turned to look at Cherry, with his bulging arms and his dyed black hair, his salon tan and his gold jewelry. After some consideration, Parson shook his head. "I can't see you fitting in out there, Cherry. Asking questions. The locals would be suspicious, and maybe a little intimidated." Parson paused to think. "No, I need somebody who would blend in. Somebody who knows the area."

"Like who?"

"I don't know. Maybe somebody who was

there, back in the day."

It took Cherry a minute. "Really?"

"Find her," Parson said.

Virgil didn't know if Montgomery Woodbine would still be at the farm. After all, he'd been selling everything off the last Virgil had seen him, almost a year earlier. By now he might have sold the property as well and moved on, to an apartment in the city or a double-wide in Florida or Arizona.

Virgil wasn't sure what it might accomplish anyway, trying to register the boat now, after it had been stolen. But Buddy Townes had said it might be a good idea and Buddy, for all his rough edges, seemed to know what he was talking about.

Claire had called last night, just as Virgil had come in from doing the chores. It was midnight in France and she was calling on her cell phone, from a bar where she said she and a couple of her cousins had stopped for a glass of wine. Virgil suspected in short order that there were multiple glasses of wine involved. They talked for ten minutes or so. She told Virgil that she missed him, and that she was sorry for pushing him that day on the river. Virgil had replied that he required a good push occasionally. While he was saying it, he was trying to decide whether or not to bring up the matter of his boat. He didn't know what to tell her because he himself didn't know what the hell had happened exactly, whether the cop had been real or phony, or what was in the cylinder, or anything else for that matter. Claire, as a cop of twenty years, would tell him to leave it alone until she got home and could look into it. Virgil didn't feel like leaving it alone. Not only that, but he wasn't sure he wanted to burden her with something as insignificant as a missing boat while she was on vacation. While he was still deliberating, the connection began to break up and Claire shouted goodbye, as if shouting might help the link, and then the line went dead. Virgil was excused from any decision making.

Approaching the Woodbine place along the dead-end road, the house appeared deserted. Of course, it had seemed that way a year ago, too. But now there was no Chrysler sedan parked in the drive, and the grass was somewhat overgrown. Virgil parked and got out, and went to the front door and knocked. When nobody answered, he came down off the porch and walked over to the machine shed and slid open the doors. Only the ancient threshing machine remained inside. The Ferguson tractor was gone and so was the Ford coupe and the stake truck.

Virgil walked back outside and closed the doors. As he was getting into his truck, he heard a vehicle and he turned to see the Chrysler approaching along the gravel road, coming fast. It turned into the lane and went around him and parked by the house and Montgomery Woodbine got out, carrying some takeout from Kentucky Fried Chicken. The old man focused for a few moments on Virgil, clearly not remembering him, and then he looked at the truck; it seemed that he recognized the vehicle.

"You bought my McCormick baler," he said.

"I did."

Woodbine chuckled. "I didn't give no warranty, if that's why you're here."

Virgil walked over to the man. "The baler works fine. I put a thousand bales through it this summer."

"Well, come on in," Woodbine said. "I got my lunch here. I go to the Kentucky Fried every Tuesday, when they got their special on. I just got enough for one though, I wasn't expecting company."

"I ate already," Virgil said, although he hadn't.

In the kitchen Woodbine made instant coffee for them both and they sat at a paint-chipped harvest table while he ate his chicken and fries. Virgil drank the bitter coffee, adding a lot of milk, and told the old man why he was there.

"I never registered the boat either," Woodbine said. "Not that I can recall. I don't believe it was required back then."

"There was a serial number on it," Virgil said. "On a plate on the dash. I never copied it down though."

"Guess you weren't planning on it getting stole." Tearing the meat from a chicken leg, the old man squinted, trying to remember. "I might of got a bill of sale. If I did, I still have it somewhere, probably in that flat-to-the-wall behind you. I never throw anything like that out."

"Where'd you buy it?"

"From a camp up in the Adirondacks," Woodbine said. "Pop's Camp, it was called. We used to rent the cabin next door every year, me and the wife, when the kids were just small. One year this camp was selling off their boats cuz they had a new batch coming in. This was about the time everybody was going to aluminum."

Woodbine finished the chicken and then the old man went into the pine cupboard and began to search for the document. Virgil waited, but he wasn't expecting much; he was going to be surprised if Woodbine came up with a bill of sale for a boat he bought fifty years earlier.

But he did. The receipt listed the boat's serial number and it was signed by the previous owner, a man named Bill Chamberlain.

"I'm not sure what good it's going to do you," Woodbine said.

"Me, either," Virgil said. "But if you can give me a bill of sale, I can at least prove chain of title. Then maybe the cops will stop pretending I invented the damn thing."

Woodbine used the same invoice book he'd used when Virgil bought the baler, and he made out a bill of sale. He was very meticulous with the document, checking and double-checking the serial number before handing Virgil the invoice.

"You got time for a beer?" the old man asked suddenly.

Virgil began to beg off but he hesitated, using a moment to look at his watch to consider. It occurred to him that Woodbine didn't have many visitors and he wondered just how often the old man's children came to see him. Virgil said yes to the beer.

They sat at the kitchen table and drank and talked about farming, which meant that they talked mainly about the weather. How there was always too much rain, or too little rain, or no rain. But never just enough rain. Woodbine told Virgil he'd raised four kids on the farm, just a hundred acres, and that his wife had never worked out of the home. Those days were gone, he noted, and Virgil agreed. Woodbine said that a man would have to be a fool to try to make a living off a hundred acres nowadays, and Virgil had agreed with that as well. When his beer was finished he got to his feet and said he had to get back to his own farm. He might have mentioned that it was a hundred acres, but he didn't.

The two men walked outside together.

"I didn't know if I'd still find you here," Virgil said.

"You figure I kicked the bucket?"

"No, but you were selling the equipment last year, thought maybe you sold the farm too. I had a look in the shed, I see you sold the Ferguson, and the old Ford."

"I sold the tractor," Woodbine said. "I gave the Ford away."

"Gave it away?"

"Not on purpose. Some guy came up from the city to look at it, right around the time you were here, I believe. Showed up with a big pickup truck and a fancy trailer. Looked the car over for maybe two minutes and wrote me a check for ten thousand dollars. Now, as a rule, I wouldn't take a check but everything looked on the up-and-up. He didn't appear to be a deadbeat, the truck and trailer had to be worth five times that. It was a Friday and he said he couldn't get to the bank until Monday and he had the trailer here and all. So I took the check."

"And it bounced."

"Like an Indian rubber ball. But I got nobody but myself to blame. I ain't hurting for money, but it galls me that I let it happen. Same with you and your boat, I guess."

"Yeah."

"Maybe I'll run into the sonofabitch someday," Woodbine said. "I won't forget him. Big colored guy, with a shaved head like a bowling ball."

Virgil opened the truck door and got in. "Thanks for the receipt."

"I hope you get your boat back," Woodbine said.

"So do I," Virgil said, and he drove off.

NINE

After thinking about it overnight, Hoffman drove to the airport early the next morning with the cylinder in the back of the car. Pulling up to the no-parking zone, he flashed his badge to a skycap and told him to load the thing onto a luggage cart. The cap looked at the badge unhappily but did as he was told, getting another porter to help him with the cylinder when he discovered how heavy it was.

Hoffman thanked the cap and said he would take it from there himself. He pushed the cart into departures and over to the first luggage drop he saw. He had to show his badge three more times before a security guard finally led him and the cart to the office of a man named Cowan, who was apparently the head honcho. Cowan was tall and lean, maybe sixty, with a hawk's eyes and a brush cut cropped close. He had a faded tattoo on his forearm that suggested he'd been a marine.

"So what is this?" he asked, looking at the cylinder.

"We seized it last night," Hoffman told him. "In the trunk of a rented Lincoln from Canada full of ragheads. We don't know what's in it and we want to X-ray it to find out. You know, before we cut it open."

"What's that got to do with us?" Cowan asked. "Get your drug squad to do it."

"They got two machines and they're both down," Hoffman said. "MIFC."

"What does that mean?" Cowan asked.

"Made In Fucking China."

If Hoffman thought that he might get a chuckle out of Cowan over that, he was mistaken. "So you're under the impression that we're here to provide you with this kind of service?" Cowan asked.

"I'm under the impression that you have an interest in our nation's security," Hoffman said. "Did I mention the rental car full of ragheads?"

Cowan took a moment to think it over. There really wasn't any way for him to say no. He turned to the guard. "Go ahead. We'll accommodate the detective." He looked at Hoffman, like a falcon eyeing a mouse. "But we won't make a habit of it."

126

■ ■ ■ ■

When he left the airport, Hoffman went back downtown, parked in an alley near the intersection of South Pearl and Alexander, and waited. He didn't know where he might find his man, but he knew he was in the right neighborhood. After a fidgety twenty minutes or so, he got out of the car and walked over to the Quik Mart tucked between two tenements and bought a *USA Today* and a pack of Camels. He continued down the block and picked up a pint bottle of bourbon at the package store on the corner. Thus fortified, he went back to the SUV and waited.

He spotted Soup wandering down Alexander shortly after eleven, blinking into the bright sunlight while he fumbled in his pants for his shades. He'd obviously just gotten up, and emerged from whatever rathole he'd inhabited for the night. He stood on the corner for a time, taking in the day, before starting out north along Morton.

Hoffman had another nip of the mash and got out of the SUV and started walking, catching up to Soup at the corner. He grabbed the skinny man by the forearm and muscled him into the wall of the building there.

"Hey, Soup. Where you heading?"

Soup turned a bad eye Hoffman's way and tried to wriggle free. "Get me some breakfast, it any of your business. I'm clean as a hound's tooth, you best let me be."

"Breakfast at fucking noon," Hoffman said, relaxing his grip but just slightly. "The life of Riley."

"I don't know no Riley."

Hoffman looked down the block and saw a diner with specials plastered on white placards on the plate glass window in front. He pulled Soup along. "Come on, I'll buy you lunch."

"Pass on that."

"You don't get to pass on anything," Hoffman said.

Inside the diner they sat at a booth against the back wall, Hoffman joking and smiling, trying to be a regular guy, while Soup was sullen and suspicious, waiting to see what this was about. Hoffman didn't get into it until after their meals had arrived.

"I need the name of a dealer," he said when the waitress was gone. "And I don't mean one of your baggy-assed homeboys selling that stepped-on shit in the alley. I need a real guy. With real coin. You understand?"

Soup had ordered a cheeseburger and fries. He was spreading ketchup on the burger as he listened. Now he put the bottle aside and stared over at Hoffman.

"I understand," he said. "I understand you out of your fucking mind. Even if I know a dude like that, I give him up to you and my black ass be in the cemetery by morning. So fuck you and your I-need-a-name shit."

Hoffman, watching as Soup took a bite out of his cheeseburger, glanced around quickly. "It's not like that. This is a business proposition."

Soup chewed and swallowed. "It's a dyin' proposition for me, what I'm saying here. What the fuck you think you get, buying somebody lunch?"

Hoffman leaned forward over the table and dropped his voice. "Listen up, you little shit," he snapped. "This is *not* a police thing, Soup. I have some serious weight to move. And you're going to help me move it."

"No chance, Hoffman. You settin' me up."

"Funny you should mention that," Hoffman said. He leaned back and smiled across the table, stirring a couple of heaping tablespoons of sugar into his coffee before continuing. "Because that's exactly what I'm going to do if you *don't* sign up for this. I'll plant about a pound of this shit on your skinny fucking person and haul you in. That makes it trafficking, and if my memory's right, that makes you a three-time loser, Soup. So you tell me what you're going to be today — a dumb fucking crackhead on his way back to stir or a savvy business-man?"

Soup sat staring at his fries for a long moment. "You a motherfucker, Hoffman."

"That's me. Now find me a guy and set up a meet. Use your brain and this could work out for you. This guy is going to be extremely grateful, trust me. He's going to *owe* you. You know?"

"All I know — ain't no such thing as a free cheeseburger these days."

By quitting time Monday afternoon, Dusty was on the common roof of the town houses, nailing the plywood sheeting to the trusses. At five o'clock she still had a few sheets to go and so, rather than quit and haul the hoses back up the next morning, she stayed an extra half hour and finished the job.

She was the last to leave the site and, walk-ing across the street to the parking lot, she pulled out her phone and checked her messages. She'd called the day camp at four-thirty to say she'd be running late. There was always someone there until six. Approaching her truck, she put her cell back in her pocket and looked up to see a vintage Camaro — '67 or '68, she guessed — parked by the fence at the back of the lot. The car was cherry red, gleaming in the fading sun, with dark tinted windows concealing anyone inside. Dusty considered that the mud parking lot was an odd place for that particular car to be, but she didn't give it much thought beyond that. She put her nailer in the back of the truck and as she did, she heard the rumble of the Camaro starting up and then approaching. She turned as it rolled to a stop a few feet away. The driver killed the engine and then sat there for a moment, obscured behind the tinted glass.

The door opened and Parson got out.

Dusty felt her heart rise into her throat. He was smiling, moving loose and easy, walking toward her. He didn't look a day older. He was like a big cat, both lazy and dangerous at the same time, his muscular arms encased in a black T-shirt with *Empire Restorations* scripted above a caricature of a screaming hot rod.

"Hello, Dusty."

"What are you doing here?"

"Why, looking for you."

"I can't imagine why," Dusty told him.

"Maybe I missed you."

"Goodbye." Dusty unslung the tool belt from her shoulder and dropped it in the box of the truck.

"Look at the carpenter here," Parson said. "They teach you that inside?"

"I learned a lot inside," she told him. "Like who to trust. And who to run from like the fucking plague."

"Now, now," he said. "I'm afraid I'm going to get my feelings hurt." He smiled. "So how you doing, girl? Looks like you're embracing the proletariat, getting it done, all that."

"Right."

"Although this truck doesn't suggest great financial success," he said, looking at the rust above the wheel wells.

"I'm getting by."

"Good," he said. "So tell me what else is new. You got a man these days?"

"None of your business." Dusty opened the door of the pickup.

Parson took a step forward and when he did he glanced inside the truck. The Iron Man action figure was on the seat. Seeing it, he paused. Dusty stepped in front of him and closed the door quickly, knowing it was too late.

"What the fuck do you want?" she demanded, upset he had seen the toy.

"They found the cylinder."

Dusty took a moment. Whatever she was expecting from him after all this time, it sure as hell wasn't this. "Who found it?" she asked.

"I'm not sure yet."

"What's it got to do with me?"

"It could have a lot to do with you, Dusty. It's a complicated situation. The people involved are acting cute."

"What does that mean?" she snapped. "Why don't you ever just say what the fuck you mean?" She waited for an answer she knew wouldn't come. "Sounds to me like somebody wants a lot of money for it. So pay it. And leave me out of it."

"It's not that simple, Dusty. They say they want to deal but they're pretty vague on the details. Like where it is, where it came from. You know I'm a details kind of guy. Apparently it turned up around Kimball's Point. But I don't know who found it, and I don't know who's holding it. I need somebody to go out there and finesse the situation. Somebody who knows the territory." He smiled. "Somebody with charm. And a winning way."

"You are so full of shit," she told him. "You think I'd help you after what you did to me? There's an old saying — burn me once, shame on you. Burn me twice — go fuck yourself, Parson."

"You sure that's how it goes?"

"Close enough."

"I'm not looking for a favor, Dusty. I'll pay you to scope this out."

"Do your own dirty work," Dusty said. "For once in your life." She opened the door and got in.

"Hold on," he said, grabbing the door handle. "You're not getting what I'm saying here. It looks as if the cops might be involved. On a certain level. Like I say, the guy's being cute."

"You're not getting what *I'm* saying here. I don't give a shit."

"You should. The last time the cops saw that cylinder, it was being tossed off a boat that was registered in your name. All they need to do is make the claim that it's the same cylinder and suddenly it's your property. You already did a stretch for trafficking. This time it would be heavy duty. You could be looking at a dime. Unless you get the wrong judge and then you could be looking at more than a dime."

He reached into his pocket and produced a business card, which he placed on the dashboard in front of her. Dusty sat staring ahead, out the windshield, to the town houses across the road. She had been very content in the belief she would never see Parson again.

"Why don't you think about it and give me a call," he said. "But maybe you're okay going back to prison. Maybe it's a better life than you have out here. Three squares a day and all that. Doesn't look to me like you're getting rich pounding nails."

"Stay the fuck away from me," Dusty said, pulling the door shut. She started the truck and gunned it out of the lot.

Driving to the day camp, she watched in her rearview, pulse pounding. Why would Parson show up now? Why would the goddamn cylinder surface? Dusty had trouble believing that it had. And maybe it hadn't, maybe it was just Parson, playing head games, trying to get back into her life. Nothing was ever a straight line with Parson, and what wasn't an angle was a curve. It wasn't so much that he lied, although he did that as easily as he breathed, it was more that he was an expert at surrounding the truth with a thousand little falsehoods, so that in the end it was impossible to know one from the other. Nobody knew that better than Dusty, and she doubted that anybody had ever paid as heavily for it as she had.

She spotted the police cars from a block away, parked in front of the day camp. Pulling up, she saw there was yellow tape stretched across the entrance to the alley beside the building. Dusty got out and went inside. Travis was in the first of the little classrooms, just him and one of the assistants who worked there, a girl of high school age. She was slumped in a chair, her legs stretched out, so fully engaged in entering a text into her cell phone that she never noticed Dusty's arrival. Travis was flipping through a picture book, looking bored. At some point in the past nine hours, he had managed to remove his T-shirt and put it back on inside out.

"Hey, buddy," Dusty said when she walked in.

"Hi, Mom."

Dusty turned to the girl. "What's going on?"

"What do you mean?" The girl had looked up briefly when she heard Dusty's voice but now she was reading something, an incoming text probably, on her cell.

"There's a dozen cops outside and they've

got the alley taped off," Dusty said. "Are you fucking stupid?"

The girl straightened up and put her phone in her jeans pocket. "They found a body in the alley."

"I found him!" Travis said.

The girl hastened to explain. "The kids found him at lunch. They were outside —"

"In the alley?" Dusty asked. "Who was it?"

"A drug addict, I guess. Overdose. They found a syringe." The girl shrugged, somewhat apologetically, although it was doubtful she knew why she might feel that way. A faint beep emitted from her pocket.

"You got a text," Dusty told her.

On the way home she stopped at the pizza place down the block and grabbed a medium for her and Travis. She didn't feel like cooking tonight. Travis was all in favor of the pizza idea.

"That's the first dead guy I ever saw," he told her when they got back to the apartment.

"Did it bother you?" she asked.

"Nope. Not a bit."

Which bothered Dusty. Quite a bit.

After putting Travis to bed, she took a shower and went out onto the fire escape with a can of Sam Adams. Inside the apartment the television was tuned to PBS; Travis had been watching *Mister Rogers* reruns earlier and Dusty hadn't bothered to turn it off. She looked out over the city and drank the beer.

It wasn't all that far from where she sat to where she had grown up. Knock down a couple of the bigger buildings and she could practically see Jefferson Park from here. She could almost smell the park — the pot and the pachouli and the urine and the vomit. The place never changed. She heard a gunshot off in the distance, or maybe it was a vehicle backfiring. One seemed more likely than the other. Inside, on the television, a man was discussing art and artists.

. . . Gauguin then struck up a friendship with Vincent van Gogh, with whom he shared more than just a talent for painting. Both men suffered at times from debilitating bouts of depression . . .

Dusty turned to look through the window into Travis' bedroom. He was sound asleep, his face angelic beneath his curly hair. He was not all that angelic when he was awake, but he was a good kid. Dusty had managed to keep him on a straight path. So far anyway. It would get harder as he got older.

She looked again at the city. She'd come a long way from her days in the park, but she

138

knew she hadn't come far enough. Today had shown her that. It was bad enough that her six-year-old son was stepping over dead bodies outside his day camp. It was worse that Parson had shown up, dragging her past with him. Dusty didn't need to hear about the goddamn cylinder after all this time. And she certainly didn't need to hear that the thing could still be connected to her. She didn't know if that was true, or just more of Parson's intrigue. But she did know, if it was true, that she would stand to lose her freedom. When that happened, she would lose her son.

And that was the one thing that couldn't happen.

Parson had dinner on the street level patio of a seafood place on Broadway and afterward he sat there watching pedestrians walk by as he drank cognac and smoked a cigar. He had left Cherry a voice message after his conversation with Dusty and he was waiting for him to call back.

His thoughts drifted to the Ford cabriolet in Argentina and when he was on his second brandy he called the dealer in Buenos Aires and offered him eight grand for the car. The dealer's English was not great, but it was good enough for him to convey to Parson how deeply insulted he was at the lowball offer.

"You show to me disrespect," the man said over the phone.

The conversation ended there, but Parson called back a half hour later and made an only slightly more respectful offer of eight-five hundred. One more phone call and they settled at nine thousand, a figure that still had the dealer whining as if he'd been held up at gunpoint, even though Parson suspected that the man had probably found the car in some backwater halfway up in the Andes, and paid whatever dumb goat farmer who owned it a hundred pesos to take it off his hands.

Parson was still thinking about routing the car through Colombia and using it as a mule, but it was a tricky proposition. Security was tighter than ever these days, and even an antique car from South America was bound to get a pretty thorough going-over. The days were gone when a man could stuff one of the tires with product and mount it back on the rim and run it through. Not only that, but if Parson loaded the car with dope, he'd be obliged to send it to someone else here at home. For a time he'd registered everything coming through customs in Jenny's name but Jenny had been gone now for over a year, having left at Parson's suggestion after he'd discovered her birth control pills hidden among her dozens of pairs of shoes in the walk-in closet. The discovery had convinced Parson that their differences were insurmountable — he had wanted a kid while she had been content to lie around the pool all day as high as a kite. She had gone to a lawyer who had made a lot of noise about Parson paying Jenny an exorbitant amount of money for their three years together. Parson had sent Cherry to discuss the matter with Jenny one night and he never heard another word from her or the lawyer.

His cell rang and he saw it was Cherry.

"Hey," Parson said. "Where are you?"

"McMahon's."

"I'll come there."

McMahon's was an upscale place up on Western Avenue, known for its steaks and its wine cellar. Cherry was sitting at the bar with a brunette wearing a tight blue dress. The woman was no more than twenty-five, Parson guessed, but then that was right in Cherry's wheelhouse. He was forty-six or forty-seven now, but Parson had never seen him with a woman over the age of thirty. He wasn't sure if women of that vintage were too old for Cherry or if they were too smart for him. Of course, women in their twenties could be just as smart, but then Parson had never seen any of those women on Cherry's arm. He would be surprised if the brunette in the blue dress proved to be the exception.

Cherry had a pathological obsession with his looks. He colored his hair an unnatural black and he was constantly checking it in any available mirror when he thought nobody was watching, as if a single gray strand might reveal to the world what the world already knew. He'd already had a couple of cosmetic surgeries, although he would never admit to them. But Parson knew that he'd had his eyes done and his chin tightened. Cherry spent time in his own gym every day, working out with the ball players and the pretty-boy cops and firemen, and he liked to brag that his regimen kept him looking young. At times Parson was tempted to ask him which workout it was that had removed the lines from around his eyes.

Cherry was drinking bourbon on the rocks and the twinkie in the tight dress was sipping some frothy concoction with what appeared to be chunks of fruit floating in it. Parson sat and ordered a brandy. Cherry introduced the woman as Zelda. While Parson waited for his drink he asked Zelda what she did and she said she was going back to secretarial school that fall, her tone suggesting she'd taken time off from her studies to find herself. A few moments after that she excused herself to go to the ladies' room. Parson suspected that Cherry had arranged for her to leave when he showed up.

"You talk to her?" Cherry asked, watching Zelda walk away, something Zelda did very well.

"Yeah."

"And?"

"She told me to fuck off."

"Sounds like her."

Parson's drink arrived and Cherry told the bartender to put it on his tab. "I'll bet she was surprised when you told her they found it," Cherry said.

"About the same as me," Parson said. He took a drink. "She's kind of bitter."

"Don't tell me that part surprised you."

"No," Parson said. "But she needs to learn how to move on. We did have some fun together. She still looks good too. Her body is tight as a dancer's, must be all that construction. Got me thinking about the good old days." He laughed. "I'm pretty sure Dusty wasn't thinking about the good old days."

"Well, she did go to prison," Cherry said.

"Am I supposed to feel guilty about it? What was I supposed to do?"

"Nothing," Cherry said. "Bad luck all around." He finished his drink and signaled to the bartender for another. "So what happens now? You want me to try to find the thing?"

"No. We'll let her do it."

Cherry turned. "I thought you said she told you to fuck off."

"She did," Parson said. "But when she was leaving I told her that the dope could still be considered hers. The boat was in her name. Which means if it happens to fall into the hands of the authorities, she's in deep shit. Deeper than before, maybe ten years deeper."

"You tell her about Hoffman?"

"No. First of all, I don't know for a fact that Hoffman has it. I got his word on it and his word isn't worth shit. But if he doesn't have it, he knows who does. And if a dumb fuck like Hoffman can figure out who found it, a smart girl like Dusty will too."

"You think she's going to tell you if she does?"

"No, I don't. But you're going to keep tabs on her, Cherry. You know where she lives and you know where she works. She'll

144

lead you to it. Remember, there's one thing we have in common, her and I. Neither one of us wants the cops to get their hands on it."

The fresh bourbon arrived and Cherry rattled the ice in the glass before taking a drink. He swallowed and nodded in agreement.

"One more thing," Parson said. "Does Dusty have a kid?"

"A kid?" Cherry asked. "I don't know. I just found her yesterday. Who knows? Maybe she got married."

"No ring."

"Why do you think she has a kid?"

Parson shrugged and let it go, as if he didn't care one way or the other. He looked past Cherry and saw Zelda in the blue dress coming down the hallway. "So, you putting Zelda through secretarial school come fall, Cherry?"

"Like I'm even going to know Zelda come fall."

TEN

Kimball's Point hadn't changed much in the seven years since she'd been there, although there were a couple of new malls off the thruway driving in, with the standard box stores — a Walmart, Best Buy, Pete's. The downtown area still looked prosperous though, despite the presence of the big chains. But then Kimball's Point had a bit of a reputation as an artsy community, and that would account for that. There were craft stores, and cafés, and a number of galleries and antique dealers.

Pulling into town, Dusty had no idea where to begin, so she drove up and down the main drag a couple of times, and then just naturally was drawn to Fletcher's Cove, back to where she'd started ten years earlier. She found Big Jim Cunningham on a trawler in his boatyard, tinkering with a sonar scanner. Dusty didn't know how she would be greeted and she was happy to see the broad red face break into a smile.

"Aren't you the stranger?" Big Jim asked. He was larger than ever, it seemed, his stomach straining the suspenders he favored, and since Dusty had last seen him he'd cultivated bushy red sideburns that made him look like a lumberjack in a television commercial.

"Hey, Jim," she said, and allowed him to clasp her in a bear hug.

They had coffee in the wheelhouse of the trawler, a forty-seven-footer Big Jim had built himself decades earlier. Big Jim sat at the console and removed his cloth cap, revealing his bald head beneath, a wide expanse of pink, freckled skin that never saw the sun.

"The cost of fuel is the big thing," Big Jim told her when she asked about the business. "You want to get rich, build a hybrid barge."

Dusty smiled and took a tentative sip of the murky coffee. She was pretty sure that Big Jim hadn't cleaned his coffeemaker since the last time she'd sat in the wheelhouse.

"So what are you doing, Dusty?"

"Working as a framing carpenter. Subdivisions, renovations. Shit like that."

"I'm gonna take credit for that. I put that building bug in you." Big Jim sat back in the captain's chair and balanced his coffee cup on his ample stomach. "You like it?"

"I like it more than prison, but less than building boats."

"Why don't you come back?"

"I don't know about that. I'm guessing my reputation is a little tarnished around here."

Big Jim had a drink of the bad coffee; he seemed blissfully unaware of its vile nature. "People know you got screwed, Dusty. I don't think anybody ever heard all the details, but nobody thinks you were alone on that boat that night."

Dusty nodded. "Well, if I told you I wasn't all that guilty, I'd have to tell you I wasn't all that innocent either. So I'm not looking for the sympathy vote. I'm doing all right. Construction is . . . well, it's constructive. You know?"

She gave the coffee one more chance before setting it discreetly aside as she stood and looked out the wheelhouse window. Big Jim's yard was at the end of the cove and all along the recess boats were docked. Fishing boats, sloops, old tugs of indeterminate years. She sensed him watching her. He was a good man, a little on the square side, and he had always treated her well when she worked for him. He'd never had kids of his own and maybe that was a factor.

"So you just out visiting?" he asked.

"Yeah. You know me — I'm a people person."

Big Jim laughed at that.

She turned. "You hear anything about some fisherman around here landing a steel cylinder?"

Big Jim took a moment, his eyes wary. "No. I haven't heard about anybody finding anything like that. What's this about?"

Dusty shook her head, as if to tell him she didn't want to burden him with the truth.

"Last time I heard anything about a cylinder like that was seven years ago, and at that time there was a bunch of police divers looking for it," Big Jim said, his eyes still on her. "You're not looking for trouble, are you, Dusty?"

She walked over and kissed him on his pink head. "Funny thing about trouble. You really don't have to go looking for it. You need a new coffeemaker, dude."

After that she hit the marinas and the launches in the area, one by one, driving south along the river and then retracing her steps and heading north. It was a small community, and the boating world in and around it smaller yet. It was hard to believe that the cylinder wouldn't be a topic of conversation. Of course, Dusty was fumbling in the dark here. She knew nothing of the circumstances surrounding the thing, the who and what and where of it all. Maybe it hadn't surfaced near Kimball's Point at all. It was at least a couple of miles from where Parson had tossed it.

And maybe it hadn't been found at all. She had only Parson's word on that, and Dusty wouldn't trade Big Jim's coffeemaker for Parson's word. All she kept getting were blank looks when she asked about the cylinder, from boaters and bartenders and sunbathers and swimmers. Maybe it was just another one of Parson's games, a way to creep back into her head. She still didn't know how he'd tracked her down.

Midafternoon she found herself just north of the town. There was a small carnival setting up in the old fairgrounds across the road from the river. Just past the grounds, to the right, she saw a sign that said Brownie's Marina and she took the turnoff.

Driving into the parking lot, she remembered the place, although it had been called something other than Brownie's back in the day. She remembered the bar Scallywags too; its name hadn't changed. She was pretty sure she'd gotten drunk there one or twice. She might even have been there with Parson.

She did a loop around the lot and parked. She sat in her truck, watching the tackle shop and the restaurant. She hoped she'd see an angler coming in off the river, but there were none. It was overcast and windy and the river was rough; there were white-caps out beyond the pier.

There was a compound, enclosed with a chain-link fence, off to the right where a number of boats were dry-docked, a lot of them basket cases. The gate was open and near the entrance a man in a dirty captain's cap was hunched over an old Mercury outboard, the motor hanging from the back of an aluminum punt.

The man gave Dusty a very thorough and somewhat lascivious once-over when she walked up to say hello. She was wearing jeans and a wifebeater and didn't feel much like an object of anyone's desire, but maybe the man's contact with the opposite sex was rare. Even from twenty feet away he was pretty ripe, which would have contributed to that.

"Getting ready to go out?" she asked.

"Yeah," he replied. "I get this damn old Merc to start."

The man had the spark plug out of the

motor and he'd been vigorously cleaning the electrodes with a wire brush when Dusty approached.

"You got spark?"

"Sure I got spark," the man said. He screwed the plug back into the block and tightened it down. "Um . . . how can you tell?"

Dusty stepped forward and grabbed the starter cord in one hand and the loose plug wire in the other. She pulled the cord several times, felt nothing from the wire.

"Dead," she told the man. "How long since this thing ran?"

"Last year."

"Probably a dirty magneto," Dusty said.

"That's what I was thinking," the man said.

Dusty knew it would be Labor Day before the guy found the magneto. She flipped open the clips on the motor's cover and removed it.

"You fish around here?" she asked.

"All the time."

"What's your name?"

"Wally," the man said.

ELEVEN

After Virgil did the morning chores he walked out into the wheat field north of the barn. The night before had been clear, leaving a heavy dew, and the heads of wheat were thoroughly soaked. It would be at least noon before the field was dry enough to combine.

Virgil walked back to the house and changed his clothes and drove into the city. First he stopped at the DMV, then drove to the police station on Arch Street. He parked again in the lot a couple of blocks from the station, the lot where he had encountered Buddy Townes on his last visit. He didn't see Buddy this time but, approaching the station along the street, he did see a man who looked very familiar scurrying out the front door. Virgil couldn't make out the face but there was something about the body language that resonated. The guy was short and squat and as he hurried across the

153

street, he put a cigarette in his mouth and tossed the empty pack to the pavement. He got into a brown sedan and drove away, but as he pulled into traffic he turned and looked directly back at Virgil.

And then it came to Virgil. The guy littering the street looked a lot like the guy who had stolen his boat. He might even have been wearing the same suit.

And he was coming out of the metro police station.

Virgil went inside and approached the front desk. The place was busy, unlike the last time he'd been there, and he had to wait ten minutes before he could talk to one of the two cops who were handling things. The officer he drew was large, red-faced with heavy jowls and wispy blond hair, which he combed straight forward from the back to cover a balding crown.

"Can I do for you?"

"I want to talk to Detective Malero," Virgil said. "But I have a question first. You notice a guy in a brown suit, just left here a few minutes ago?"

"Did I notice a guy?" the red-faced cop asked.

"Stubby little guy in a brown suit. He just walked out."

"I don't know, pal," the cop said. "I'm up

154

to my ears. What about him?"

Virgil turned to the other cop at the desk, a woman with short dark hair. She was the one who had taken Virgil's story the first time. She was writing something on a pad but she had clearly been listening.

"You see the guy?" Virgil asked.

The woman finished whatever she'd been writing and slid the paper out of sight below the counter. "What's this about?"

"I was here a couple of days ago, reporting a stolen boat," Virgil said. "I talked to you. You remember?"

"I remember."

"The guy in the brown suit — I think that was the guy who took it."

The woman shrugged. "I never got a look at him. We have people coming and going."

Virgil could see how it was now. He regarded the woman a moment longer, long enough to make her uncomfortable, then he turned back to the red-faced cop. "Is Malero here?"

They made him wait another half hour before leading him upstairs, to the large open office with the bank of desks where he had last talked to the detective. Malero was drinking coffee, his feet up, joking with two other cops in suits. When Virgil approached, he gave him a look that suggested he didn't recognize him, and kept on talking. Vigil sat down without being asked and took his brand-new boat registration from his pocket and placed it on the desk in front of the cop. Malero never gave it a glance. When the other two detectives moved away, he leaned back in his chair to regard Virgil. He was very close to smirking.

"You're back," he said. "Has your attitude improved any?"

"Last time I was here I was pissed off because somebody pretending to be a cop stole my boat," Virgil said. "My boat is still missing so I guess my attitude is about the same."

Malero nodded, staring absently across the room, as if already bored with the conversation. "What can I do for you to-day?"

Virgil picked up the registration and pushed it toward the cop. "Registration for my boat. You know, so you can start looking for it."

Malero glanced briefly at the paper but didn't pick it up. "That's today's date. How can you register a boat you don't have?"

"All you need is the serial number and eighteen dollars," Virgil told him. "I got the number and a bill of sale from the previous owner. I can give you his address if you want

156

to talk to him."

"What the hell is this?" Malero said angrily, flipping the registration back across the desk. "You're up to something. Is this an insurance scam?"

"If it is, it's not a very good one," Virgil said. "The boat wasn't insured."

Malero made a point of looking at his watch. He took a pen from his pocket and hastily scrawled out the serial number from the registration. "All right, buddy. We'll keep an eye out for your boat. We'll put our best men on it."

"Don't you want a description?"

The cop shook his head, clearly aggravated at this disruption of his day. "Yeah." He sighed.

"Cedar strip. Sixteen-foot Peterborough, built in the fifties. Got a twenty-horse Johnson on it."

After watching the detective write *wooden boat* on the paper, Virgil got to his feet and leaned over to retrieve the registration. He folded it carefully and put it in his shirt pocket. Malero smiled up at him, an unctuous little grin that told Virgil that no one would be looking for his boat.

"One more thing," he said to the cop. "The guy who took it was here at the station a little while ago. Kind of an interesting development. Maybe you should put your best men on *that.*"

It was noon when Virgil got back to the farm and by then the wheat was dry enough to harvest. Virgil had a quick lunch and then headed out into the north field. The clutch plate in the combine blew apart a half hour later, after he'd made a single pass through the crop. Virgil climbed down from the cab and walked to the machine shed, where he loaded his tools in the back of his pickup and returned to the combine. It took him almost two hours to remove the damaged clutch and he spent the better part of an hour on the phone before he finally located the replacement parts at a dealer east of Red Hook. The parts man said he could courier it out the next morning and it should arrive sometime in the afternoon. Virgil thought about it and then said he would drive over and pick it up.

The combine, with the drive train now in pieces, remained stalled in the middle of the field, a couple hundred yards behind the barn. By the time Virgil returned with the new clutch plate, it was six o'clock. He spotted the note pinned to the milk house door when he pulled up to the barn. He walked over to have a look and saw it was a page torn from a notebook, with *Ulster Veterinary Clinic* across the top. The note was from Mary Nelson:

Sorry to spring this on you but I was in a bind. Where are you anyway? Those two newbies in the field were rescued this morning from some asshole who used them in plowing competitions when he wasn't starving them. I might have someone interested in them. I'll call you later. Don't be mad at me, Virgil.

The vet had drawn a happy face at the end of the note. If Mary thought that was going to improve Virgil's mood, she was mistaken. She'd been talking him into taking possession of abused horses for a few years now and every time she showed up with another sad case in her trailer, Virgil told her it was the last one. Today he didn't even get the satisfaction of doing that.

He walked around the barn to have a look in the front field and saw, among the small herd of horses that had been there when he'd left a couple hours earlier, two huge draft horses, chestnut with white markings. They might have been Percherons but Virgil was no expert. They were mangy-looking and filthy and bone thin, standing by themselves in the far corner of the field, picking at the pasture at their feet.

"Jesus H. Christ," Virgil said, and headed out to the field to fix the combine.

If things went smoothly, he would just have time to do the repairs before dark. He could be back combining when the dew burned off the next morning. Of course, that was assuming that things ran smoothly, and they rarely did. Hell, a man couldn't even go to pick up combine parts without a couple of unwanted horses being dumped on him in his absence.

He was halfway up inside the Massey, with just his legs showing, trying to align the pilot bearing, when he thought he heard a vehicle up near the house. Thinking it might be the person allegedly interested in the two draft horses, he ducked down to have a look between the drive pulleys but didn't see anything, although the driveway was partially concealed by the barn. He watched a moment and went back to work, where he was having no luck fitting the clutch and the pressure plate together. The parts man at the dealership had tried to sell him an alignment tool, but for sixty-five dollars Virgil had declined. He was beginning to regret the decision when everything suddenly fell into place. Then he heard the woman's voice.

"I'm looking for Virgil Cain."

So apparently there had been a vehicle in the drive.

"Yeah?" he replied.

"You Virgil Cain?"

"You come for the horses?"

The woman hesitated. "Um . . . no."

"What can I do for you?"

"Police."

Virgil smiled. It was about time. Apparently somebody had been listening to him after all. Malero said he'd put his best men on the case. Maybe his best man was a woman. Virgil snugged down the bolts on the plate and came out from under the combine.

"I was hoping that somebody —" he began, and he stopped.

The woman standing in his wheat field was early thirties, he would guess, medium height and very fit, with short dirty-blond hair and beautiful green eyes. She had a tattoo of a serpent on her right forearm, and another, this one a panther, on her shoulder, the back legs of the cat disappearing into her tank top.

"Thought you said you were a cop."

"I am," she said. "Undercover."

161

Virgil took a rag from his pocket to wipe his hands. "I'm Indiana Jones."

"Don't get smart with me," she said. "I'm tracking the cylinder you found. I got some questions for you."

"You got a badge?" Virgil asked. "Last phony cop showed up, at least he had a badge. Why don't you take a hike?"

He went back under the combine and picked up the wrench. He didn't have enough daylight left to get everything back together and would have to finish in the morning. At least he could tighten down the clutch so it remained in place.

"Okay, I'm not a cop," he heard the woman say.

"And you're obviously not familiar with the phrase *take a hike,*" Virgil said as he worked.

"I still need to talk to you."

"About what?"

"The cylinder. I told you that."

"You also told me you were a cop," Virgil reminded her. "You should realize that when the first thing out of your mouth is a lie, then I'm probably gonna be a little skeptical about the second thing out of your mouth. You're not running for office, are you?"

"Jesus Christ," the woman said. "Just that

I'd heard you'd been to the cops the other day and —"

Virgil was interested enough now that he came out from under the combine again. "Who'd you hear that from?" he asked.

The woman shrugged.

"I said who'd you hear that from?"

"You know a guy named Wally, doesn't know shit about outboard motors?"

"I know Wally. I didn't know he was so loose-lipped. I guess a pretty girl shows up and he starts to babble."

"If she can clean a magneto, he does," she said, letting the pretty-girl comment pass. "Wally says you were out fishing and you hooked the cylinder with your anchor. Off Kimball's Point."

"Wally's just a fountain of information, isn't he?"

"The man could use a bath."

Virgil smiled. "What's your name anyway? You know mine."

"Dusty," the woman said after some consideration.

"Dusty who?"

"All you need to know," she told him.

"All I need to know," Virgil scoffed. "Is that the same as that other peckerhead saying he'd be in touch? What the hell is going on here anyway? I'm the only one minding his own damn business and look what I get. One day I'm out fishing and I pull up this cylinder — that I'm pretty sure is not full of Jell-O pudding — and the next thing I know, I got a phony cop who sticks a gun in my face, tells me I'm a criminal, and then steals my boat. And now I got you. Whoever the hell you are."

"I'm not trying to pull anything," Dusty said. "I'm looking for the cylinder. Simple as that."

"What's in it?"

"Doesn't matter," she said. "What's in it has nothing to do with you."

"Yeah?" Virgil asked. "Did you hear the part about the guy stealing my boat?"

"Okay," Dusty said. "You're right. You got fucked on that count. Maybe I can help you out. Tell me about the guy who did it. He claimed he was a cop?"

Virgil glanced toward the sky to the west. The sun was gone and it would be dark in fifteen minutes. He exhaled, resigned to having a conversation with the woman. "Let's start back to the barn. I'm going to get the third degree, I might as well be drinking a beer while I'm getting it."

They walked across the field together. At the barn the woman stood by as Virgil filled the water trough for the horses and gave them a half bushel of feed. He carried extra grain to the two draft horses, still in the corner of the field. They didn't look as if they'd been properly fed in weeks. The woman's truck, an older Ford with rust issues and mud splattered on the doglegs behind the wheel wells, was parked halfway between the house and the barn. After he shut the tap off Virgil went into the old milk house, where he kept his beer in a round-shouldered fridge that was over fifty years old but miraculously still running.

"I'd offer you a Budweiser, Officer," he said, "but I assume you don't drink when you're on duty."

She smiled at him. "Wally never mentioned you were a comedian. I'll take a beer." She was standing in the doorway, her hip against the jamb, arms crossed. She'd been following him since they'd left the field and every time she'd tried to engage, he'd held up his hand, as if telling her to wait.

Virgil gave her the beer and pulled an old vinyl-and-chrome kitchen chair around and sat. He indicated another chair to the woman but she stayed on her feet. There was something cautious about her, like a stray dog, even though it had been she who had shown up uninvited. But stray dogs did that too, always on the prowl for scraps of

165

something, while poised to run away. It seemed as if the woman was no different. Virgil leaned back against the wall, lifting the chair's front legs off the concrete, and took a long pull on the beer before smiling at her.

"So you're what a drug dealer looks like these days," he said.

"Nice try," she said. "But you're not even close. What makes you think there's drugs involved anyway?"

"The fact that I wasn't born yesterday?"

She drank from the bottle. "I was you, I think I'd be assuming that the less I know, the better. I can see you wanting your boat back. I'll try to help you out with that — if you tell me what I want to know."

Virgil smiled. "I got a feeling you already know a lot more than I do."

"Maybe not. All I heard was basically what you told me. You found the thing and brought it into dock, then an hour later somebody shows up, flashes a badge, and takes it away from you."

"*And* my boat."

"Yeah, yeah. We won't forget about the boat. The part I don't get is how it happened that fast."

"Somebody made a phone call."

"I figured that," she said. "But that's still

pretty fucking fast. I could see the dude showing up the next day maybe. Takes time for word to get out, especially out here in the boonies. So who made the call? And who was the guy that showed?"

Virgil shrugged. "Claimed to be Albany police. But I went to the station the next morning and they say they had nobody out that way seizing a boat or anything else. They seemed pretty damned sure of it, since they have no jurisdiction out here. So I have to think that the guy was a phony. The badge looked real, and the gun sure as hell looked real, but I guess you can fake anything nowadays. All I know for certain is that it was somebody who was real interested in that cylinder. You know — somebody like you."

She tipped the beer bottle up, glancing at the whitewash where it was peeling away from the ceiling. It occurred to Virgil that she was thinking of what to ask next.

"He did *look* like a cop," Virgil added. "You don't."

"And what do I look like?" she asked. "I mean — to a guy like you?"

"Like somebody running from the cops."

"Well, I'm not. If that's what you're worried about."

"Did you think I was worried about something?"

"No," she admitted after a moment. "So you got no idea who the guy with the badge was."

"Nope. But I saw him today."

"What? Where did you see him?"

"I drove into the city to see how the cops were doing with their make-believe investigation of my boat. And the guy walked out of the station, just before I walked in."

"You talk to him?"

"No. He was too far away and he jumped into a car and left."

The woman drank again, then wiped her mouth. She had intelligent eyes, and they moved constantly; she was like a pool player trying to figure the angles. "You tell the cops?"

"I tried. They made out like they had no idea what I was talking about. They kind of made out like *I* had no idea what I was talking about."

"So who the fuck is this guy?" the woman asked. "Something doesn't fit here. Is he a rat? Is he undercover? What's he up to?"

"I can't help you with that," Virgil said.

"I know somebody who can," the woman said. "The guy that dropped a dime on you. You got any idea who did it?"

"I got more than an idea," Virgil said. "I know exactly who called it in. Brownie, the guy that owns the marina. You know, where you and Wally share secrets."

"Wally did all the sharing. Not me."

"Now that I believe."

"Why do you think it's this Brownie?"

"He's a nosy ex-cop who was standing there inside the tackle shop watching the whole thing that day. And what he didn't see he heard from his little buddy Mudcat. Wasn't hard to figure out who made the call. The next day I asked them about it and they both lied. But they weren't very good at it."

"What's a little buddy Mudcat?"

"It ain't much, I can tell you that."

Dusty frowned but let the subject pass. "So — you always know when people are lying to you?"

"I've been right on the money with you so far."

"You're kinda fucking rude, you know that?" Dusty said. "I told you — the less I tell you, the better off you are. I'm trying to protect you, man. You should be grateful."

"Gee, thanks," Virgil said. "So you going to tell me what's in the cylinder?"

"I don't think so," Dusty said. "But I'll tell you this — I'm not all that interested in the contents, I'm just interested in who has it. My life would be much better if you'd never hooked the thing."

"And why is that?"

"Long story. I don't want to bore you."

"That's one thing you haven't done."

She took a moment, as if she might tell him more, but then shook her head. "Let's just say that I have to find it."

"Before the bad guys do?"

"Maybe," she said. She looked at the beer bottle in her hand. "Maybe I need to find it before the good guys do."

"Which side you on?"

The woman tipped the bottle back, finishing it. "I guess I'm somewhere in between. Thanks for the beer." She put the empty on top of the fridge. There was a notepad there from the vet, dust-covered, with a couple of pens alongside. She thought for a moment, then scribbled on the paper until she got one of the pens to work and wrote down her name and a number. "Here's my cell. If the guy decides to return your boat, give me a call, will you?"

Virgil took the slip of paper from her and looked at it before putting it in his shirt pocket. "I have a feeling he won't be bringing my boat back."

"You never know," Dusty said. "Maybe I

should get your number too."

"You know where I live," Virgil said. "Where you going now?"

"Find out who it was that Brownie called that day."

"And who do you figure is going to tell you that?"

"Who do you think?" she asked and she left.

Driving back to Kimball's Point, Dusty called home to check on Travis. The sitter, a teenager from across the hall, said he was sleeping, and that she was doing her homework. Dusty told her she wouldn't be late, and hoped it was true.

It was after nine o'clock and fully dark when she got back to the marina. The carnival she'd seen setting up across the road earlier was now in full swing. There was a small Ferris wheel and a tilt-a-whirl and a midway featuring various other rides and roadside attractions. A bingo game was in progress on the infield of the old fairgrounds, with a man in a tuxedo and top hat calling out the numbers. Dusty could hear the familiar loop of the calliope as she drove past.

The farmer named Virgil Cain wasn't at all what she'd expected. Growing up in the city, she and her friends had always looked down on people living out in the country, as if their rural upbringing somehow meant they lacked intelligence. It was a generalization and, like most generalizations, it didn't hold up very well as Dusty got older. Living in Kimball's Point, she'd gotten to know a lot of the locals and she'd soon discovered that they were just as smart or stupid, or together or fucked up, or honest or deceitful, as everybody else she'd ever known. Not only that, but Dusty was the one who spent three years in Albion Correctional because of some pretty stupid decisions of her own. Who was she to pass judgment on anybody else?

Virgil Cain was no rube. He actually had mocked her when she claimed to be a cop, although she probably deserved that. For somebody who was obviously pissed off about losing his boat, he was getting a kick out of the whole situation, at least to a certain extent. There was something about him she couldn't put her finger on. She thought about him, how relaxed he was in spite of her showing up under rather odd circumstances. She pictured him, leaning back in the old kitchen chair, Budweiser in hand, wearing brown twill pants and a blue cotton shirt, sleeves rolled up to reveal large ropy forearms, deeply tanned. The toes of his work boots were worn through, the steel showing.

Maybe it was that he was an ordinary guy, she decided, and the only one in the whole scenario who might fit that description. She'd been surrounded of late by people like Nick Santiago, with his leather coat and his two-hundred-dollar fedora. She doubted Virgil Cain owned a hat like that and, even if he did, she doubted he would do anything that might result in someone nailing it to a table. She found herself liking him, although he'd made it quite obvious that he didn't trust her as far as he could throw his tractor.

The lights were still on in the tackle shop when Dusty pulled up. She parked on the far side of the lot and walked over. When she entered, a sandy-haired man with a ruddy complexion and a humongous gut overhanging his belt was busy emptying out the till. Dusty could tell at a glance that the man was drunk. When he looked up at her, it seemed he needed a moment to focus. There was a glass with liquor and ice on the counter beside the till.

"Hey," Dusty said.

The man looked her up and down quickly and went back to his till.

"What do you need?"

Dusty took a couple of steps toward a display of Rapala lures. "Looking at some tackle."

"Well, I'm closing," Brownie told her. He gave her the judgmental look again. "This is pretty high-end stuff anyway."

Dusty stopped at the display and glanced over at him. "What does that mean?"

"It means I'm closed. They got tackle at Walmart."

Dusty smiled and moved away from the lures, toward him now. "You giving me a shopping tip — or is that, like, a sociological observation?"

"You take it any way you want. I'm tired and I'm going home. You carnival people been in and out of here all day and never bought shit."

Dusty stopped at another wall display and picked up a chain-link fish stringer. "You Brownie?" she asked.

"That's what the sign says."

"Brownie — used to be a cop?"

"What of it?" Brownie finished his counting and took a drink from the glass. His speech was thick with liquor.

Dusty held onto the stringer as she moved on to an array of filleting knives. She picked one up, slid it out of its sheath, and ran her

174

thumb across the edge of the blade. "Word I'm hearing — you're the guy made the phone call about the dude finding the cylinder."

Brownie set the glass down. "Who the fuck are you?"

Dusty held the knife to the light, sighted along its edge. "Just a carny, like you said. So who took the cylinder, Brownie?"

Brownie squinted through his little pig eyes, and she could sense his whisky-laden brain putting the pieces together. "Shit — I know who you are now. You're no carny. That'd be a step up for you. So they let you out, did they?" He began to mumble as he turned away. "Problem with the prison system in this country. We can lock the scum up, we just can't keep them locked up."

He continued to mutter as he knelt down to open a small safe encased in the concrete wall above the baseboard. He fumbled with the code a moment, entering it twice before swinging the door open. He put the money inside and closed the safe, tugging at the door to make sure it was locked, and was turning his head when Dusty slammed him from behind, hammering the side of his face into the concrete. She jerked his right arm behind him and wound the stringer around his wrist. He pulled back from the wall and she drove him forward again, this time smashing his nose into the cement block. While he was off-balance, with all his considerable weight forward, she got hold of his other wrist and wrapped it tight with the stringer, hog-tying him.

"Jesus!" he yelled.

Dusty pulled hard on the chain link, jerking his arms up behind him. "You know, for somebody in retail, you have a pretty surly attitude," she told him.

Brownie's nose was gushing blood. He tried to struggle to his feet and when he did, she yanked on the stringer and pushed him down. "I don't know anything about it!" he screamed.

"Try again," Dusty said.

Brownie went limp, gasping for breath. The blood from his nose was running into his mouth, and he spit it out onto the carpet. "The guy brings the cylinder in and then the cop shows," he said. "That's all I know."

"Really?" Dusty said. "That's what you want to tell me? I mean, if that's all you got for me I just might tie you off and leave you here for the night, you fat drunken fuck. You saying you're okay with that?"

"It's the truth!"

"The truth," Dusty said. She held the

176

stringer with one hand and glanced behind her. The filleting knife was where she'd left it on the counter. "I heard somewhere recently that art is truth."

"What?" Brownie's face was an inch from the concrete wall. He was sweating heavily, his hair already soaked.

"What do you know about art?"

"Art who?"

"Art, you fucking idiot," Dusty said. "Like paintings and stuff."

"What are you talking about? Let me go!"

"Who's your favorite painter?"

"What the fuck is wrong with you?"

"I like van Gogh. He was friends with Gaugin, you know. They both suffered from depression."

"Let me up, you fucking bitch!" Brownie attempted to break free and Dusty pulled on the stringer with one hand and drove her palm into the back of his head with the other. "Okay!" he whimpered.

"But you know, van Gogh was crazy," she said. "Maybe that's why I like him. I've always been attracted to crazy people. Works against me, often as not. You're not crazy, are you, Brownie?"

Brownie shook his head, the blood dripping from his nose.

"Didn't think so. Because I'm not attracted to you in the least. Drunks and liars don't really do it for me." Dusty reached for the filleting knife. "But van Gogh — dude was nuts. Cut off his own ear, you know that? Cut off his own fucking ear."

She leaned forward and, holding onto the stringer with her left hand, she showed Brownie the knife in her right. "I'm glad to hear that you're not crazy," she said. "Only a crazy man would lose an ear rather than tell me what I want to know. So who took the cylinder?"

"I don't know!"

"Okay," Dusty said, and she pulled the knife back, sliding the razor edge back along the fat man's temple and stopping it in the ridge above his right ear. "Let me know when you remember."

The blade went through the skin and into the hard cartilage and Brownie began to scream.

TWELVE

Hoffman knew the place from years earlier, but just vaguely, when it had been known as Filbert's Pool Hall, even though he didn't recall there ever being anything out front identifying it by that name, just a large green generic sign, *Billiards*. The kids and the local wiseguys had called it Filbert's; maybe that had been the name of a past owner. Hoffman had probably been in the place at one time or another — he'd been in most of the dives in the city — but he couldn't remember anything specific about the interior. It was on Third Avenue, a half dozen blocks from Jefferson Park, and smack in the middle of what the locals called the C Zone, the C standing for crack, the zone standing for either what zone usually stands for or the fact that the dopers in the area were usually zonked into another zone of one kind or another.

Hoffman was driving his sedan and Soup

was in the passenger seat, giving directions. Soup was still acting sullen about the whole thing and Hoffman had feared that he might bail on him, but he'd been there at the coffee shop that morning, as arranged. Soup's brain was still functional, when he wasn't high, and he would know that he really had no choice but to cooperate. He could leave the city but Hoffman knew he would never do that. Where the hell would he go?

Soup told him to park in the alley behind the pool hall. There was a small space there, just long enough and wide enough for two vehicles. There was a black Dodge Ram 4×4 backed into the one spot and Hoffman parked beside it. The pickup truck had a pair of steer horns fastened to the hood, reaching across the full width of the truck.

"This better be good," Hoffman said, looking at the horns as he and Soup got out.

They made their way to a steel-barred door, propped open, and a second door, made of wood, that was locked. They had to wait a few moments after Soup knocked. Then the wooden door was opened by a huge cowboy. At least he looked like a cowboy — he wore a Stetson, pushed back to reveal blond curly hair and blue jeans with black cowboy boots, along with a fancy white shirt with piping stitched diagonally toward each shoulder and a belt with a large buckle with a rearing bronco etched inside a rope corral. The man's shoulders were nearly as wide as the doorway. He showed them a wide smile, revealing perfect white teeth, in fact too perfect and too white to be his own.

Hoffman turned to Soup. "This is the guy?"

"Yeah."

"Jesus, you found me a white guy," Hoffman said. He stuck his hand out and the cowboy took it and shook it like he was working an old pump.

"This Hoffman," Soup said to the cowboy. "Yuri."

Soup hadn't mentioned a name before, and Hoffman hadn't asked. Thinking about it now, he would have preferred not to know it at all. Too late for that; he should have told Soup up front. But the cowboy was named Yuri. It didn't sound like a cowboy name, and the man who owned it didn't sound like a cowboy either.

"I am happy to meet you, Mr. Hoffman," he said in a thick accent. "Come into office."

Hoffman glanced into the poolroom out front as he passed down the narrow hallway. There were only a half dozen tables, with maybe twice that many video machines. An old man sat at the counter by the till up front, reading a magazine or maybe a racing form. There were seven or eight kids scattered about the room, playing the machines. Nobody was shooting pool. The place was a front if Hoffman ever saw one.

Yuri's office was a shit kicker's dream. The walls were covered with movie posters — *Shane, The Searchers, The Outlaw Josie Wales,* and a dozen others. A bronze sculpture of an Indian on his pony sat on a scarred wooden desk. A lasso hung from a coatrack and there was a real Western saddle, resting on a Navajo blanket, across the back of a sagging couch against the wall.

The cowboy named Yuri walked around the desk and sat down, laced his fingers behind his neck, and smiled at the two men. Hoffman sat in a chair opposite. Soup hung by the door, uncertain what to do.

"I just as soon be going now," he tried.

"You're not going anywhere," Hoffman said. "You signed on for this."

"I didn't sign on for nothing."

"Take load off, Mr. Soup," Yuri said, indicating the couch with the saddle. "Sit a spell, and we see what Mr. Hoffman has to say for himself. We see what this cop has for me."

Hoffman hesitated. It almost seemed as if the Russian, if that's what the fuck he was, was taunting him. "I got a hundred pounds of pure cocaine for you," he said defiantly. "That's what I got."

Yuri's expression did not change, although one eyebrow cocked, and he glanced quickly at Soup, who was staring at the floor, wanting only to be gone. Yuri turned back to Hoffman.

"Is my understanding that cocaine is illegal in this country," he said. "Yet here you are cop telling me this. I am just a poolroom operator." Yuri extended his long arms straight out to the sides, his palms raised, then he shrugged his shoulders in an exaggerated manner.

"I'm an ex-cop," Hoffman said. "If you really need to know, let's just say the cocaine is part of my severance package. The legality of this situation is not something we need to worry about." He made a point of taking in the shabby office before he continued. "Unless Soup found me the wrong guy. That's the case, I'll be on my way."

"Hold on to your horses, Mr. Hoffman," Yuri said. "You just get here. You are in big hurry all of sudden? Maybe I want to help with this severance package. Maybe I am civic-minded citizen. Where is this cocaine?"

"Not far."

Yuri's eyes went to the door that led outside to the alley. "You realize that I must see it, to know it is real deal, before we can discuss transaction."

"I realize that," Hoffman said. "But that's where it gets a little tricky." He hesitated, then he got to his feet. "Come on."

He led the way outside, into the alley, with the cowboy trailing and Soup bringing up the rear. Hoffman opened the trunk of the sedan to reveal the cylinder there, nestled on the bed of blankets he'd made for it that morning before carefully lowering it inside. Yuri stepped forward for a better look. He took the cylinder by one of the steel handles and tipped it forward, obviously looking for a lid or some sort of access point.

"What are you doing, cop — trying to sell me pig in a poke?"

Hoffman started to speak but then he gave Soup a look. He pulled a five from his pocket. "Soup, run across the street and get me a coffee, will you? Double, double."

Soup, chafing at being designated a gofer, took the five reluctantly, eyeing Hoffman in contempt. He turned and started out of the alley.

"And Soup," Hoffman said, "don't you get lost, boy."

When Soup was gone, Hoffman reached farther into the trunk and pulled out a manila envelope that had been tucked beneath the blankets. He retrieved an X-ray from inside and handed it to Yuri the Russian cowboy, who held it up above his head to have a look. The image was obviously of the cylinder, and inside were a dozen or so packets of something, along with a lumpy mass connected by a jumble of wires to a small rectangular device. A small rectangular device that could very well be a keyboard.

"Whoa, doggie," Yuri said. "Is little surprise in here. Like Cracker Jack."

"Rumor has it this thing's been booby-trapped," Hoffman said. "Rigged to blow if the wrong person opens it."

"Is something in there, darn tooting," Yuri agreed. "One way to find out."

"You want to open it?"

Yuri smiled and handed the X-ray back to Hoffman. "I think is maybe something you contract out, a job like this."

"Who can you trust though?"

"Maybe I know a man," Yuri said. "But let's hold up for one minute. First you are telling me you have pure cocaine and now you are telling me you have never seen it. This gives me trouble."

185

"Let's just say its reputation preceded itself," Hoffman said. "This shit came straight up from Colombia. It's been in cold storage for seven years. Waiting for you, cowboy. So what's it worth?"

Yuri shook his head. "Until I have the powder in my hand, it is worth nothing. All you have shown me is a piece of steel. I can buy steel at the junkyard." He turned to watch Soup, entering the alley with Hoffman's coffee.

"You're not going to be disappointed," Hoffman said.

"I believe you," Yuri said. "For now. I don't think a cop would come to me with bogus shit. I think this is real deal." He watched as Soup handed the coffee over. "However. If this is the cops setting me up — then I kill you and I go to jail. You are dead and I am in jail. Not good situation for anybody." He paused. "Oh, I kill you too, Soup, for bringing this to me. Did not mean to leave you out. Is bad deal for everybody. Do you agree?"

"Shit, got nothin' to do with me," Soup said. "This ain't my deal."

"It's not a setup," Hoffman said.

"Then we have no problems," Yuri said. "So we go, we find a man to cut open the thing."

186

Hoffman's cell rang and he answered it to hear Brownie barking at him. "Slow down," he said. "What's going on?"

"You still got the cylinder?" Brownie asked.

"I'm looking at it right now," Hoffman said. Yuri was watching and listening.

"Well, somebody's on your trail, and they're fucking serious."

"Who?"

"The original owner. Or one of them."

Hoffman considered this. "You at the marina?"

"Yeah."

"On my way."

He hung up the phone and turned to Yuri. "We're going to have to postpone this. I got something to take care of."

"Wait one dang minute here," Yuri said. "You are suddenly going to vamoose? You show me this, and tell me story about pure cocaine from Colombia, and now you leave? Are you cock-teasing me, Mr. Hoffman?"

"No," Hoffman said. "There's not a problem."

"But you get phone call just now and you are talking about cylinder," Yuri said. "This I know because I am eavesdropping. And I hear you say who? And then you say you are on your way. How do I know you did

187

not just receive other offer? Tell me how do I know this?"

"It's nothing like that." Hoffman closed the trunk lid. "Just somebody sticking their fucking nose in where it doesn't belong."

Yuri thought for a moment. "You know what, Mr. Hoffman? I did not go looking for you. *You* came looking for me. But now I think your business is my business. I think I will stick to you like glue. Until we see what we have here." He paused, glancing at Soup. "I think we are a team, the three of us."

Hoffman wasn't happy with the new partnership, but the Russian made it clear that it wasn't up for discussion.

"Ain't it funny how things turn round, Hoffman," Soup said. "Bottom rail on top now."

Brownie's right ear was still attached to his head, but that was the only positive he could take from the incident. He'd gone to emergency and had things stitched back together, after concocting a story about a mast from a catamaran falling on him. The doctor who had sewn him up, a young woman who had been summoned to the hospital from some social event, questioned the story but only briefly. It seemed as if she didn't believe it for a minute, but also that she didn't care. The fact that Brownie had a noseful of dried blood and was reeking of scotch and fear-induced sweat might have affected her bedside manner. She put in forty-odd stitches, taped some gauze over the wound, and returned to her party.

Brownie was back at work the next day, running the tackle shop and managing his pain with aspirin and vodka. Before opening the shop he'd spent a good half hour cleaning his own blood from the glass counter, the carpet, the concrete wall, and even the front of the safe. The woman's fingerprints would be in evidence all around the shop, he knew, but he didn't need them. He knew exactly who she was. If he wanted her arrested, all he had to do was call the police. But the police would want to know why the woman had attacked him. Brownie knew the answer to that too, but he didn't feel like telling it to the local cops. So he called Dick Hoffman instead.

Hoffman showed up a little past noon, with a large grinning cowboy and a shifty-eyed skinny black kid who was either an addict or a refugee from some ghetto hell or both. Mudcat McClusky was sitting there when the trio arrived, finishing his lunch. He had a dab of mustard on his nose, the result of attempting to ingest in two gulps a foot-long hot dog from the carnival across the road. When Brownie saw Hoffman and his little crew walking across the parking lot, he told Mudcat to wipe off his nose and go check the cash box at the boat launch.

Mudcat met the three men as he was going out and they were coming in, and he slowed at the sight of them, glancing back toward Brownie before leaving; Mudcat was a nosy man and it was clear he wasn't happy about being dismissed. When he had quizzed Brownie earlier about his ear, Brownie had snapped at him and advised him to leave it alone.

When Hoffman entered, he walked directly over to Brownie, standing behind the counter. The cowboy commanded the middle of the room while the junkie held back by the door. Hoffman indicated the bandaged ear.

"They did that?" Hoffman asked.

"Forty fucking stitches' worth," Brownie said.

"And it was Parson?"

Brownie didn't reply for the moment. He looked at the cowboy, who was standing spread-legged, still smiling at God knows what. Maybe he was an imbecile. If he was, why was Hoffman traveling with a druggie

190

and an idiot? Whatever his reasons, Brownie would have preferred he had left them both outside. He was embarrassed enough to tell Hoffman the story, let alone tell it in front of a couple of strangers.

"No," he said. "It wasn't Parson. Somebody working for him, is my guess."

"Well, who?" Hoffman asked.

Brownie had a vodka and orange juice tucked down below the register, out of sight of any customers, and he reached for it now and took a drink. "It was the girl," he said, almost in a whisper.

Hoffman didn't hear. "What?"

Brownie looked up, his lips tight. "It was the girl," he said, a little louder this time.

"The girl?" Hoffman repeated. "What girl? Wait a minute — you mean the fucking girlfriend? From the boat that night?"

"Yeah."

"How the fuck did that happen? She's back running with Parson?"

Brownie thought for a moment he'd say she hadn't been alone. But he knew he'd look even worse if the truth came out. And it would. "She got the jump on me," he said. "I'm half in the bag, and she's got . . . a fucking machete or something. I'm locking up and she jumped me from behind."

"What did she want?"

Brownie took another drink. He'd gone through half a quart of Absolut and it wasn't one o'clock yet. "Asking about the cylinder. I told you on the phone."

"Asking what?"

"Who found it. Where. All that shit. What I want to know is — how the fuck does she even know about it? Why don't I get a heads-up? Maybe I could have been ready for her. I never knew the fucking bitch was even out of jail. Is Parson behind this?" He stopped, staring defiantly at Hoffman. "Lot of questions here, Dick."

Hoffman ignored them all. "Did she ask what happened to it?"

Brownie exhaled heavily. "What do you think?"

"What did you tell her?"

Brownie shook his head, disgusted at what he'd done, and pissed off that he was being forced to admit it.

"What did you tell her?" Hoffman asked again.

Brownie exploded. "What do you want me to say? That I spilled my guts? Well, I did. She was cutting my ear off! Did you some-how miss that part? She was cutting my fucking ear off!"

"What did you say?"

"I told her. All right? I told her you took

the cylinder."

"My name?"

Brownie had another drink, his nose in the plastic cup like he was inhaling the contents. He nodded his head.

"That's nice, Brownie," Hoffman said. "That's real nice."

The cowboy spoke for the first time. "I suggest you cut off his tongue too," he said to Hoffman. "To prevent further indiscretions."

"Who the fuck are you?" Brownie snapped.

"I am associate of Mr. Hoffman," the cowboy said. He smiled. "In charge of tongue removals. If he so wishes."

"Jesus Christ," Brownie said. He turned on Hoffman and indicated the other two. "What the fuck is going on here?"

"What else did you tell her?"

"Nothing."

"Nothing?"

"Listen, you better take care of me, Dick. Wasn't for me, you wouldn't have the thing to begin with. I got an idea what it's worth. You owe me."

"You're fucking right I owe you. What else did you tell her?"

"I don't know," Brownie said. He tried to remember. "I told her it turned up a couple of miles upriver. It was like she was trying to figure out if it was the real thing. She was asking about the guy who hooked it."

"Why him?"

"I don't know. I got the impression she'd talked to him."

"What's his name anyway?"

"Virgil Cain."

"And she'd been to see him?"

"Maybe. I got no idea," Brownie said. He grew defiant. "I didn't get a fucking chance to follow up because I had to go to the fucking hospital because some crazy cunt tried to cut my fucking ear off. Okay?"

The cowboy with the Russian accent got a kick out of Brownie's tirade. He actually slapped his knee. Even Hoffman smiled.

"Glad you're enjoying this," Brownie said. "Next time I'll call somebody else."

"You'll heal," Hoffman said. "What we need to know is how *she* knows. And whether she's working as a free agent or if Parson sent her."

"How would Parson know about it?"

Hoffman hesitated for a long moment. "No idea. But if she's working for him, then we know she's not going to involve the police. Because we don't want the police involved, Brownie. They don't and I don't and *you* don't. You do understand that."

"Yeah, I get that," Brownie said.

"But if she's on her own, I got no idea what she's up to," Hoffman said. "And we need to find out. So where does he live?"

"Where does who live?" Brownie asked.

"Virgil Cain."

THIRTEEN

Dusty worked until three the next afternoon and then told the foreman she needed to leave early. She could tell that he was curious. She had taken yesterday off to go to Kimball's Point and now she was asking for more time, even if it was only a couple of hours. She was still new on the job and taking time off, especially without giving good reason, was not a good idea. He told her to go ahead, but she could tell by his tone that he wouldn't tolerate her making a habit of it.

She wasn't all that thrilled about walking into the Arch Street station but there didn't seem to be any other way. Besides, it wasn't as if she hadn't been there before. In fact, she'd been there a number of times in her past, usually under arrest. She hadn't been back since the night things turned to shit on the river, and she was hoping she wouldn't run into any of the cops who had known her back then, or even earlier. Her Jefferson Park days. Cops come and go, but then seven years really wasn't a long time.

She parked along the street and walked over to the station. On her past visits to the place, she had never entered by the front door before. Under arrest, she had always been driven into the rear parking lot and brought up into the station from below.

It was a different feeling, walking through the front door, and not just because she wasn't wearing handcuffs. The place was a little cleaner out front, and the walls were covered with posters showing cops in various acts of serving the community — a smiling cop directing traffic at an intersection while a parade passed by, another helping a child on the playground, and a third tending to a wounded puppy. Apparently somebody on the force had a Norman Rockwell fixation, and that somebody had been put in charge of sprucing up the department's image. She noticed that there were no posters of clean-cut cops kicking the shit out of crackheads down by the river, or of jolly patrolmen pocketing bribes from the bar owners selling to underage students. Maybe those posters were still being made.

A woman of about fifty, in uniform, was behind the front counter, talking to an older man, who was complaining about being ticketed for something or other. There was another cop, a man also in uniform, sitting at a row of desks just beyond the counter. Dusty didn't recognize either of them.

After the woman finally convinced the man that he had to go to traffic court to vent about the horrific injustice inflicted upon him by some bylaw officer, Dusty approached her. She was taking a chance even being there but she needed to eliminate certain scenarios, and this was the first. Maybe she'd get lucky and it would be the last as well.

"Would Detective Hoffman be in?" she asked.

"I'd have to check," the woman said. As she spoke she was writing something on a pad in front of her. Dusty wondered if she was making a note about the irate old man who'd just left, in the event he really lost it and ended up on a roof somewhere with a hunting rifle. All over a parking ticket. "What's this about?" the woman asked when she finished.

Dusty shrugged. "Just need to talk to him."

The woman nodded. "And just him?"

"Yeah."

"Hold on then." The woman picked up

the phone and hit a number.

"Who's she looking for?" the man at the desk behind her asked. "Dick Hoffman?"

"Yeah."

"He's gone."

The woman put the phone down. "What do you mean — gone?"

"Took his pension. As of yesterday, I believe."

The woman turned to Dusty. "There you go. You want to talk to somebody else?"

Dusty shook her head. "No."

Walking back to her truck, she decided to take a stroll down to the farmers market, a few blocks away. She bought strawberries and tomatoes and fresh corn on the cob. It was the first corn of the season. Travis was going through an anti-vegetable stage and she would use the strawberries as a reward for his eating the corn. She would even stop for ice cream to go with the strawberries. She walked back to her truck but instead of starting it, she sat there and ate a few strawberries from the basket while she thought about what she knew, even though it wasn't a hell of a lot at this point.

On one level, things made less sense than ever. It had bothered her that the guy who had shown up at the marina and taken the cylinder had not asked Virgil Cain for any identification, or even for his name. He had taken the boat and left. That didn't sound like something a cop would do. Dusty had encountered her fair share of police and she knew that most of them would go to the other extreme, take down the names of everybody within five miles of the place, ask a bunch of stupid questions that had nothing to do with anything, and make note of the temperature and wind direction to boot. And all in that formal language they like to spout in front of a judge. Saying "persons of interest" instead of suspects, or "I attended to his residence" instead of just saying they went to somebody's house. But that hadn't been the case with the cylinder. This was strictly a hit-and-run. It was only natural for Cain to assume the guy wasn't a real cop.

But Dusty knew two things now that she didn't know before. One was that the man who seized the cylinder *was* a real cop, not a phony one. And two, it was now obvious why he'd acted the way he had at the marina. One day he seizes the cylinder and two days later he decides to retire. He had no intention of turning the dope over to the drug squad.

Or did he? What if the retirement story was bogus? If Dusty knew one thing about the police, it was that lying was their stock-in-trade. Maybe the two cops she'd encountered at the front desk were in on it. One playing ignorant and the other in the know.

One of two things could be true. The first was that Hoffman was dirty. He'd stumbled on a shitload of cocaine and decided to go free agent with it and sell it to the highest bidder. Which would explain his sudden retirement, and which meant that nobody would be trying to connect the drugs to Dusty. Whatever this cop Hoffman was going to do with the coke, he was doing it for his own benefit.

Which would mean that Dusty was out of the picture.

The second scenario wasn't as rosy. Maybe the police were running a sting. Right now they had a hundred pounds of cocaine they couldn't connect to anyone. They could dump it down the drain, but flushing it without busting anybody wasn't going to give them any satisfaction. They knew damn well it was Parson who brought the shit up from down south. And they knew Dusty had been the legal owner of the boat that brought it. So what if this was all a scam? They'd invented the story about Hoffman retiring and sent him underground. An unhappy cop looking to make a deal.

Dusty wondered now if it was Hoffman who had contacted Parson in the first place. Parson hadn't said it was a cop, but then that was Parson's way. Tell half of what he knew, and make sure half of that was bullshit. But who else could it have been, if it wasn't Hoffman? It sure as hell wasn't Virgil Cain.

She needed to find out. She really wanted to learn that Hoffman was on the take, that he was the dirtiest of cops. Then she would be out of it. She could go back to work and hope she never heard from any of them again.

Parson's business card was on the dash of the truck, where he'd tossed it that day at the construction site. She reached for it, taking note of the address, out on Van Wies Point Road. He'd moved since becoming a vintage car expert. She put the truck in gear and started across town.

The house was large and impressive and old, with leaded windows and a circular drive out front. A second driveway curled around the house, past an inground pool and down to a large brick garage that sat overlooking the river. The garage was of a more recent construction, and it had six doors across the front. It looked as if it could house a dozen vehicles.

There was a blond woman sunbathing topless on a lounge by the pool, with a cool drink by her elbow. She had pouty lips and large gold hoops in her earlobes. When Dusty drove past her in the old truck, she sat up and stared, removing her shades for a better look.

Two of the garage doors were open and a black Escalade and the red Camaro Parson had been driving at the site were parked out in front. There was a navy blue Mercedes convertible there too, new or close to it, with the top down. As Dusty pulled up, she could see Parson inside, carefully polishing the hood of a '67 Corvette.

Dusty had picked up a takeout coffee on the drive across town. She got out, coffee in hand, and walked into the garage. Once inside, she sensed another presence and glanced to her left to see Cherry leaning against a workbench, drinking a Coors Light. Cherry, with his dyed hair, his gold chains, and his pumped-up physique. Drinking that horse piss because he was worried about his waistline. Dusty hadn't seen Cherry since before she'd gone to prison. But his name had come up, and quite recently. She was surprised to see him there.

"Hey, there's my girl," Parson said, straightening up from his work.

"Your girl's over by the pool, sunburning her fake tits," Dusty told him.

Parson laughed at that, then nodded past her. "You remember Cherry," he said.

Dusty never gave Cherry a glance. "Yeah," she said.

"What do you know?" Parson asked.

"I know you're fucking with me, as usual," she said. "Why didn't you tell me the guy who's got the cylinder is a cop named Hoffman?"

"I didn't mention that?"

"No, you didn't. What the fuck is going on?"

Parson tossed the cloth onto the hood of the 'Vette. "I really don't know. How did you find out it was Hoffman?"

"I had a long conversation with the guy who phoned it in when the thing came off the river," Dusty said. "An ex-cop named Brownie, a fat fucking lush with a low threshold for pain."

"He gave Hoffman up?"

"Oh, he told me all kinds of things," Dusty said. Now she glanced at Cherry, without wanting to. He dropped his gaze to the concrete floor, as if something of interest had suddenly caught his fancy. She quickly turned back to Parson. "He told me this Hoffman has money problems, and he's looking to sell the coke to get himself square. Which is what he would tell me if that was true, but it's also what he might say if the police were trying to set somebody up here."

"Somebody like me?" Parson asked.

"That'd be good by me," Dusty said. "They nail your ass and I'll go home and sleep like a baby. No, it's me I'm worried about."

"You didn't used to be so selfish."

"I don't have time for your bullshit, Parson," she told him. "What's this guy saying? Is he trying to sell you the coke?"

"Yeah."

She exhaled. She glanced out the big doors. The blonde was again reclining on the lounge, stretched out in the sun like a lazy hound. "So you have two choices," she said as she watched the woman. "You can buy it and hope for the best, which would bite you on the ass if it turned out to be a setup. Or you could tell him to fuck off, and then you're out of it." She had a sip of coffee before turning back to Parson. "Now doesn't door number two sound like the smart choice?"

"It's my property, Dusty."

"I don't need to be reminded about whose property it is," she told him. "You forget who you're talking to? All I want is to be kept out of it. You can understand that, can't you? I did three fucking years for this."

"He was asking about you," Parson said.

The words rolled off his tongue so easily, so matter-of-fact, and yet she was almost positive he was lying. Almost. She turned and walked away from him, toward the back of the garage where a large window overlooked the river. She stood there a moment, trying to gather herself. There was no reason to believe him. He would do anything or say anything. She knew that better than anyone.

She looked past the manicured lawn to the water beyond and then she saw the boat. It was moored alongside an elaborate dock of cedar and stainless steel. At first she thought it was another Chris-Craft, a similar model, but looking closer she realized it wasn't. And when the current suddenly shifted, blowing the boat sideways slightly, she saw the name etched in gold along the bow.

Down Along Coast.

She knew that Parson would be watching her, knowing what she was seeing, and she spoke without turning. "How'd you manage that?"

"Bought it at the police auction," he said. Proud of himself. "Should've seen their faces. They had already torn it to pieces once, looking for more dope, and after I bought it they did it again, just to make sure."

"Why would you buy it?"

"I'm a sentimental guy, Dusty."

"No, you're not," she said. She turned and walked back toward him. "You have no idea how badly I want to be clear of all this."

Parson shrugged. "Technically it's your dope. You want to hide your head in the sand and pretend it doesn't concern you, go ahead. I were you, though, I wouldn't put much faith in that. I'd try to find it. Take it out of circulation and you know you're safe."

"You mean give it to you," Dusty said. "Or are you just worried about my well-being?"

"Little bit of both, Dusty."

Dusty glanced at Cherry, who had been strangely quiet the entire time. She knew why. Turning back to Parson, she removed the lid from the paper coffee cup and dumped the contents over the hood of the gleaming Corvette.

"You missed a spot," she said, and left.

FOURTEEN

There wasn't a lot of conversation leading up to it. Virgil had combined wheat all afternoon, the new clutch working like a dream, and after he'd emptied the last hopper and done the evening chores he walked up to the house, where he found a brown Taurus sedan parked in the driveway and the three of them waiting for him in his kitchen. It was nearly dark when Virgil walked in and saw them, the chubby little poser who had taken his boat under the pretense of being a cop, along with a very big drugstore cowboy and a skittish black kid who looked as if he was about to jump out a window.

The poser seemed to think he was in charge. He wanted to know if the woman named Dusty had been by to see Virgil and although Virgil wasn't at all sure about the motives of the woman named Dusty, he knew in a heartbeat he wasn't about to turn her over to this bunch.

"Never heard of her," he said. "Where's my boat?"

"Never mind your boat," the man said. "And never mind the bullshit. I know for a fact that the woman was here. What did she want?"

"She wasn't here. Where's my boat, fuckhead?"

"This man and his boat," the cowboy said, sounding amused. He had a heavy accent, Eastern European maybe.

"Tell me what the woman wanted and we'll talk about your fucking boat," the poser said. "Who's she working for?"

"I got no idea who you're talking about," Virgil said.

The cowboy began to emit grumbling sounds from his chest. Grumblings of impatience, Virgil suspected. There was a baseball bat in the back kitchen, near the door, Virgil's version of home security. If he had known what was waiting for him after seeing the sedan in the driveway, he would have picked it up on his way in.

"Why would you want to do this the hard way?" the poser asked.

"You got hearing problems?" Virgil asked. "I told you I never heard of the woman. So why don't you take your little road show here and go away? Come back when you have my boat."

"Talk, talk," the cowboy said. "Too much talk."

"You can go piss up a rope, Duke," Virgil told him.

"Duke. I like that," the cowboy said, and he hit Virgil in the temple with a hard right hand.

Virgil was expecting it, but he wasn't expecting it to be that quick. He rolled away from the punch but it still got him pretty good. He fell backward but remained on his feet, still thinking about the baseball bat, but the poser stepped in behind him, blocking the entrance. Virgil half turned and drove his work boot into the cowboy's knee, causing him to howl in pain. Virgil turned and slugged the poser flush in the face with a looping right cross. The poser went down on his back, his stubby little legs flying up in the air. For a moment he resembled a turtle on its shell, arms and legs flailing.

The cowboy was on Virgil at once, grabbing him by the shoulders and slamming him face-first into the refrigerator, rocking it back against the wall. For some reason Virgil found himself wondering if anything had spilled inside. Falling to one knee, he brought his elbow up into the cowboy's

211

balls, freeing himself from the man's grasp, then turned and hooked the big man in the jaw. But the cowboy returned the punch, snapping Virgil's head back against the fridge. Virgil lowered his shoulder and drove the cowboy backward, across the room, and up against the kitchen counter. He pounded the man in the kidneys several times with his right hand, while the cowboy hammered at him from above with both fists. He could hear the cowboy grunt in pain from the body blows and Virgil stepped back and fired a vicious uppercut to the man's jaw. The cowboy made a sound like a man about to lose his lunch and Virgil thought for a moment that he had him, and then he felt something come down hard on his skull above his left ear, dropping him to the floor. The poser, still holding the gun he'd used on Virgil's head, began to kick him, and the cowboy joined in.

"Motherfucker!"

Virgil, covering up, heard someone yell and he assumed it was the black kid, who was presumably still in the far doorway, not joining in on the fun. The two other men grew bored with kicking him after a while, it seemed, and the cowboy grabbed Virgil by the hair, pulling his head up while the poser leaned down to talk to him, the semiautomatic hovering a couple of inches from Virgil's face.

"Okay, smart guy. What did she want?"

"She wasn't here," Virgil said. He was gasping for breath and he could feel the blood oozing out of his scalp, running down his neck into his shirt collar.

The cowboy brought his large Western boot down on Virgil's left forearm. The cracking of the bone sounded like a firecracker going off. Virgil howled, cursing the man.

"Leave the dude alone!" the black kid yelled. "He just some farmer. He don't know nothin'."

"Shut up, Soup," the poser said.

"What the fuck, you 'bout to kill the man."

"I said shut up. Unless you want the same, you little prick. Take a look around, will you?"

"Look for what?"

"Phone numbers, names. Anything. She was here, she might have left a contact. Just look, Soup, make your black ass useful."

"I'll look. Leave the dude alone. He ain't done shit to you. His fucking arm done broke already."

"Maybe we break the other," the cowboy said. "Make a match."

Virgil, his teeth gritted against the pain in

his arm, knew that the woman's phone number was somewhere on the kitchen table, where he'd tossed it when he had come into the house the day she'd been there. It was probably buried in among some newspapers, junk mail and flyers. But it was there.

"Sticking to your story, asshole?" the poser asked him. He was leaning over Virgil again, his face close, his breath reeking of tobacco and bad food.

"She was never here."

The poser stood up and watched as the black kid went through the motions of searching the room. Virgil, relieved not to be looking at the gun anymore, rolled onto his side, cradling his left arm with his right, and managed to sit up, his back to the kitchen cupboards. The pain in his arm was disorienting and he thought he might be sick. He looked up to see the cowboy smiling down at him. Virgil found himself wanting to smile back, just to fuck with the man, but he couldn't quite pull it off.

The poser was ransacking the place, knocking over pots and pans, rifling through cupboards; it seemed he was more concerned with creating havoc than with actually finding anything. But the kid was going through the stuff on the table now. Virgil watched him, knowing what he was about to find, and then watching as he found it. The kid's eyes flickered over what Dusty had written and then the kid gave Virgil a quick look, no more than a flash, and slid the paper under a John Deere calendar Virgil had picked up at the co-op the previous Christmas and not gotten around to hanging up yet. The kid made a show of going through the rest of the stuff on the table, even sweeping some magazines onto the floor, probably to impress upon the poser that he was doing his job.

"Ain't nothin' here," he said finally.

"Time to break other arm?" the cowboy suggested hopefully.

The poser came back over, took the gun from his holster, and pushed the barrel against Virgil's cheek. "Was she here or not?"

"No."

The man thought for a while. "You're either telling the truth or you're the stupidest fucker I've ever seen."

The cowboy laughed. "Maybe he is both."

The poser straightened up. "Maybe. Either way I guess we're done here." He raised his voice. "Listen up, you fucking hillbilly. I'm going to find this broad and when I do, the first thing I'm going to ask her is whether or not she came to see you. If she says yes, then we'll be back. And you're not going to like it. You understand that, dummy?"

"Where's my boat, dipshit?" Virgil asked.

The poser kicked him in the jaw and he fell over, onto his left side, his weight pressing down on his broken arm. He screamed. He remembered hearing the cowboy laughing as they left.

FIFTEEN

It was after ten o'clock when they got back to the city and Yuri told Hoffman that it was too late to see his main man, as he phrased it, about cutting the cylinder open. Apparently the events of the day had convinced the Russian that Hoffman had no alternative plans with regards to the dope and so Hoffman was allowed to go home for the night. He'd had disturbing visions of the cowboy insisting on coming home with him. They agreed to meet the following day at the pool hall. Hoffman dropped Soup off on South Pearl.

"Don't you get antsy before morning and take off," Hoffman told him. "You've come this far. You might as well see it through. You gotta assume that fucking Russian is going to want to make this right with you. Give you a taste."

Soup hadn't said a single word since leaving the hick's farmhouse and he didn't say anything now. He gave Hoffman a look that suggested that he wasn't too thrilled with the taste of things so far then got out of the car and went off down the block without a word. The truth of the matter was that Hoffman didn't require Soup's presence anymore. But until he opened the cylinder and sold what was inside, he didn't want some halfwit crackhead running around the city telling everybody about it. The story just might filter back to the department. Once the thing was out of his possession, Hoffman didn't care who knew about it. Nobody was going to believe Soup over Hoffman at that point.

When he got home the light on his phone was blinking. Rather than check his messages he scrolled down the display list. His ex-wife had called once, and his bank three times. Hoffman didn't feel like listening to the messages just then, especially since he knew they were all about the same subject. Money owed.

He poured himself a rum and Coke and sat down in the dark, turned the TV on and turned it off, realizing there was nothing he wanted to watch. There never was. The only time he watched sports was when he had a bet on the outcome, and he usually lost. The eleven-o'clock news depressed him, particularly the local news, which only reminded him that the city where he worked was a cesspool. Spending a long day with the likes of Soup and Yuri the cowboy only reinforced that notion. Soup was a child of the city, and the Russian was a recent arrival and obviously a nutjob that the immigration people had typically waved through; between the two of them they represented all that had gone wrong over the recent years. The local politicians were always talking about the city making a comeback. There would be no comeback. When a thing is totally fucked, it is *totally* fucked. It wasn't a damaged car you could pound the dents out of and rebuild the engine and bring back to respectability. This city was ready for the boneyard.

There was nothing for him here anymore. He had few friends and no hobbies. He didn't golf, or fish, or spend time out in the garage building little model airplanes to display in his rec room or fucking birdhouses to sell on the front lawn. He owed a lot of money to a lot of people. There were bars he couldn't walk into because of gambling debts.

After tomorrow, he knew he was going to have to make a choice. If he made a deal with the Russian, he was only going to have enough money to get himself clear of debt. He would be back to square one, with only his pension to support him. And that monthly check wouldn't go far, not when he wasn't working, when he had nothing to do all day but go to the track, or hang out at Dunnett's.

There was another option. He could tell them all to go fuck themselves. Call the bank and inform the snotty little shit with the glasses and the blond tips that he and his bosses were the proud new owners of Hoffman's house. And tell Jackie that the alimony express was off the tracks. Her new boyfriend was supposed to be a hotshot who sold some wireless Internet gizmo to people out in the boonies. He drove a new Audi. Well, let him keep Jackie — who'd never worked a day in her life — in clothes and hair color and red wine. He hoped for Mr. Wireless's sake she'd rediscovered her sex drive, because when she was married to Hoffman it was missing in action for about ten years.

He mixed another drink, warming to the idea of cut-and-run. He could move south, to Florida, or even Arizona. Rent a place there, a one-bedroom, and live off his pension. Whatever he managed to pry out of the cowboy tomorrow would be gravy. The bank wouldn't chase him. They'd take the house, which might fetch three hundred grand on the market, and put it against what Hoffman owed, which was closer to four hundred. But they would eat it, they did it all the time. Jackie might track him down and demand a cut of his pension, but he would fuck her around as he had for years and eventually she would give up. She had basically given up on him in every other way a long time ago.

He went to bed happy with his decision and slept better than he had in months. When he got up the next morning he finally listened to his messages. There were no surprises from Jackie or the bank, but there was one that he had missed on the display. It was from the department, telling him he had to come in and sign some documents in order to initiate the processing of his pension. Hoffman took a shower and found a semiclean shirt and drove downtown.

They had the papers waiting for him at the front desk. He'd come in off the street, rather than from below. He didn't want to walk through the bullpen and listen to the comments from everybody there about his sudden retirement. He was fully aware that he wasn't well liked anyway, especially by the younger cops, the ones who believed they could make a difference by writing traffic tickets and busting street-level users and ugly hookers. The older cops understood, most of them, but then they were nearly all gone. Guys like Brownie, who for thirty years had squeezed every nickel from every situation he encountered. Brownie had figured out early on that the system didn't work so he had invented his own system. It was pay as you go, and most of the money ended up in his pocket. He would make enough righteous busts to make it appear that he was doing his job, but the rest of the time he was always willing to give a perp a break, as long as the perp was willing to show his gratitude. Hoffman had to figure that the criminal element in the city lost a good friend when Brownie retired. He was sitting out there even now, in his little bait-and-tackle shop, waiting for Hoffman to show up with a thick envelope as his reward for calling him about the cylinder. Hoffman wasn't entirely sure how he felt about that at the moment either, after Brownie had spilled his guts to the girl. Brownie might find himself in the same column as Jackie and the bank.

The woman at the front desk knew him by name and he should have remembered hers, but he didn't. She was tall and had red hair, pulled back in a ponytail. Apparently she was the one who left the message, which meant Hoffman didn't have to explain to her why he was there. He wanted to be in and out, quick as possible.

"Any idea how long this takes to kick in?" he asked her when she handed over the papers. He was thinking now that he might leave town sooner rather than later. Maybe even this week. After his business with the Russian was done, why wait around for things to go sour? There was no reason that they should, but then that's usually when they did.

"Not really," she said. "I was just told to get your signature."

They were little yellow Post-its on the pages showing Hoffman where to sign and he went through them with the pen as he talked. "I might need to know how to get in touch with a change of address," he said. He glanced up from his signing. "Thinking about downsizing, selling my house. Who would I call about that?"

"If you want to wait, I can check," the woman said.

"No," Hoffman said. "Could you leave it on my machine at home?"

"Sure."

Hoffman signed the last sheet and pushed

the papers across the desk.

"Oh, there was somebody here looking for you yesterday," the woman said as he turned to go.

He stopped. "Who?"

"Some woman. Wouldn't give her name."

"What'd she look like?"

"You know, one of those tough girls. Tats, short blond hair. Somewhere around thirty, thirty-five."

"What did she want?" Hoffman asked.

"She wouldn't say that either. She didn't want to talk to anybody but you."

Hoffman stood, thinking for a while. She was getting around. At least this time she hadn't cut anybody's ear off.

"She leave a contact number?" he asked.

"No. I told her you were taking your pension and she left."

"You told her that?"

"Yeah."

Great, Hoffman thought. Didn't anybody know how to keep their mouth shut?

"Okay," he lied. "I know who it was now. Some little snitch always trying to sell me useless information."

He walked outside onto the sidewalk, where he lit a cigarette and glanced around nervously. He wondered if she was in the area. Maybe she was sitting in her car along

Grand Street, watching him this minute. What the fuck did she want? She had a lot of nerve, chasing down a metro detective. At the station yet. She could go back to jail for what she did to Brownie, but apparently she'd known that Brownie wouldn't be reporting her. If she knew Brownie wasn't straight, then she would have figured out the same about Hoffman, especially after she found out that Hoffman had suddenly retired. But what was her angle? Was she working for Parson, or was she on her own this time, looking to score? She probably figured the cylinder owed her something after doing the stretch in prison.

What Hoffman did know was that the quicker he pawned the dope off on the Russian cowboy, the better. If the little bitch got in his way before that, she was going to regret it. Hoffman wasn't Brownie, getting caught with his guard down. It was a pretty good bet that he'd been drunk when the woman found him. It would be a different story if she came after Hoffman; he would shoot her in the fucking face. Nobody had invited her to the party.

The guy from Rochester showed up at five thirty to look at the Corvette and twenty minutes later, after taking it for a drive, he offered Parson $55,000 for the car. Since it was fifteen grand less than the asking price, Parson thanked him for stopping by and wished him a nice drive home. They settled ten minutes later for $68,000. The man had a cashier's check for the fifty-five — in case he got lucky on the first offer, Parson assumed — and he paid the remainder in cash from a wad of new hundreds he'd brought along as backup. They did the paperwork at Parson's desk and then had a shot of Woodland Reserve to seal the deal. The man said he would be back in the morning, with his own plates, to pick up the car, and left.

When he was gone Parson began to tear down the Hemi from the 'Cuda convertible he bought at the auction. After draining the oil and removing the pan and pump, he rotated the engine on the stand and removed the dual carbs, the intake manifold, and the heads. There was almost no ring ridge on the cylinders, meaning that the mileage showing on the odometer was probably genuine. After pulling the crankshaft and the pistons, he wiped down his tools, put them away, and decided to call it a day.

He was sitting at his desk, in front of his laptop, drinking another bourbon while he watched one of his cars close on eBay when Cherry walked in. Parson indicated the bottle and Cherry poured himself a shot. He was acting a little nervous but Parson knew that he got that way from time to time, especially back when he'd been heavily into the steroids. Parson suspected he still cycled from time to time.

Cherry angled his chair so he could see the computer screen. It was the Jaguar roadster and the bidding had eight minutes left. The current bid was at $41,000 and it had cleared the reserve.

"What's she been up to?" Parson asked, watching the screen.

Cherry shrugged. "After she left here she went home. Went to work the next day. I drove by the site at noon."

"What does she do at night?"

"Not much, looks of it. Her truck's always outside her place."

Parson logged onto the site, entered one of his alternate membership names — NYC03 — and upped the bid a thousand dollars. "Where's she living?" he asked.

"Arbor Hill, crummy apartment building on Clinton," Cherry said. He indicated the laptop. "You're going to scare that boy off."

Parson sat watching the screen. "Nah, he's got the hook in him." He clicked on the bid history to get the name. "MIKEY42 has got the fever."

The bid went up another thousand. Six minutes left. Parson waited thirty seconds and bid again.

"She got a man?" Parson asked.

"Not that I've seen," Cherry said, still watching the screen. "One of these times he's not going to bite. Then what?"

"Then I've bought my own car. I'll wait a couple of weeks and relist, claim that NYC03 is a deadbeat buyer. No harm, no foul. But this guy isn't going anywhere."

"Doesn't mean that he'll overpay."

"He will though. If he was sitting here with us, the car parked across the room, he probably wouldn't. But this Internet buying is a drug." The bid went up another grand. "See — it turns into a pissing contest. *Mano a mano*. MIKEY42 doesn't want to get his ass kicked by NYC03." Parson bid again and it bounced right back. "Boy's ego just cost him another two grand."

In the end, the Jag sold for $48,000. Parson exited the site and poured more bourbon for himself.

"What about a kid?" he asked.

"What?"

"Does Dusty have a kid?"

"Yeah. I thought I told you that."

"I would have remembered," Parson assured him. "How old?"

"Shit, I don't know. Little fucker. She leaves him at some day camp on Lark."

Parson was quiet for a time. "What's he look like?"

"He looks like a little kid. I've only seen him from a couple of blocks away."

Parson left it alone then, sat nursing his drink.

"I don't trust her," Cherry said.

"Dusty?" Parson said. "No, she's okay. She might hate me but she would never roll over. She was going to do that, she would have done it when she was looking at time. You can bet they offered her a deal back then. She wants nothing to do with this and that's why she'll come through. To get herself clear." Parson glanced over at Cherry. "Especially if she's got a kid."

"She wants out of it, let her go. I'll take Hoffman out myself. Pop him and take the dope and that's it."

"Sure." Parson reached for the bottle. "By the way, where is it?"

"The dope?"

"Yeah."

Cherry shook his head. "I got no idea."

"There you go. Pop Hoffman and we might never find it. Dusty'll find it because she believes she *has* to find it. And when she does, we'll make it straight with Mr.

Hoffman. I hope he's taking good care of my inventory. It won't go well for him if he isn't." Parson laughed as he thought about it. "Actually, it's not going to go all that well for him either way."

"That happens, I think we should eliminate Dusty too," Cherry said. "Why leave her walking around? It's loose ends, Parson, and you don't leave loose ends. You never have."

Parson turned an eye on Cherry. "No. Dusty gets a pass. I told you — she's straight up. Maybe she hates me, but keep in mind she has good reason to. She gets a pass, Cherry."

Cherry fell silent as he finished his drink. A few minutes later, he got up to leave, saying he had something to do. Parson stood and watched him drive away, then he sat down and logged back online. Maybe he'd find a bargain out there tonight.

Sixteen

Virgil had put the number in his pocket before leaving for the hospital and since then he had gone back and forth in his mind about calling her. There was no question that his arm was broken, but he'd left home thinking that he could go into emergency, have a cast put on, get a scrip for some painkillers, and be back home by midnight or so. It hadn't worked out that way. The doctor on duty had taken one look at the X-ray and told Virgil he was going to need surgery, and probably a rod inserted in his arm to keep the bone in place while it healed. That wouldn't happen until the next day so they stitched together the cut in his scalp and admitted him, loading him up with Demerol for the night. The doctor who did the stitching, an attractive young woman named Stone, asked how he injured the arm and when Virgil told her he fell out of the hay mow she shook her head in disgusted dismissal and walked away. Virgil got the impression she'd been lied to before.

He had surgery at nine the next morning and an hour or so after his head cleared from the anesthesia he called the woman named Dusty on the phone in his room. He had decided against it at one point, thinking he didn't want to involve her any further, but he was worried that she was already in deeper than she knew. After all, they had shown up at his place looking for *her*.

Her cell rang once and went to voice mail. That was fine by Virgil; he could give her the bare bones of the thing and avoid going into detail. He left a short message, telling her that the three men had paid him a visit and advising her to be on the watch. He hoped his tone would convince her that these guys meant business, but at the same time he didn't want to scare her too much. Virgil didn't think she scared all that easily anyway. He didn't mention the fight, or the fact that he was in the hospital with a broken arm. The information wasn't going to do her any good.

The surgeon came in around four o'clock in the afternoon to check on him. Dr. Stone was with him. After the surgeon examined the arm and left, she told Virgil he could probably go home the next day. What she didn't know was that Virgil had a herd of orphan horses and three dozen head of beef cattle that needed tending. Not to mention another fifteen acres of wheat to come off. When she left, Virgil got out of bed and found his clothes in a locker and got dressed. He was sharing the room with a kid of about ten or eleven who'd had his appendix removed the day before. The kid watched as Virgil tossed the gown on the bed.

"You can't leave," the kid said. "The doctor said."

"She did?"

"Yeah. Like, five minutes ago."

There was a tray of food beside the bed, which Virgil hadn't touched. "I'll give you my pudding," he told the kid.

"That stuff is crap," the kid said.

"Why do you think I'm leaving?"

Nobody bothered him as he made his way to the elevator and down to the ground floor and out the rear entrance to the parking lot. From forty yards away, he could see his truck had a ticket on the windshield. He'd only figured on being there a couple of hours. Beside his pickup was a dark blue F150, the same one he'd seen at his farm a couple of days earlier.

Dusty was behind the wheel, watching

him walk across the lot. When he got close, she climbed out and stood there looking at him. She was wearing jeans and work boots and a faded green tank top. He watched her taking him in, the cast on his arm, his right eye swollen half shut, the stitches in his scalp.

"Aren't you pretty?" she said.

"I've been prettier."

"I would hope so."

"How'd you know I was here?"

She pulled her phone from her pocket, flipped it open and shut. "Call display, dude. You called from the hospital and your truck's in the lot."

"So you really are a detective."

"You didn't mention that you got the shit kicked out of you," Dusty said.

"Must have slipped my mind."

"Right. What did you do to piss them off?"

Virgil shook his head, dismissing the question, and walked over to pick the ticket from his windshield. Thirty dollars.

"I asked you a question," she said, standing behind him.

He turned. "You want to get something to eat?" he asked. "I couldn't warm up to that hospital food."

She hesitated a moment. "I'll drive," she said.

They went to a takeout place called Ben's Best Burgers a couple of blocks away. Dusty called it the Triple B, and vouched for the food. They both got burgers and fries, root beer for Dusty and water for Virgil. They ate in her truck.

"So three guys?" she asked.

"Yeah," Virgil said. "The phony cop who stole my boat, and a big galoot in a cowboy hat. Had a thick accent, Russian or something close. And a skinny black guy, wasted-looking. The phony cop called him Scoop or Snoop, something like that. But he was just a bystander. He did you a favor though; they were searching the place and I saw him hide your phone number."

"Why would he do that?"

"No idea. But he did it."

Dusty took a bite of the burger and chewed it, thinking. "So they showed up looking for me?"

Virgil shrugged and ate some fries. The inside of his mouth was cut and it made chewing difficult. It was too bad; the food was good and he had a feeling he was going to end up throwing it away.

"Did you tell them I'd been around to see you?" she asked.

"I don't recall mentioning it."

"So they got rough," she said. "Why didn't

you just tell them?"

"I didn't like the way they were asking."

Dusty sipped her root beer. "You're pretty fucking loyal to somebody you don't even know," she said. "Shit, I might be ten times as bad as them."

Virgil smiled. "That would make you pretty bad."

She seemed to think about that as she wrapped up her garbage and stuffed it into the bag the food had arrived in. She wiped her mouth and put the napkin in the bag too. She sat quietly for a time, looking out the windshield, before finally speaking.

"He's not a phony cop," she said. "He's a real cop, a dirty detective named Dick Hoffman. I got no idea who the other two are."

"How do you know this?"

"Brownie told me. The same Brownie who dropped a dime on you."

"He wouldn't tell me shit," Virgil said.

"I found him to be very forthcoming," Dusty said. "We bonded over a discussion of nineteenth-century Dutch post-impressionist painters."

"I'm not even going to ask."

"Well, it was Brownie who made the call. Hoffman grabbed the cylinder. And your boat. And the next day he retired from the force. Which *maybe* means he has no intention of turning the cylinder in."

"Where's the maybe in it?" Virgil asked. "If he was on the level, then my boat would be in a compound somewhere and the police would have some knowledge of all this. It's not, and they don't. Which means that this Hoffman guy is as crooked as a dog's hind leg."

"You're pretty smart for a farmer."

"Then I'd hate to see stupid. Look at my face."

Dusty sighed. "I don't know what the fuck is going on. The police could be involved still, looking for somebody to pin this on. The only one I trust is you, and that's because I think you know less than me. That, and you took a beating because you're too dumb to tell these guys what you know when you don't know anything."

"I'm not sure if that was a compliment or an insult."

"Both," she decided.

She drained the last of her root beer, staring at the burger joint across the parking lot. A kid came out the back door, carrying a bulging green garbage bag, which he stuffed into an already overfull Dumpster. Glancing around, he lit a joint that he fished from his shirt pocket, took two long tokes on it, and went back inside.

Dusty turned to face Virgil. "All I want is for things to go back the way they were before you found that cylinder. You couldn't have just cut the fucking rope? I'd have bought you a new anchor."

"Next time," he said. He'd only managed to eat half the burger and so he wrapped it up to take home with him. He needed to go soon; he had chores to do. "Where were you when I called you?" he asked.

"At work."

"Where is work?"

"Right now at a new subdivision over in Rensselaer," she said. "I'm a carpenter. Framing mostly."

Virgil nodded and tried one more french fry before giving up.

"What I can't figure is why Hoffman and his little posse are looking for me," Dusty said. "It's like he's running scared."

"Scared of who?"

"I don't know. Parson maybe."

"I'll need a scorecard pretty soon," Virgil said. "Who is Parson?"

"The guy who owns the cylinder."

"Is he somebody to be scared of?"

"If you're Hoffman, he is."

"What about you — you scared?"

"Nah," she said. She started the truck and

they pulled out of the lot and headed back toward the hospital. Virgil watched her as she drove but she never looked over at him.

"So what's your connection to Parson?" he asked.

"True confessions is over," she said. "I just figured I should tell you what you're up against. I was you, I'd forget about the boat."

"Well, I'm not going to forget about it," Virgil said. "Tell you the truth, I'm beginning to take this personally."

Now she did look at him, her eyes going from the cast on his arm to the arc of stitches in his scalp. "I could see how that might be."

She pulled into the hospital lot and parked beside his truck. She waited a moment before putting it in park, something clearly on her mind. "I really need to find that cylinder."

"To sell?"

"No," she said adamantly. "I'd toss it off the Dunn Bridge. In a heartbeat." She exhaled before glancing over. "You wouldn't have a piece, would you?"

"A handgun?"

"Yeah," she said casually. Too casually, Virgil thought. "Might come in handy with Hoffman and his boys looking for me. I could score one in my old neighborhood, but it's kind of tricky."

Virgil shook his head.

She waved the notion aside. "Just a thought."

"Right," he said. "But you're not scared?"

She smiled at him. "You gonna finish those fries?"

SEVENTEEN

After leaving the station, Hoffman drove over to the poolroom. Soup was already there, sitting on the overstuffed couch in the Russian's office, drinking coffee. Yuri was wearing the clothes he'd worn the day before. Hoffman could see flecks of blood on the white shirt, blood from the hick they had kicked around the kitchen of the farmhouse the night before. Why couldn't the man change his shirt? When Hoffman walked into the office, the Russian took his cowboy hat from the chair and put it on. He was ready to go.

They drove north on 787 out of the city, then swung around to an industrial complex, wedged between the railyards and the thruway. Yuri provided the directions. On a side street the Russian pointed to a Quonset hut with a hand-painted sign above the front door, which read *D&R Collision*. Hoffman parked in a fenced-off compound beside the building, the yard scattered with wrecked vehicles, some missing front ends, bumpers, windshields. Hoffman opened the trunk and he and the Russian grabbed the duffel bag containing the heavy cylinder and lugged it over to the side door of the building with Soup trailing after them.

Inside the building a man of about thirty-five was kneeling down beside a van, MIG-welding a new quarter panel into place. Off to the side a young guy, no more than a teenager, was water-sanding the hood on a Pontiac Sunfire. They waited for the welder to flip his shield up to examine his work. Only then did he notice them.

"Yuri," he said. "When you get here?"

"Dante, my friend. Is good to see you."

The man named Dante stood up, looking for a brief moment past Yuri to Hoffman and Soup. He didn't appear to expect or particularly want an introduction, and either way, Yuri didn't provide one. That was fine with Hoffman. Dante looked at the cylinder in the open duffel, on the concrete floor at Yuri's feet.

"I have little job for you," Yuri said.

"Yeah?"

"Have steel cylinder here full of goodies. I need for you to cut open."

Dante walked over and knelt down for a

look. He didn't ask after the nature of the goodies. Hoffman figured that he probably had a pretty good idea what was inside, or didn't want to know, one or the other.

"Stainless," he said. "But I can cut it. I'll just cut a square out of the side. You know, to protect the goodies."

"Good," Yuri said.

"I'll get at it this afternoon."

Hoffman shot Yuri a look, and the Russian removed his cowboy hat and pushed his thick hair back. "Is good, but I have slight problem. Is somewhere I have to be. I was thinking maybe I would give you two hundred dollars to cut open cylinder. However, if you could expedite the job, I could double that."

Dante stood up and shrugged. "Sure."

Yuri smiled and put his hat back on. He clapped Dante on the back. "How long does it take, this job?"

"I'll have to change my tanks," Dante said. "I don't know, twenty minutes."

"Good. My friend and I here, we have other business in the area. We will come back in thirty minutes. Mr. Soup, you will stay here and keep Dante company?"

"Like I got a choice," Soup said.

"Is promotion for you, Mr. Soup. I am putting you in charge."

"Right," Soup said unhappily.

"We will be back," Yuri said.

Walking back to the car, the Russian gave Hoffman a sideward glance. "You will pay the four hundred, Mr. Hoffman."

"I don't have it."

"Well, we have thirty minutes," Yuri said as they got into the car. "We can find ATM, or whatever you need."

Hoffman started the engine. "I can't get my hands on it. Not right away." He paused. "My money's tied up."

Yuri was quiet for maybe thirty seconds, then nodded his head slowly. "I think I see now how it is with you, Mr. Hoffman. I think I see now why cop suddenly decides to get into this business."

"You don't know fuck-all about me."

"I know enough. I also know that I will pay to Dante the four hundred, and you will pay me back. If cylinder is as advertised, is not a problem. If not, then this money you have, this money that is tied up, you will find way to untie it. Pronto."

Hoffman jerked the car into gear and they drove out onto the street. "Where we going?" he asked.

Yuri pointed to a McDonald's a few blocks away, the arches rising above the houses. "Go there first. I need to buy Big

Mac breakfast. Then we come back and find place to park, to watch building. I trust Dante, but you can never trust a man completely. Temptation is powerful thing. Do you agree?"

"Whatever."

"You sound like surly teenager," Yuri said, smiling. "You are mad because I make comment about the untying of your money." He watched Hoffman, waiting for a reply, but Hoffman wouldn't give him the satisfaction. "Like I said, we come back and park," Yuri said after a moment. "Close but not too close, you understand?"

Yuri got his breakfast and they drove back and parked along the street a couple hundred yards away from D&R Collision, at a spot where they could watch both doors of the building. Hoffman sipped his McDonald's coffee and listened as Yuri downed the eggs and pancakes and sausage and hash browns like a man who hadn't eaten in a week. When the carnage was complete, he tossed the wrappers in the backseat and wiped his mouth with his sleeve, then pulled out an antique pocket watch to check the time.

"Eighteen minutes," he said. "And no boom-boom. So far, is so good."

Hoffman watched as the Russian began to

wind the watch, turning the stem without looking at it, like a character in an old movie. The man was a walking cliché. Hoffman was looking forward to being clear of him, his stupid jokes, and his superior attitude. A couple more hours and that would be it. He turned his attention to the Quonset hut. He wished he could see inside.

"He better be fucking doing it right now," he said. "I don't want to walk in there in the middle of things."

"Is good boy, Dante," Yuri said. "I knew his father. We did business together in Europe when I was a young man." Yuri thought for a moment. "Of course I am still a young man. Especially compared to you. I am forty-one years. How many are you — sixty maybe?"

"Fuck off," Hoffman said.

"You are younger?"

"I'm fifty-two," Hoffman snapped.

Yuri laughed. "You must have had rough life."

Hoffman heard the rumble of a diesel engine and looked in the rearview to see a garbage truck come motoring around the corner a block behind them. There were no residences on the street and most of the businesses, like the body shop, had Dumpsters, so there wasn't much to pick up, just

246

a few bags here and there. Hoffman was in a no-parking zone but they could go around him. He still had his badge if he needed to show it.

"Maybe it's time we discussed money," he said to Yuri.

"And why would I discuss price when I have yet to see what it is I am buying?" Yuri asked. "If I say to you, Mr. Hoffman, would you like to buy a car? You would not say, Why yes, Yuri, I give you ten thousand dollars for this car. No, you would say, What kind of car, what year, how many kilometers does it have? You follow?"

"Miles."

"What?"

"Miles, not kilometers," Hoffman said. "You're in America now. You should speak American."

"Okay, wave the flag if you wish. Hooray for red, white, and blue. My point is — first I see what you are selling, then I *taste* what you are selling. And then maybe we talk price. Who knows — maybe I walk away."

"You won't walk away." Hoffman took a cigarette from the pack on the dash. As he was lighting it, there was a sudden —

BOOM!
247

The noise reverberated through the car and caused Hoffman to break the cigarette in half. Panicked, he looked anxiously at D&R Collision, then heard Yuri laughing, and the sound of the diesel engine accelerating again. Hoffman realized that the garbage truck had backfired.

"What is wrong, copper?" Yuri said, trying to catch his breath. "Did you poop in your pants?"

"Sonofabitch," Hoffman said. He glared at the departing truck. "Fucking asshole."

"Maybe you should arrest him," Yuri said. "For making backfire. Hurry before he is too many *kilometers* away."

"Fuck you," Hoffman said. His pulse was racing. He took another cigarette from the pack and lit it. He inhaled deeply, glancing again at the body shop across the street. "What the fuck are we going to do if that place suddenly blows sky-high?"

"I cannot speak for you but it is the highway for me," the Russian said. He began to sing. "Happy trails to you. Until we meet again . . ."

Hoffman sat smoking the cigarette while Yuri sang. Apparently he knew the words to the entire song. He sang them all, and when he was finished he continued to hum the tune. He was driving Hoffman crazy. Finally the Russian pulled the pocket watch out again.

"Is time."

Hoffman started the car and they drove into the compound once more. As they were walking toward the building, the side door burst open and Soup came flying out at a run. Hoffman had to grab him by the arm and throw him to the ground.

"You motherfucker!" Soup screamed.

"Settle down," Hoffman said.

"Fuck you!" Soup shouted. "That fucking thing is booby-trapped and you knew it!"

"Relax," Hoffman said. He looked toward the building, wondering how much time had passed. Parson had said sixty seconds. "It didn't blow."

"You didn't know," Soup said, squirming to get free of Hoffman. "Get your fucking hand off me. You didn't know. Me and the dude in there coulda been blown to pieces. You a evil motherfucker, Hoffman."

Hoffman lifted Soup roughly to his feet. "Nothing happened, right? Just relax, you little shit."

"My life you fucking with, Hoffman."

"Enough of this," Yuri said and started for the door of the building.

"Come on," Hoffman growled, dragging Soup by his shirt.

They walked inside. The cylinder was on a steel table and a neat rectangle, maybe a foot long, had been cut out of the side of it. Several plastic packages, tightly packed and secured with duct tape, were on the table beside the cylinder. Still inside, nestled among more packages, was a mass of gray putty from which a tangle of wires ran. Beside the putty was a standard keypad used for alarm systems. Dante was standing beside the table. He did not look happy.

Hoffman hesitated when he saw the putty and the keypad but Yuri reached in, pulled the putty out of the cylinder, and lifted it to his nose for a sniff. Smiled.

"Is Plasticine," he said. "Like children use to play. Plasticine! Hey, copper, someone is having fun with you. Is joke."

"What's going on here?" Dante said, his voice flat.

"Is nothing," Yuri said, tossing the putty on the table. "Someone is having a joke on my friend here and I was playing along. Is just Plasticine and keypad."

"You thought it was going to blow?" Dante asked.

"Of course not, Dante," the Russian said. "I would not put you in position of danger."

"Fucking bullshit, man," Soup said. He was hanging back, eyeing the cylinder like it was still about to detonate.

"Shut your fucking mouth," Hoffman told him. "You people do nothing but whine."

Dante let it go, but his eyes were guarded. Hoffman was pretty sure that he wouldn't be doing any favors for the Russian in the near future, if ever. Yuri pulled a black trucker's wallet from his pocket and counted out the four hundred and handed it to Dante, who put it in his coveralls without a word and walked away, clearly pissed off. Yuri and Hoffman packed the dope into the duffel bag and the three of them headed for the side door, leaving the cylinder behind. Yuri told Dante that he could sell it for scrap but Dante never replied.

Outside, they put the bag in the trunk and got into the car.

"Pool hall, copper," Yuri said, like a wealthy man instructing his chauffeur. He smiled at Soup in the back seat. "Now we are getting close to nitty-gritty, Mr. Soup."

Soup remained quiet. He was still fuming, twitching in the backseat. Hoffman wondered how bad he was jonesing; they had been together for the better part of two days, and if he had been getting high over that time, he was awfully good at hiding it. Well, his reward was coming soon. Maybe Yuri would give him an ounce, or even two.

Of course, if the shit was as pure as it was reputed to be, Soup would probably kill himself with it. But that wasn't Hoffman's problem. He just didn't want to stiff the little bastard; if he did that, there was always the chance Soup would shoot his mouth off to a cop. Half the cops in the city knew him by name. He wouldn't have any trouble getting one of them to listen, and with Hoffman's luck, it would be a cop who didn't much care for him. So Hoffman needed to keep Soup happy until he could get out of town. After that, Soup could tell anybody anything he wanted.

They drove to the alley behind the pool hall and Hoffman parked again beside the big pickup truck, the one he assumed was Yuri's. Who else in the city would have a pair of horns on the hood of their vehicle? For somebody in the drug trade, he wasn't exactly inconspicuous. They got out and Hoffman opened the trunk and as he did he heard police sirens, approaching fast.

"What the hell?" Yuri said, staring at Hoffman.

"It's nothing," Hoffman said. But he was wondering. It seemed a little too coincidental.

Yuri took a few steps toward the street. The sirens grew louder; the cruisers were apparently heading toward them, coming down South Pearl to Third Avenue, which ran out front of the pool hall. Yuri looked down the side street toward South Pearl, listening, then he turned back on Hoffman.

"Nothing?" he asked. "Is cops and coming this way. What is this?"

"Got fuck-all to do with us," Hoffman assured him.

Yuri was not convinced. He pointed a large forefinger at Hoffman. "You will wait here."

He disappeared into the rear of the building. Hoffman turned to Soup, who had been edging along the alley, seconds away from flight. The sirens were now almost on top of them.

"Get back here," Hoffman told him. "It's nothing, I tell you." He took a cigarette from his pack and lit up. "You want a smoke, Soup?"

"You want a smoke, Soup?" Soup mimicked. "Fuck you, Hoffman. One minute I'm a whiny nigger and the next I'm your homey. Fuck you, man. I rue the day I met you, motherfucker."

"Take it easy," Hoffman said, but he was distracted, his mind beginning to work, even though he tried to fight it. How could anybody know? Dante at the body shop was pissed, but Hoffman doubted he would make a call on Yuri. Besides, how would he know where they were heading? Hoffman took a long look at Soup, who had moments ago been on the verge of running. Soup, who they had left alone for half an hour while the cutting was done.

"You didn't make a phone call, Soup?"

"What? Who the fuck would I call?"

Hoffman thought about it. "I don't know," he admitted. "But if you did, you're one dead crackhead."

"I didn't make no call."

Hoffman decided to walk out to South Pearl and have a look. As he did, he saw two cruisers come down the street, slowing down as they passed to turn onto Third Avenue. Hoffman stood on the sidewalk and watched as they stopped after making the turn; he could still see the rear fenders of both cars, and he heard the doors open and close. They were practically right in front of the pool hall. Hoffman turned and walked back to the car. Soup was leaning against the rear fender, his head down, his expression dark and devoid of hope at this point.

Hoffman paced the alley, smoking. What if the police were raiding the pool hall for some other reason? The place was obviously a front for something. Numbers, drugs, guns; the Russian could be into anything. Hoffman knew nothing about the man. He could have checked him out, but it wasn't as if Hoffman had been looking for a Boy Scout. However, if the police were in the pool hall right now, Hoffman sure as hell didn't want them wandering out here in the alley. No matter what they were looking for, they'd be real interested in the duffel bag in Hoffman's trunk.

He walked back and forth a couple more times, waiting for the Russian to come out, and then he decided he'd had enough. He started for the door, then thought about the coke in the trunk and walked back along the side of the car and reached over to slam the lid shut, not thinking to grab the keys from the trunk lock. He turned and headed inside.

The Russian was not in his office. Hoffman kept moving, down the narrow corridor and into the poolroom, where he found him standing at the front counter, talking to the grizzled old man who ran the cash register. Hoffman could see the cruisers out front, through the plate glass. There was also an ambulance there now, parked in front of the restaurant across the street. One of the uniforms was standing on the sidewalk by the front door of the restaurant, talking to a woman who appeared to be a waitress.

Yuri turned when Hoffman approached. "Someone is having heart attack at restaurant across the street." He laughed at the thought. "Is not good advertisement for your restaurant." He assumed the voice of a circus barker. "Eat here, then have heart attack!"

Hoffman shook his head, but he was relieved.

"You have no sense of humor, copper," Yuri said. "That is your problem. Every day you must laugh."

"I don't think you and I find the same things funny," Hoffman said.

"Maybe not," Yuri said. "So then back to business." He began to walk to the rear of the room and as he did he spoke to Hoffman over his shoulder. "Is time to find out if this dope you bring me is as good as you are bragging. All the time I have heard of pure cocaine but never have I seen it."

They went through the room and down the narrow hallway, past Yuri's office, to the back door. They stepped outside into the alley, expecting to find Soup there waiting for them. But Soup was gone.

And so was the car.

EIGHTEEN

It rained all night and it was still raining when he got up the next morning. Virgil had intended to harvest the rest of his wheat today but that would have to wait now until things dried up. He was also going to have to learn how to manage with just one arm for a few weeks. Fortunately, he was right-handed and the Russian cowboy had been considerate enough to stomp on his left arm, although Virgil recalled he'd been all in favor of breaking them both.

The pain wasn't too bad this morning. The disapproving doctor had supplied him with some Percocet and he'd taken one before going to bed the night before. Getting up at dawn, he'd gone without. The arm was uncomfortable but tolerable. His head hurt where the crooked cop had whacked him with the gun, but he could live with that too.

Taking a shower had been difficult, trying

to keep the plaster cast out of the spray. Drying off took some contortions but shaving, strictly a right-handed exercise, was not a problem. He had cereal for breakfast and sat at the kitchen table for a while, drinking coffee and watching the rain as it came down, forming puddles in the driveway and filling the ditch out front. The horses were gathered beneath the large chestnut tree in the corner of the pasture field. The two Percherons, if that's what they were, appeared to be slowly growing accustomed to their new home and were grazing beneath the tree with the others. Virgil wouldn't bother feeding them grain this morning since they wouldn't walk up to the barn in the rain to get it and the trough would just fill with water, ruining the feed. They had plenty of grass.

Watching them, Virgil realized that Mary Nelson hadn't called, as she had promised. It was true that he hadn't been home much in the past couple of days. He had no answering machine or voice mail so in all likelihood she had phoned and been unable to leave a message. She wouldn't worry; she knew that Virgil, in spite of his reluctance, would take care of the draft horses.

It bothered him not getting the rest of the wheat off. The rain would make the grain tough, but there was nothing he could do about that, just as there was nothing he could do about the weather. That didn't stop him from thinking about it. And worrying about his wheat crop was easier than worrying about the woman named Dusty. She had seen the stitches in Virgil's head and the cast on his arm, so she was aware that the men looking for her were serious, whether she wanted to admit it or not. The fact that she had asked about a gun told Virgil that she was more frightened than she let on. It was obvious that she knew a hell of a lot more than Virgil. There were things that she'd told him, but he was pretty sure there was more that she hadn't.

He was tempted to call the Albany police and tell them who it was who had taken his boat. But he had no way of knowing who he could trust, or if in fact anybody would believe him. If this Hoffman had just retired a few days ago, he would obviously still have friends in the department. Virgil needed more information and sitting there, watching the rain come down, he couldn't think of who might provide it.

It took another couple of cups of coffee and an hour of boredom before the obvious person came to mind.

He headed out just before noon, driving

east to the Hudson River. He didn't have much to go on; all Buddy had said was that he was renting a place on the water near Coeymans. Fortunately for Virgil, the beat-up Cadillac was conspicuous, and so was the guy who owned it. Virgil decided he would travel up and down River Road, hoping to spot either the car or the man.

He reached Coeymans, a town of seven or eight thousand, around one o'clock. There was a shopping area, a few bars and restaurants, and a large boat launch on the river. After driving through the town a couple of times, Virgil flipped a coin and took River Road south, checking out the seasonal cottages and cabins along the shore. Buddy said he fished every day, but it was still raining heavily and Virgil doubted that Buddy would be out in the weather, not in a little aluminum boat. Virgil suspected that Buddy was a man who liked his creature comforts.

He drove south as far as Coxsackie and then retraced his route to Coeymans, where he headed north. The rain finally began to let up and the clouds to the west broke into large chunks, which the wind pushed off to reveal blue skies beyond.

When he found the Cadillac, it was parked just where he might have expected — outside a bar. The place, called The Flats, was a low-slung stucco building on a narrow lane a couple of hundred yards from the Hudson. Buddy, of course, was inside, drinking draft beer and playing shuffleboard with a very tall blond woman of about forty-five wearing artfully torn blue jeans and a tight tank top. The blonde was attractive, in a weathered way, and her breasts were impressive, quite large and very round, probably not original equipment. Original or enhanced, she was apparently proud enough of them that she had decided not to hide them in the constraints of a bra. Looking at Buddy's beaming face as he fired the rocks down the hardwood table, Virgil was quite certain that Buddy was okay with that.

Virgil said hello to Buddy, who seemed more surprised at Virgil's battered appearance than he was to see him in the area in general, then sat at the bar and ordered a beer. The place was pretty busy for a weekday afternoon and Virgil assumed that the weather was a factor. There were a few vacation properties and campgrounds in the area and sitting inside a cottage or a tent, watching the rain come down, was not what people had in mind when they were on holiday. If the outdoors was not an option, the bar was a good substitute.

Buddy finished his game with the woman

and Virgil overheard him proposing steaks and beer at his place later on. Buddy, it seemed, had access to the best porterhouse cuts in the entire state. As a pickup line it was pretty effective, at least with the lanky blonde. The woman went off to run some errands and told Buddy she would see him at seven o'clock. As she was walking out the door, Buddy suggested she pick up a couple of bottles of wine.

"What the fuck happened to you?" he asked, walking over to Virgil at the bar.

"Fell out of the hay mow," Virgil told him.

Buddy took a quick inventory of Virgil's injuries. "Looks like you hit a few bumps on the way down."

Virgil smiled and turned to the bartender and ordered another beer for himself and one for Buddy, who sat down on the next stool over.

"I tried to find a number for you," Buddy said. "You don't have a phone?"

"I got a phone."

"Unlisted?"

"No. It's in Tom Stempler's name. Used to own the farm."

"He died, right?"

"Yeah. Five, six years ago."

"Ever think of putting the number in your name?"

"Then people might start calling me."

The bartender brought the beer and Virgil paid. Buddy took a long pull, the foam clinging to his mustache, and put the glass on the bar. He looked at Virgil, then he smiled like a horny teenager and nodded toward the door through which the blonde had disappeared.

"You see her?"

"You're like a puppy with two peckers, Buddy."

Buddy nodded. "Her name's Mimi."

"French girl?"

Buddy laughed at that. "And to think I wanted to stay in Florida. I could fall in love with that woman."

"That why you were looking for my number?" Virgil asked. "Tell me that?"

Buddy laughed again — it seemed he was in a hell of a mood — and took another drink, this time remembering to wipe his mustache. "Got some information for you," he said. "You caught yourself a big one, man. That cylinder's full of cocaine. That is, if it's the cylinder I think it is, and with all the commotion it's caused, I'm guessing it is."

"How did it end up at the bottom of the Hudson River?"

"It got dumped during a bust," Buddy

said. "I talked to a couple of cops who were in on it. Said it happened out from Athens, deep spot in the river. A dealer named Parson brought the dope up from the Caribbean on a boat called *Down Along Coast.* Stuff came from Colombia originally, supposed to be the best of the best. But somebody with knowledge of it coming into the country got into a mess over kiddie porn and rolled over like a dead carp, patched the information to the metro drug squad. They kept tabs on the boat while it came up through the intercoastal and raided it in the middle of the night, out in the river. But this Parson got spooked at the last minute and threw the cylinder overboard and then he went with it. Seven years later and a little farther south, you hook it with an anchor. How's that for a needle in a haystack?"

"Yeah, I'm a lucky guy," Virgil said. "So Parson got away?"

"They pulled him in for questioning after the fact. But they had nothing on him. They did find a few grams of coke on the boat, pleasure snort, but they couldn't tie it to him. Apparently the guy's made of Teflon. When he bought the boat down in the islands he registered the thing in his girl-friend's name. She took it on the chin for the coke they did find. She wouldn't give up Parson so they made it trafficking and made it stick and she did three years in Albion Correctional. Parson walked. And just to thumb his nose at the cops, he bought the boat back at police auction. It's a forty-four-foot Chris-Craft, all mahogany and teak, nice-looking boat. I saw it yesterday, moored in the river outside Parson's pad."

"What were you doing out there?"

"I wanted to have a look. Cops told me where he lived, out by Van Wies Point. I saw Parson himself. He drove up in a white Corvette, gave me the stink-eye when he saw me parked across the road."

"What's he look like?" Virgil asked. "Don't tell me he's a Russian in a cowboy hat."

"Nah, he's a black dude," Buddy said. "He's put together, probably a gym rat. As fit as a butcher's dog."

Virgil's next question was technically not a question at all. Not when he already knew the answer. "You get the girlfriend's name?"

"Dusty Fremont."

Virgil nodded and tipped back his beer. "These cops you talked to. They heard anything about the cylinder recently?"

"Far as they know, it's still at the bottom of the river."

"I guess they're out of the loop then," Virgil said.

"I guess they are," Buddy said.

"That's surprising," Virgil said. "Or maybe not. I found out who took the cylinder, and my boat. Albany detective named Hoffman."

"So the Albany police have it?"

"I don't think so. Hoffman was a cop the day he took it. He retired the next day."

"Ah," Buddy said. "Which leads you to the conclusion that he's probably not going to turn the coke over to the proper authorities. Which leads you to further conclude that he's not going to bring your boat back."

"That's where it leads me."

"How did you find out his name?"

"A woman told me."

"What woman?" Buddy asked and when Virgil didn't answer he figured it out quick enough. "Shit. How did she find you?"

"She's a smart girl," Virgil said. "She was looking for Hoffman and now it turns out Hoffman's looking for her. He's traveling with a big mean cowboy with a Russian accent and a scared junkie."

Buddy took his cigarettes from his pocket and lit one. He sat thinking. "Why would she want to deal herself back in? She already did time for this."

"She seems pretty conflicted about it," Virgil said. "Told me she wished I'd never found the thing."

"And you say Hoffman's looking for her?"

"Yeah. Matter of fact, he somehow got wind that she'd been to see me and he and his band of merry men showed up at my place a couple nights ago, asking questions."

Buddy pulled on the cigarette. "Was that the night you fell out of the hay mow, Virgil?"

"Yeah."

Buddy took a moment, then nodded. "So you never told this Hoffman she'd been to see you."

It was a statement and not a question, so Virgil never replied. He watched as Buddy Townes smoked the nonfilter and tried to figure the angles. It was interesting to watch; the man went from eager horndog, giddy with thoughts of thick steaks and voluptuous blondes, to private investigator in a matter of minutes. Like an old beagle laying on a porch, catching the whiff of a cottontail on the wind.

"Why would Hoffman be looking for her, when he's got the dope?" he asked.

"I've been wondering that myself," Virgil said. "She thinks he's afraid of something."

Buddy drained the last of his draft and pushed the mug across the bar in the general direction of the bartender, who was at the far end, mixing drinks for a waitress who stood by. Only the two of them were working and they were kept hopping, serving the customers who'd come in out of the rain. Virgil's second beer was still half full but he didn't hurry it along. He wasn't about to get into a guzzling contest with Buddy Townes.

"All right," Buddy said after he'd gotten the bartender's attention. "There's a third party missing here and I have to assume that third party is Parson. I guarantee you he knows that somebody found the cylinder. I don't know how, but he knows."

"Dusty mentioned him."

"She did?"

"Yeah. She didn't say anything about being his girlfriend, and she didn't say he knew about the cylinder." Virgil paused, thinking back to the conversation in the hospital parking lot. "But she did say he owns the thing."

"Like I said, he knows."

When the bartender brought the beer, he told Buddy to put the cigarette out. Buddy did so reluctantly, and gave him a twenty.

"Parson still in the business?" Virgil asked.

"Allegedly not," Buddy said. "According to the cops, he restores high-end cars for a living. Vintage stuff. There's a theory it's a front. But Parson's been clean since that night on the river. He'd actually been pretty clean in general, even before that. He took a fall once twenty years ago on a conspiracy rap, did eighteen months. After that, he became an expert at keeping his own fingerprints off everything. You know what I mean? Like getting the girl to put the boat in her name."

"You think Dusty's working for him now?"

"Do you?"

Virgil shrugged. "Like I said, she seems pretty reluctant to be involved at all. It's almost like she has no choice. That make sense?"

"Hard to say, without knowing the whole story. But you can bet your ass that Parson wants that powder. There was rumored to be a hundred pounds of pure cocaine in that cylinder. You know what that's worth on the street? You're talking a couple million dollars minimum. A man loses fifteen, twenty grand on a deal and he'll chalk it up to experience. This is a different kettle of fish. If Parson knows that somebody found that cylinder, he's going to want it back."

Virgil absently rotated the beer mug on the bar. "If Hoffman didn't turn it in, you have to assume he's going to sell it. Why not just sell it to Parson?"

"If Hoffman called you up and offered to

sell you your boat back, would you buy it?"

"No."

"There you go. Parson might be thinking the same way." Buddy considered this a moment, then nodded, as if agreeing with himself. "And that's why Hoffman would be afraid of him. *If* Hoffman knows that Parson knows. This thing goes round and round, doesn't it?" Buddy reached for another smoke, and stopped. "And . . . maybe that's why Hoffman's looking for the woman. If she's out asking questions, then he's going to think she's working for Parson, whether she is or not. Why wouldn't he think that? She was the girlfriend, she was on the boat, she served the time. You could say she's invested more in this than all the rest of them put together." Buddy took another drink.

"She works construction," Virgil said. "Drives an old pickup. She doesn't look like any kind of a drug dealer to me. But I think she's nervous about Hoffman. She knows now that he's looking for her." Virgil indicated the cast on his arm. "And she knows he's playing rough."

"What's this about a Russian?" Buddy asked.

"I don't know how he fits in," Virgil said. "Whether he's just muscle for Hoffman or something else. Big bastard. I got a feeling he's seen too many Clint Eastwood movies. A little on the mean side, I'd have to say."

Virgil saw Buddy look at his watch, and in that instant he could see Buddy's focus shift. He knew that Buddy was thinking about the tall blonde again.

"She could be in a shitload of trouble," Virgil said.

"Mimi?"

"Dusty."

"Right," Buddy said. "And you're thinking about riding to her rescue?"

"No. I just want my boat back."

"Bullshit." Buddy laughed. "You're going to get yourself in shit, you know that? Why fuck around with these people if you don't have to? You can buy another boat. Go back to your farm, let them fight it out among themselves."

"Okay."

"You're not even listening to me."

Virgil finished his beer. "Sure I am. Thanks for the information, Buddy. I hope you have a nice dinner."

"I hope I have a nice dessert."

Virgil got to his feet. He was nearly to the door when Buddy called out to him. Virgil turned.

"Stay out of it, Virgil. These guys aren't

271

fucking around. People like this will kill you just to make a point. And we're talking about a couple million dollars here."

Virgil nodded.

"How do you know this girl's not playing you?" Buddy asked. "Shit — she might be the baddest one of the lot."

Virgil smiled. "She told me the same thing."

As he headed for home, hitting Route 385 at Coxsackie and driving south, Virgil considered what Buddy Townes had said. And he knew that Buddy was right. He knew nothing about the woman named Dusty Fremont, other than that she was acquainted with a nasty bunch of people. She had shown up at Virgil's farm telling half-truths, trying to get him to reveal things that he didn't know, that he would have no way of knowing. No matter how Virgil tried to paint her in a positive light, the fact remained that she was looking for a ship-ment of cocaine that was apparently worth a small fortune. She wasn't a cop, so it seemed unlikely she was looking to get the dope off the street. In spite of her insisting otherwise, it was easy to assume that she wanted the coke for the same reason every-body else did. To get rich. Either she was on one side or the other.

Still, there was nothing about her that suggested that she was driven by greed. Virgil wanted to believe her when she said she'd rather not be involved in the situation at all, that she wished he'd never found the thing to begin with. But there were things she wasn't telling him, something she was protecting. And, on a certain level, in spite of her tough talk and her street swagger, Virgil knew she was scared.

He was approaching Kimball's Point now, and as he drove past the entranceway to Brownie's Marina, he glanced over to see several police cruisers in the parking lot. The tackle shop was encircled with yellow tape. He continued on for another mile or so, and then turned back.

Mudcat McCluskey was sitting on the steps of the shop, his head in his hands. Cops, both in uniform and plainclothes, were milling about. A number of rubber-neckers were gathered in the parking lot, and the outside deck of Scallywags was full of drinkers, watching the proceedings like spectators at a sporting event. Virgil rolled to a stop on the far side of the lot and sat there for a moment until he spotted Wally farther off to the right, smoking a cigarette and leaning against the chain-link fence that

273

surrounded the boat compound. Virgil drove over and got out.

"What's going on?"

Wally took one last pull off the cigarette and flicked it with his forefinger into the compound behind him. "Oh, looks like Brownie had himself a little trouble last night."

"Somebody rob him?"

"I don't know that they robbed him," Wally said. "But they strangled him and stuffed him under the dock there. Mudcat found him floating this morning when he came to open up."

Virgil turned toward the activity around the tackle shop.

"Mudcat's taking it hard," Wally said. "You would, too. Brownie was the only guy who liked him even a little bit, and now he's dead."

Virgil could see that Wally wasn't taking things nearly as badly as Mudcat. A police van pulled in off the highway, then did a half circle in the lot before backing up to the tackle shop. A guy and a woman, both wearing white coveralls with *County Police* on the back, got out and went inside.

"What happened to your arm?" Wally asked.

"Fell out of the hay mow," Virgil told him.

"Shit. That farming is dangerous work."

"So is running a tackle shop, apparently," Virgil said. "You say it wasn't a robbery?"

"I got close enough earlier, before they ran me off, to hear a couple of the cops. They were saying nothing was touched inside. Kind of looks like whoever did it waited for Brownie to close for the night and then grabbed him. Strangled him with some fishing line, according to Mudcat." Wally laughed. "That ten-pound test is good stuff."

Virgil shook his head and waited for Wally to stop chuckling. "Well, you have an opinion on most things, Wally," he said. "You got any ideas on who did it?"

"I got one, but it's half-assed," Wally said. He pointed his chin toward Scallywags. "There was a guy showed up last night about eight o'clock. Driving a blue Mercedes convertible. I was shooting pool. Guy comes in and sits at the bar alone, drinking Jack. Doesn't say shit to anybody. He left just after dark. Drank a lot of bourbon and never left Suzie a tip, she was some pissed."

"So?"

"So nothing," Wally said. "There was just something off about him. Not tall, but really put together, like a body-builder or something. Jet-black hair. Gold jewelry. Fucking

275

guy kept looking at himself in the mirror behind the bar. One of those guys."

"You tell the cops?"

"Nope," Wally said. "If I'm wrong, then I got no reason to tell them. If I'm right, then I might be the next guy in line for a ten-pound test necklace. If the guy's strong enough to strangle a big fat fucker like Brownie, he'd have no problem with a little shit like me. I'll keep my mouth shut, thank you very much."

As Wally was talking, Virgil watched as Mudcat suddenly looked their way, then moved at once to point Virgil out to a couple of plainclothes cops who were standing on the dock, having a smoke.

"Something else going on with Brownie this week," Wally said. "He had a big bandage taped over his ear and his face was all marked up. Looked like somebody laid a beating on him."

"Yeah?" Virgil said absently, still watching Mudcat. "I wonder who would do a thing like that."

Now Wally followed Virgil's gaze. "Look out," he said. "You can bet Mudcat's spouting off about your problems with Brownie. You better take a hike, Virgil."

"Why would I take a hike? I didn't kill Brownie. If I did, I probably wouldn't be hanging around here, talking to you."

Virgil started across the parking lot, his eyes still on Mudcat, who was indeed enthusiastically expounding on something as he approached. Virgil was almost to the dock before he noticed that one of the detectives standing there listening was Malero. Mudcat didn't see Virgil until the last moment, and when he did his eyes went wide and he clammed up at once.

"Well, well," Malero said, turning. "Look who we have here."

"You find my boat yet?" Virgil asked.

"Never mind your goddamn boat, smart guy. We got a few questions for you."

"What are you even doing here?" Virgil asked. "I thought this was out of your jurisdiction."

"An ex-cop from Albany PD is dead," Malero said. "My jurisdiction is wherever I say it is."

Virgil shrugged. "Fire away."

"Mr. McCluskey here tells us that you threatened Gordon Brown a few days ago. You want to tell us what that was about?"

"I'd have an easier time doing that if it was true," Virgil said. "I never threatened Brownie. I did threaten Mudcat here. I told him I was going to kick the shit out of him if he didn't stop lying. Apparently he didn't listen to me because here he is lying again. And this time he's lying to the cops. Hey — why don't you guys kick the shit out of him?"

"You seem to think this is a laughing matter, Mr. Cain," Malero said. "A man has been murdered here. A man you had words with a few days ago. Are you going to deny that?"

"We had words, yeah," Virgil said. "You see, Brownie was the one who called the guy who came and towed my boat away. You know — the boat you're allegedly looking for. You having any luck with that?"

"Mention that boat again and I will arrest you," Malero said.

"And charge me with what — mentioning?" Virgil asked.

"This fucking guy," the other cop said. He stepped forward, pushing his way in front of Virgil. He was big, with a blond brush cut and breath that stank of cigarettes. "Listen, asshole. This isn't a fucking comedy club. You are a person of interest in a murder. Now suppose you tell us where you were last night."

"I spent most of the day in the local hospital, getting this," Virgil said, offering up his cast. "You can check with Dr. Stone down at the ER. Last night I was home, eating painkillers. If you think I came out of surgery and came down here and with one arm strangled a guy who had to weigh two hundred and fifty pounds, then you'd better go ahead and arrest me right now. Otherwise I'm heading home. I was you boys, I'd start looking elsewhere for whoever killed Brownie. Shouldn't have any trouble rounding up a few suspects — I can't imagine there's any more than a couple hundred guys in the area that didn't like him."

The two cops were stymied. Virgil thought for a moment they were pissed enough that they might take him in and keep him overnight, just to inconvenience him, but they obviously decided not to waste their time with him. He turned to walk away and as he was stepping off the dock, Malero called to him.

"Hey, shithead. What makes you think that Gordon Brown called about your boat? Why would he do that?"

Virgil hesitated for just an instant. He had almost told Malero about the cylinder the last time they talked, and he'd decided against it. This time, he didn't even consider the option.

"I don't know *why* he did it," Virgil said. He smiled, indicating the tackle shop. "You could ask him, but it looks to me like you're about a day late."

NINETEEN

The weather cleared overnight and the new day arrived cool and crisp, with a good breeze from the southwest. The temperature climbed throughout the morning but the air remained dry and by eleven o'clock the remaining fifteen acres of Virgil's wheat was ready to come off. He combined right through lunch, finishing the field just after three. He emptied the wheat into the GMC stake truck with the racks and went into the house to call the co-op about bringing it in. They were swamped for the day and he was advised to wait until morning, so he backed the truck into the machine shed, out of the weather, although the forecast called for clear skies the next couple of days.

He walked to the house and scrambled up a couple of eggs, which he ate at the kitchen table, covering the eggs with hot sauce. He washed the frying pan and his plate, opened a beer, and walked out to sit on the side porch, taking with him the weekly newspaper that had arrived with the mail. He read the front page twice without really seeing it and then set it aside.

He'd been thinking about Dusty ever since he'd gotten out of bed that morning. Actually, he'd been thinking about her since he'd left Brownie's Marina the day before. And even before that, he realized. Buddy Townes was right. These people were dead serious. Of course, Virgil had known that, to some extent. He had a cast on his arm and a stainless steel rod in the bone as evidence of that. But somebody had taken it a step further with Brownie. When Wally had mentioned that someone had put a beating on Brownie a few days earlier, Virgil was quite certain that somebody had been Dusty. After all, she'd told him that she'd persuaded Brownie to talk. But Virgil couldn't believe that Dusty had come back and killed him. He'd already spilled his guts, so what would have been the point? Besides that, Virgil wasn't ready to believe Dusty was a killer. Or she might be the baddest one in the bunch after all.

It occurred to him that maybe the fact that Brownie had talked to Dusty had something to do with Brownie now being dead. But why, Virgil had no way of knowing. There

282

were people involved who seemed very willing to go that far, and the Russian cowboy who had broken Virgil's arm was big enough for the job. As for the guy who Wally had seen in Scallywags the night before, well, he was just another wild card in the deck. Wally had an active imagination. Chances were the man admiring himself in the mirror behind the bar had nothing to do with any of it. Of course, that didn't change the fact that *somebody* had killed Brownie.

At one point during the day, while running the combine, Virgil had decided that he was done with the whole damn mess. Now, thinking about it again, he knew it was absolutely the right decision. Since the day he'd hooked the cylinder with his anchor off Kimball's Point, things had gone as wrong as they could go. He had lost his boat, been stonewalled by an uncooperative police department, and suffered a good old-fashioned shit-kicking in his own kitchen. As unhappy as Virgil was with those developments, compared to Brownie, he'd gotten off pretty easy.

So far.

Time to cut his losses, stay on his own ground, and be finished with it. It was what a wise man would do, and from time to time Virgil liked to think he fit the description.

He knew nothing about drugs and drug dealers, and he was happy to keep it that way. The only drug he'd ever tried that still appealed to him was Budweiser. Back when he was playing ball, they practically had to tie him down to force him to take a cortisone shot. He had never tried cocaine, but then, the situation at hand wasn't really about the cocaine, it was about the people surrounding the cocaine. Well, they could have it, and all the shit that came with it.

Having made his choice, he began to feel better about things. He regretted losing the cedar strip but, like Buddy said, he could always find another boat. Cutting his losses was the smart move, and — given what happened to Brownie — the healthy move. He finished off his beer and went inside for another. Back on the porch, he put his feet up on the railing and watched his herd of horses.

Technically they weren't his horses; they were animals that had been rescued from various abusive situations by Mary Nelson. He had finally talked to her last night; the phone had been ringing when he walked into the house after his encounter with the cops at the marina. Mary was apologetic about leaving the two draft horses, which she confirmed were Percherons, and she was more apologetic when telling him that the home she'd thought she'd found for them had fallen through.

"But they're workhorses," she reminded him. "You could do your plowing with them."

"I'll keep that in mind," Virgil said. "You know, when the world finally runs out of fossil fuel."

"Besides, you would never admit it, but you like to take care of things," she said before hanging up.

That wasn't quite true. Virgil didn't even like horses all that much, but he liked the notion of saving them from the type of assholes who would mistreat them. Thinking of those faceless bastards caused him to consider the people surrounding the goddamn cylinder he'd found, the people he had decided just a short time ago not to consider anymore. And so he pushed them from his mind again. The only one he could say he was concerned about was Dusty, and she was going to have to handle whatever came up on her own. It was her bed; she could lie in it.

He wondered, though, if she knew that Brownie had been murdered. If not, somebody should tell her. But not Virgil, of course. He was done with it. At this point all he needed to do was to stop himself from thinking about it. He had made his decision and that was that.

The afternoon sun was warm on his face and after he finished the second beer, he began to doze in the chair. He was almost asleep when he remembered what she had said to him in her truck the night she had shown up at the hospital.

The only one I trust is you, and that's because I think you know less than me.

Virgil straightened in his chair, his eyes open.

The only one I trust is you.

He sat and looked at the front pasture, at those damn horses. The horses he hadn't asked for, but which had somehow come under his care. They wandered about, at their graze, oblivious of Virgil and of everything around them.

"Shit," Virgil said. He walked down off the porch and got into his truck and headed for the city.

Hoffman's car was behind a thrift store in Arbor Hill, rammed into the block wall there, the headlight broken and the driver's-side front fender collapsed against the wheel. Hoffman had had no idea where the car was until a beat cop called him with the information. The cop knew who he was, even addressed him as Detective, and Hoffman, who quite obviously couldn't introduce Soup or a hundred pounds of cocaine into the conversation, was obliged to make up a story about the car being taken by his wayward nephew, who had accidentally crashed the vehicle while out joyriding. Hoffman told the cop that he'd known that the car was there, and was in fact on his way to pick it up when he received the call. He further assured the officer on the phone that he would be disciplining his nephew in his own way. He didn't want the city police out trying to hunt down a nephew who didn't exist.

He took a cab to the alleyway and, after prying the fender off the wheel with a tire iron, drove the car to a nearby garage to have the headlight replaced. Then he went back to the Third Avenue pool hall to talk to Yuri. He had considered the possibility that the Russian might just pull out of the whole venture after Soup ripped Hoffman off, but to the contrary, Yuri had called Hoffman twice already that morning, and he seemed more determined than ever to make the buy. Of course, at the moment, there was nothing for the Russian to buy. Maybe it was true after all — everybody wants what they can't have.

Hoffman included. Now he was truly bent on finding the coke, selling it to Yuri, and getting the hell out of the state. He'd left a careless trail these past few days and it was likely to come back and haunt him if he was to stick around. Associating with Soup and Yuri had been a dicey proposition from the start, and now, with Soup on the run with a couple million dollars' worth of cocaine, the situation seemed even more likely to blow up in Hoffman's face. Crackheads not being known for their discretion; if Soup was to get busted with the haul, he would roll over on Hoffman in a heartbeat. And Hoffman would be the one looking at time. There were judges out there who just loved to throw dirty cops in jail. Hoffman needed to find the coke and he needed to find it fast.

Yuri was waiting in the back office when Hoffman walked in, still wearing the black hat and the jeans and the boots, although now he'd switched to a red Western shirt, this one featuring looping lariats on each shoulder. He was behind the scarred desk, the size 12 boots propped on some scattered papers and magazines on the desktop. Hoffman sat opposite him.

"All right, where we going to find him?"

he asked.

"You have other clothes?" Yuri asked.

"What?" Hoffman was wearing his brown suit.

"Every day you wear the same thing."

"I wore a blue suit yesterday. What're you talking about?"

"I don't care the colors," Yuri said. "Is still the same thing. You look like cop. We need to find Mr. Soup, and yet everywhere we go you might as well be wearing a sign that says, 'I am cop!' "

"So I'm conspicuous?" Hoffman said. "You looked in the mirror lately?"

Yuri regarded his own attire with obvious admiration. "Ah, but I do not look like cop. Unless this is Dodge City in olden days. Then I look like U.S. marshal. But today, no one mistakes me for cop. So first thing we do, we go to your house and you change duds, partner."

Hoffman threw his hands up. "All right, all right. If it makes you happy. We'll go there first. What I want to know is where we're going second."

"Is good question," Yuri said. "Mr. Soup is crackhead. If he is looking to *buy* drugs, he is easy to find. But we both know this is not the case. I think we can say that Mr. Soup has sufficient product. He is stoned and he is scared, yes? This means that he is holed up. We must flush him out."

"And how do we do that?"

Yuri got to his feet. "I have no plan, not yet. But for flushing, I think we first must find birds of a feather."

They walked out back, to where Hoffman's car was parked beside the black pickup with the horns attached to the hood. Yuri indicated the sedan with the dented fender and shook his head. "We leave this car here. Is like your clothes, it screams cop."

They got into the pickup and drove to Hoffman's house in the suburbs. Hoffman went inside and changed into khaki slacks and a golf shirt he'd won at a police stag once, bearing the Kraft Foods logo across the breast pocket. Even untucked the shirt didn't adequately cover the Glock on his belt, so he pulled on a windbreaker as well, despite the fact it was seventy-five degrees outside. He put his shield in his pocket, thinking he might find it useful where they were going, wherever the hell that turned out to be.

Before leaving his bedroom, he glanced out the window to see Yuri out of the truck, leaning against the front fender while he rolled a cigarette. Another cowboy cliché.

Hoffman was sure his neighbors were getting an eyeful. They were a pretentious bunch of assholes and right now they were probably making jokes about the circus being in town. Not that he cared at all; he'd lived on the street for fourteen years and he never knew any of them well enough to call them by name.

He stopped in the kitchen and took down a bottle of rum from the cupboard above the fridge and drank a couple of ounces straight from the bottle. He was tired. He hadn't slept much the night before, lying awake thinking of how stupid he had been not to remove the keys from the trunk lock, and then planning on what he would do to Soup when he found him. The scenarios varied, depending on whether he found him with the coke, or without. Either way, it wasn't going to be a happy time for the thieving black fuck.

He took another drink, put the bottle away, and went outside. Yuri pulled on the rolled cigarette, exhaled as he watched Hoffman coming down the drive.

"Now you look like salesman," he said. "At conference. All you need is silly hat." When Hoffman got close, Yuri leaned toward him. "You even smell like booze, like salesman at conference. You have no normal clothes?"

"Fuck you," Hoffman said. "This is it. We can't all dress like a rodeo clown."

Yuri laughed out loud. "Rodeo clown! See — you have sense of humor after all. Okay then, is no use. I think we could put you in bathing suit and still you would look like police."

From Hoffman's quiet neighborhood in Colonie they drove downtown. The Dodge truck towered over the cars on the street. Hoffman, sitting in the passenger seat, looked down into the vehicles they passed. He watched for women drivers with short skirts, the skirts hiked up to operate the pedals. Sitting at a light, one woman caught him gawking, and she gave him the finger. Stupid bitch.

They made their way along South Pearl, a few blocks from Jefferson Park, and Yuri pulled over to the curb. He indicated the various diners and greasy spoons on either side of the street.

"Whatever he is up to, Mr. Soup still has to eat," he said. "Maybe you should check these fine establishments, see if he has been in for chow. I will go to Jefferson Park."

"You mean you don't want me with you," Hoffman said.

"Now you are catching on," the Russian

said. "Even in your salesman outfit, you are sticking out like you have sore thumbs. So maybe it is best if you are still cop after all, maybe you find something that way. Is more than one way to skin cats, right?"

"Right," Hoffman said, and got out.

"Leave your cell phone on," Yuri added, leaning over to talk out the passenger window. "You find Mr. Soup, I am the first person you call. Is understood?"

"Yeah."

But Hoffman had a disturbing thought as Yuri pulled away. What if it worked the other way around and Yuri found Soup? Would Hoffman be the first person Yuri would call? Or would Yuri call Hoffman at all?

Hoffman wasn't convinced. He had no claim of ownership on the dope — after all, he had stolen it himself — and even if he did, there was nothing about the Russian to suggest he would honor a claim, bogus or otherwise. When Soup had first introduced Hoffman to Yuri, he had expected his status as a cop would carry some weight with the man. The opposite was true; Yuri seemed to enjoy putting Hoffman down — because he was a cop, not despite the fact. He obviously considered himself superior to Hoffman, and he wasn't hesitant to show it. It was almost as if Hoffman was working for the Russian. He didn't seem to care that Hoffman, with a quick phone call, could bring his world crashing down around him. Not that Hoffman had witnessed anything overtly criminal in his dealings with Yuri, but he was quite certain that the pool hall on Third Avenue wouldn't stand up to a protracted search-and-seizure.

If the coke didn't show up, if it was gone forever, then Hoffman would make that call before he left town. See if the Russian shit kicker thought that was funny.

Until then, he decided he needed to keep Yuri close. The black truck was still visible a couple of blocks away, idling at a stoplight. The Russian would park nearby, Hoffman assumed, and make his way into the park on foot. Ironically, Jefferson Park was the one place in the city where Yuri wouldn't stand out. The place was a cesspool of freaks and addicts and other assorted losers. A mad Russian in a cowboy costume wouldn't rate a second glance.

Hoffman started to walk toward the park, but he did take the time to check out the diners he passed along the way. Wouldn't he love to stumble on Soup in one of them, having a little lunch before returning to his stash, wherever it was? It occurred to Hoffman again that Soup could very well overdose, if the coke was as good as purported. But Soup was a crackhead; he'd be smoking the stuff, not shooting it. Hoffman had never heard of anybody OD'ing from smoking cocaine. He hoped that was true. If Soup killed himself, Hoffman would never find the coke. Some homeboys would stumble on it and it would be scattered to the four winds. The only positive to that scenario is that maybe it would take a bunch of them out too. But that wouldn't help Hoffman's retirement plans any.

Yuri was right about one thing. Even in his casual clothes, Hoffman wasn't fooling anyone. He was known in the neighborhood, so the punks and the gangbangers and the junkies knew him by sight anyway, but even to others, it seemed, he was an easy man to make. He went with it, flashing his shield a couple of times when asking waitresses or proprietors if they'd seen Soup. Nobody had, or at least nobody was talking, not yet anyway. But somebody would. A man sitting on that much product couldn't keep it quiet for long, no matter how hard he tried. Somebody would talk, somebody with an ax to grind, or an old score to settle. Soup had been a fuckup his whole life, and Hoffman was counting on him to come through again.

It took Hoffman the better part of an hour to walk the three blocks to the park. Jefferson Park took up most of a small block off South Pearl and on a warm July day it was crowded with people of all stripes — reckless skateboarders, mothers pushing strollers, teenagers shooting hoops or tossing footballs, girls sunbathing. And hustlers and creeps and users and perverts, all doing their thing. Homeless men with snot running down their faces, their pants stained with piss. Teenage girls, bad complexions covered with makeup, who would turn a trick for a pipe. Hoffman hated the place. It was everything that was wrong with the city and society in general. He'd spent too much time there when he worked drugs, and back then he'd been fond of saying that if he was running the city he'd bring the bulldozers in and turn the entire block into a parking lot. And he wouldn't bother evacuating the place first.

Walking across the grass toward the pavilion at the park's center, he knew that he drew looks. Not that he gave a shit. These people could smell a cop from a mile off, and it wouldn't be hard to smell Hoffman anyway, sweating in the windbreaker in the summer heat. He didn't see Yuri anywhere, but then he could be at the other end, or he might not even have come into the park yet. The surrounding neighborhood was a rat's nest of drug dens and shooting galleries. Hoffman suspected that Yuri knew his way around the area. The notion only led to his anxiety over the possibility that the Russian would find Soup first and cut Hoffman out. The best solution, as Hoffman saw it, was to track Soup down himself. He even considered cutting Yuri out, but Yuri was the only buyer he had on the line. He could go back to Parson, but that really wasn't an option. Not that Hoffman believed for a moment that Parson had forgotten about the coke.

That's where the woman came in. Hoffman wondered if he might run into her down here. After all, she knew the territory too. That would be a bonus. He could remove her from the equation and send Parson a message in the process. Better yet, have Yuri do it. Hoffman suspected it was the type of thing Yuri enjoyed. Not only that, but if Yuri were to kill her, it would excuse Hoffman from any retribution from Parson.

Approaching the pavilion, he saw a large black woman selling peanuts and popcorn and other assorted snacks from a cart. The woman was familiar to Hoffman, yet it took a moment for him to place her as he approached. There was, on the other hand, no hesitation on her part. She turned to him and he saw the recognition come to her immediately; her expression went from neutral to one of pure hatred in the blink of an eye.

Hoffman remembered her then. He couldn't recall her real name but she was known as Shell, a junkie who had operated as a dealer, strictly small-time, a decade or so earlier. It seemed to Hoffman she'd come from Jamaica originally; he remembered that she had an accent. It took him a little longer to figure out what it was that would make her look at him the way she was at this moment, and then it came to him. He'd busted her with a gram of smack one night, along with a couple hundred in cash. She'd been heading somewhere to fix and she was in a bad way. Hoffman had made a deal with her, letting her keep the dope while he took the money. But there had been a kicker to the deal — he'd also made her give him a blow job in the front seat of his cruiser.

He smiled at her now. "Shell," he said. "Long time."

"Fuck you."

"What?"

"You heard me," the woman said.

Hoffman shook his head, disappointed

that she would carry a grudge after all these years. "So it's nuts these days, is it?" he asked. He reached into the glass container and helped himself to a handful of cashews. "I hope that's all you're dealing, Shell."

"That's all," she said. "You got your cashews, you can keep moving. Cuz I don't want none of what you dealin'."

"Telling me you're clean, Shell?"

"Goin' on three years now."

"How'd you manage that? Once a junkie, always a junkie." Hoffman smiled again. "Or is the city's methadone program propping you up?"

"Maybe it is. None of your business."

"Isn't welfare a wonderful thing?" Hoffman asked. He ate a couple more cashews and then looked around, checking to see who might be within earshot. "I'm looking for Soup. You seen him?"

"I don't know no Soup."

"Don't you fucking lie to me," Hoffman said casually, still looking away.

She fell silent, admitting nothing. Her breathing was heavy, like she'd just climbed five flights of stairs.

"Okay, maybe you don't know him," Hoffman said, turning back to her now. "I just remembered you're not from here originally, are you? You're from Jamaica or the Dominican, one of those shitholes that sends us their criminals by the boatload." Hoffman popped another cashew into his mouth. "Tell me, Shell. How's your status these days? Did our government decide that a woman selling peanuts in a cesspool of a city park is providing an essential service and therefore issue you a green card? Is that what they decided?"

"My husband an American," Shell said quietly, her voice so soft Hoffman had to lean closer to hear.

"That a fact?" he said. "And this marriage — is it for real? You didn't just marry some junkie friend of yours from the hood in order to stay in the country, did you? Are you living with this *husband,* Shell? Because I can check it out. And while I'm checking it out, I'm pretty sure I can shut off your methadone until you can prove you actually belong in this country. That program is not for foreigners. That methadone is for honest-to-God red, white, and blue American junkies. You good with that — you okay to do without your daily shot for a week, or maybe two?" Shell blinked quickly, in an effort to stop the tears that were forming in the corners of her eyes. She took a breath, then exhaled. "I ain't seen Soup for some time, maybe a week or more. That the truth."

"Where would you find him, if you were looking?"

"I can't say. That ain't my world no more."

"Bullshit," Hoffman said. "Look where you're standing, smack in the middle of it. So I'll ask you once more and if you can't come up with an answer, then I'll just head over to the station and do what I need to do."

She wouldn't look at him. She picked up a cloth and wiped the glass on the cart, working the rag vigorously, as if trying to wipe away Hoffman's very presence. She stopped, as if realizing the futility of it, and tossed the cloth aside. "His sister Janelle live over on Delaware. The walk-up beside the drugstore. I know sometime he crashes there. But that's all I know."

"Well, well," Hoffman said. "That wasn't too hard, was it?" He reached in and helped himself to more cashews. "Can I pay you for the nuts, Shell?"

"You can leave me the fuck alone."

TWENTY

She had said she was framing town houses over in Rensselaer. At least that's how Virgil remembered it anyway. He'd been fresh out of surgery and loaded up on painkillers when she told him, sitting in her truck in the hospital parking lot. Even if his memory was accurate, it wasn't going to make it easy to find her. Virgil didn't know the area east of the Hudson all that well.

Virgil would have called Dusty but he couldn't find the scrap of paper with her phone number on it. He was pretty sure it was still on the nightstand at the hospital when he'd left. If he could remember the number he wouldn't have to make the trip; he simply needed to tell her that Brownie had been killed, and a phone call would suffice for that. She at least deserved a heads-up on that account. What she chose to do with the information was up to her. Virgil would finally be done with it.

It was after four thirty when he crossed the Dunn Memorial Bridge to drive into Rensselaer. It was a town of maybe ten thousand, the houses spread scattershot along the bank of the river, the roads running up and down steep inclines. Virgil promptly got lost in the meandering backstreets, came out of the maze, got lost again. He knew what her truck looked like, but that was all he had to go on.

After a half hour, he came upon a couple of new subdivisions on the north edge of town, close to where Interstate 90 dipped down, heading east. The developments were, typically, pushing out into the countryside, eating up what appeared to be good farmland.

He was driving past the second site when he spotted the familiar blue Ford 150 parked in a mud lot across the road to his left. To his right was the work site itself, a number of half-constructed town houses with a large sign out front that read *Murphy Construction.*

Virgil missed the entrance to the lot and had to drive past. At the next intersection he turned around in a little strip mall, approached the parking lot again, and saw Dusty as she walked out of the half-constructed town house complex and crossed the street to where her truck was parked. She was wearing khaki pants and a T-shirt and a blue hard hat. Over her shoulder she carried a carpenter's apron and in her right hand she held an air nailer. As Virgil approached, behind a line of cars, she got into her truck and drove away.

Virgil followed, watching as she drove through the town and crossed over the bridge back into Albany, where she made a right on Broadway and drove over to Clinton Street, turning left. Virgil was well back in the heavy traffic and he had trouble keeping the old pickup in sight. Once he was forced to stop at a stoplight and he thought he'd lost her but he spotted her a couple of minutes later, waiting at the next light. A few blocks farther along the F150 turned left onto Lark Street. By the time Virgil got there and made the turn, the truck was parked alongside the curb a hundred yards away and Dusty was walking into a building that looked like a community center, with a playground alongside and a small soccer field.

Virgil pulled up behind the pickup. Dusty was gone only a few minutes and when she returned she was leading a boy of about six or seven, a cute kid with dark skin and a mound of wild curls tucked beneath an

Orioles cap. He was carrying a new baseball glove and a ball.

Virgil got out of his truck and Dusty saw him. She should have been surprised but if she was, she didn't show it.

"Hey," she said, looking past him. Checking to see if he was alone.

"Hello."

"What are you doing?" she asked.

"Following you."

"I figured that. What's going on?"

Instead of replying, Virgil looked at the boy. The kid probably didn't need to hear the details of Brownie's demise. "Hi," Virgil said.

"This is Travis," Dusty said.

Virgil put his hand out and the little boy put the ball in the glove so he could free his right hand. "I'm Virgil."

The boy said hello quite seriously; he didn't seem at all shy of the stranger. He was looking with interest at the cast on Virgil's left arm. Dusty regarded the busy traffic, then told Travis to get into the truck. She watched as he did, and it seemed she was deciding what to do next. She would know that Virgil hadn't been looking for her without a reason.

"We'll go to my place," she told him, and before he could answer she got into her

305

truck and drove away.

It was easier keeping up now, although she made no particular effort to help Virgil in that regard, twice running yellow lights. She hadn't seemed all that pleased to see him, but why would she be?

Below North Swan she took a left onto a narrow side street, turned again after a short block, and parked along the curb behind a clapboard five-story walk-up. She and the boy got out as Virgil pulled up behind her. She indicated a sign between her truck and Virgil's.

"They'll ticket you," she said.

Virgil looked around. There were no other parking spots along the street.

"Well, you won't be here long," she said.

The apartment was small and somewhat messy, with toys and clothes strewn here and there. But it was clean enough in general, and felt very much like a home. Dusty removed her work boots when she entered but told Virgil he could leave his on, her tone again suggesting that he wouldn't be staying. That fit into his line of thinking too. She went down a hallway and into a bedroom, leaving Virgil alone with Travis, who had removed his ball cap and was now tugging at the laces of his glove.

"So you're an Orioles fan?" Virgil asked.

"Not really. My aunt Julie bought me this cap."

"Who do you like?"

"I don't have a favorite," Travis said. "You want to see my glove?"

Virgil took it from him. "You need to loosen this up," he said. "The leather is stiff because it's new."

"I know," the boy said, his eyes on Virgil's cast again. "The ball keeps popping out when I play catch."

"You need to get some neatsfoot oil," Virgil told him. "Work it into the leather and when you go to bed at night, put the ball in the glove and tie it there with string." He took the ball from the boy and demonstrated. "Wrap it tight like that. Do that every night and it'll make a good pocket."

Virgil heard a step and glanced up to see Dusty watching from the hall. She'd changed into clean jeans and a loose cotton shirt, the sleeves rolled up.

"Mom, we have to buy some neats oil," Travis told her.

"So I hear," she said as she walked past.

She set Travis up in front of the television with a glass of juice and some crackers, and told Virgil they could talk out on the tiny balcony off the back of the apartment, where there was a steel table and a couple of lawn chairs. The balcony overlooked the side street where they had parked. Without asking, Dusty brought out two cans of Sam Adams and gave one to Virgil.

"So?" she asked.

"Somebody killed our friend Brownie last night," Virgil said.

She didn't say anything for a while. She pulled back the tab of the beer can, glancing inside the apartment, where the boy was sitting on the floor with his back against the couch, out of earshot, watching cartoons.

"How?" she asked.

"Strangled him with some fishing line."

She nodded. "Something ironic about that."

"I guess so."

She fell quiet again after that, sipping at the can while she considered the information. Virgil drank the cold beer and watched her. She had strong arms and hands, her fingers banged up from her work, her nails lined with dirt. Her face and neck and arms were deeply tanned. It appeared she wore no makeup, at least to go to work.

"Was it a robbery or something?"

"Apparently not," Virgil told her. "Somebody had it in for him."

"Might have nothing to do with the other," she said after a moment. "Guy like that probably had a few enemies."

"That's what I told the cops."

"You talked to the cops?"

"Yeah," Virgil said. "They heard that I had a little problem with Brownie. You know, because of my boat."

"But you didn't kill him."

"Nope."

She smiled, balancing the beer can on her knee. "I didn't think so. You don't look the type. And if you did kill him, I kind of doubt you would go to all the bother of tracking me down to tell me he's dead."

"Probably not. I can't say for sure, seeing as this is all hypothetical."

"So why did you track me down?"

"Because I thought you should know. I would have called you but I lost your number. But I think you need to consider whether or not Brownie told anybody that it was you who remodeled his ear last week. The cops might want to talk to you."

"What makes you think that was me?"

"I'm pretty smart for a farmer."

"Right." She tilted the can back. She was feigning nonchalance but her eyes wouldn't rest, darting one way then the other, as they had done the first time he'd met her, the first time they'd had a beer together.

"So the cops figure you for a suspect?"

she asked at length.

"I don't think so," Virgil replied. "As much as they'd like to."

She nodded, not looking at him. Virgil watched as she drew a deep breath and then took a long pull from the can of beer before setting it aside.

"Well, thanks for letting me know," she said and stood up.

Virgil knew he was being dismissed and he was fine with that. He'd felt some odd obligation to her and now that he'd honored it, he could go home. And stay there. He got to his feet. Turning toward the sliding door to the apartment, though, he remembered something.

"You know a guy drives a blue Mercedes convertible?" he asked. "Dark hair, maybe in love with his own image?"

She almost pulled it off. Her hesitation was so slight, so nearly indiscernible, that Virgil could have missed it. If he hadn't been standing so close to her, he was sure he wouldn't have seen it. But her eyes betrayed her. There was something in the instant she heard what he had asked, a flash of recognition — and quite possibly fear — that gave her away.

"No, I don't," she said. "What about him?"

"He was drinking at Scallywags last night."

"Wouldn't there be a lot of people drinking at Scallywags last night?"

"Good point," Virgil said.

They went into the apartment. Travis, in front of the TV, was wrapping his baseball in the glove, the way Virgil had shown him, his tongue clenched between his teeth as he concentrated on the task. Virgil drained the beer and turned to Dusty, handing her his empty can.

"Mind if I use your bathroom?"

She told him where it was and he went down the hallway. He had a leak and as he was washing his hands, he could hear Dusty talking to someone on the telephone. He heard her say she'd be there shortly. There was a sense of quiet urgency in her voice. After she hung up, she told the boy he was going to his aunt's for the weekend. She stopped talking when Virgil came back.

She was scared.

"Well, I'll see you around," Virgil said.

"Sure."

Virgil pointed his finger at Travis. "Neatsfoot oil."

"I'll remember. Bye."

Dusty opened the door to let him out. Virgil hesitated there, and turned back to her. Not wanting to, but doing it anyway.

311

"So what are you going to do now?"

"What am I going to do about what?"

"You said you needed to find the cylinder."

"No," she said. "That was before. These people are playing too rough for me. I'm done with it."

The first day he had met her, Virgil had told her she was a lousy liar. She hadn't gotten any better at it.

But it had nothing to do with him.

"Me too," he said.

He went down the steps to the sidewalk out front, and as he walked around the block to his truck, he knew he was doing the right thing in getting the hell out of there. Only a damn fool would involve himself in a situation with crooked cops and sadistic Russian thugs and stone-cold killers. Only a damn fool would even consider it.

But of course, only a damn fool would walk over to Dusty's truck and open the hood. And only a damn fool would remove the rotor from the distributor and stash it beneath the front seat of his own truck.

Only the most foolish of damn fools would do a thing like that.

When Dusty and Travis walked around the corner ten minutes later, with Travis carrying a backpack, Virgil was sitting behind the wheel of his own truck, his arm out the open window, listening to Patsy Cline on the radio. Dusty gave him a look of warning as they walked by, just enough to let him know once more that she didn't want him around. By her wary expression, though, she knew that something wasn't right.

She turned the truck over for maybe a minute and she got out and popped open the hood. She apparently knew a little about engines because in very short order she slammed the hood shut. She stood looking at him for a moment, and then she opened the passenger door and got Travis out of her truck and brought him over to Virgil's passenger side. They both got in. She was so angry she wouldn't look at Virgil.

"So much for you being smart," she said. "Where's my rotor?"

"Threw it in the storm sewer."

"Fuck," she said.

"You said a bad word," Travis told her.

"Sometimes it's okay to use a bad word," she told him. "Me . . . not you."

"Hey, I just want my boat back," Virgil said.

"Your boat," she repeated. She sat fuming for a moment longer, then gestured out the windshield with the back of her hand. "Drive on, Galahad."

TWENTY-ONE

After talking to Shell, Hoffman did a walking tour of the park, asking here and there if anybody had seen Soup. Nobody was talking, of course, and he knew he was wasting his time. Soup could have been standing five feet behind him, and the dregs he was asking would deny having seen him. Just the way it was down here. Garbage protecting garbage.

But at least he had one lead, and that was one more than he'd had an hour ago. He went looking for Yuri and found him at the north end of the park. In his bright red shirt and his cowboy hat, the Russian wasn't hard to spot, behind the remains of a screen that surrounded a basketball court, smoking dope with some of the players, a rag-ass bunch of teenagers and other assorted stoners, dressed in baggy shorts and torn NBA jerseys. Yuri was sitting on a picnic table and they were gathered around him like he was the Pied-fucking-Piper, due to the fact that he was passing around a couple of joints the size of Cuban cigars.

Hoffman stopped when he saw what was going on. If he walked over, the kids would make him at once and disappear into the streets. Whatever Yuri was working, Hoffman decided to leave him to it. He did stand there long enough for the Russian to notice him; he wanted him to know that he was still in the picture. He saw Yuri smile and nod his head as if agreeing with Hoffman on something, and Hoffman turned and headed out of the park. It was after five o'clock; if Soup's sister was a working woman, she should be home by now. He could walk to Delaware Street from there.

He knew the building, and he knew that Soup had some sort of connection to the neighborhood, simply because he'd seen him there often enough. On his rap sheet Soup was usually listed as no known address, but that was true of most of these skids. They had their welfare checks mailed to their friends or their aunts or a post office box, but they themselves never had anything like a home address. They were no better than hoboes, which was why it was always hard to track them down.

He went into the front foyer to check the

names on the mailboxes, but he knew it would be an exercise in futility. The apartment numbers were listed, and a couple had names alongside, but most were blank. Just another quirk of a neighborhood where nobody wanted anybody else to know their business. The inner door to the lobby was locked. Hoffman could have rung the super's number and shown his badge, but chances were pretty good that the super was tight with the tenants and in no time the entire building would know there was a cop on the premises. And Soup, if he was hunkered down somewhere inside, would be gone.

Hoffman went back outside and around to the alley at the rear of the walk-up. The back entrance was a steel fire door and it was locked, too. There was an overflowing Dumpster nearby and garbage scattered around the entranceway — fast-food wrappers, liquor bottles, condoms. The whole alley stunk of rotting food and piss.

Hoffman stood there for a couple of minutes, deciding what to do, and just as he resigned himself to going back out front and buzzing the super, the steel door opened and a chubby kid of about fifteen walked out. Hoffman collared him and pushed him back inside, against the brick wall of the

317

stairwell. He flashed his badge and told the kid he was looking for Janelle's apartment. When the kid, typically, feigned ignorance, Hoffman took the Glock from under his jacket and slammed the butt of the gun across the teenager's face, opening up a cut on the bridge of his nose. The kid folded like a cheap tent and gave him the apartment number.

Hoffman went up the stairs to the second floor and made his way down the dim hallway to the apartment. He could hear a TV playing inside, what sounded like cartoons. Hoffman knocked and waited. The door opened a couple of inches, held there by the chain, and a woman's face appeared. Hoffman showed the tin again and he heard the chain unlock and the door opened a little wider, but not much.

The woman resembled Soup slightly, although she was a hell of a lot healthier-looking. When he realized she wasn't about to willingly let him in, Hoffman shoved the door with the flat of his hand and entered. The woman was forced backward a couple of steps.

"What do you want?" she demanded.

"Looking for Soup," Hoffman said. "You're Janelle, right?"

When the woman made no reply, Hoffman

left her there and did a quick search of the apartment, moving through the living room, where a girl of about five was watching television, then in and out of the two bedrooms, checking the closets and under the beds. Last he had a look in the bathroom, pulling back the shower curtain, before returning to the kitchen. The woman stood in the open doorway to the living room, anger clear on her face. The little girl was still on the couch, watching, her eyes wide. Hoffman took in the surroundings, looking for signs of a male presence — shoes, a jacket, anything. The apartment was clean, and there was the smell of something baking. Cookies maybe.

"Do you have a warrant to search my house?" the woman asked.

"I don't need a warrant," Hoffman told her. "I got some questions."

"Since when you don't need a warrant to barge into my house?"

"Listen to the lawyer here," Hoffman said. "All right. I can make a fucking phone call and have a warrant here in twenty minutes. And you better believe I'll find some reason to take you downtown, lady. And then that little girl goes to children's services. Now tell me — is that how you want to play this?"

The woman looked at Hoffman with

contempt. "No," she said.

"Where's your brother?" he asked.

"I haven't seen him."

"And you would tell me if you had?"

"I guess that would depend on what this is about," the woman said.

Hoffman ignored the question. "When was he here last?"

"More than a month," the woman said. "He knows not to come here if he's using. Sets a bad example for my little girl."

"Soup sets a bad example for the whole human race," Hoffman said.

"I wouldn't know about that. I guess you'd be the expert on that."

"What?" Hoffman snapped.

The woman hesitated. "Nothing."

Hoffman gave her a look of warning and went past her, his shoulder brushing her on the way by. There was mail on the kitchen table, a few bills and some magazines. He went through the letters, tossing everything carelessly aside when he didn't find anything related to Soup. Some of the mail fell to the floor. When he walked back into the living room, the woman picked the letters up and put them on the table again. Hoffman turned to the little girl.

"What's your name?"

The little girl hadn't taken her eyes off

him since he'd arrived but now she looked away, her eyes on the cartoon show. "Maya," she said.

"Please," her mother said, but Hoffman held his hand up to silence her.

"Has your uncle been here?" Hoffman asked. "Has Soup been here? Do you call him Soup?"

"She calls him Trevor," the woman said. "I told you he hasn't been here."

"He hasn't been here," the little girl said softly.

Hoffman stood watching her for a moment, wondering if she was lying, even at that age. It was inherent with these people. He turned back to the woman.

"Why do you want him?" she asked when he did.

"He took something that belongs to me. He *stole* from me."

"Stole what?"

"None of your business," Hoffman said. "Where would he go? I mean, say he was in trouble or something, and he needed a safe house. Where would he go?"

"I got no notion."

"Yeah, you do. This isn't the first time Soup's been in the shit, major-league fuckup that he is. Where would he go?"

"Please watch your language."

"Answer the question."

"I have no idea," the woman said. "I have no control over him. I'm just looking after my own."

"Looking after your own," Hoffman said. "What a fucking fantasy. You people couldn't look after a kitten. And the cycle just repeats itself, doesn't it?"

"Please don't use that language in front of my little girl. Please."

"Yeah — like she never heard that word running in the park."

"This isn't the park," the woman said. "It's my home."

"Yeah, whatever." Hoffman took a pad from his pocket and wrote his cell number on it. "Listen — Soup shows here, you tell him to do the smart thing and give me a call. Tell him —" Hoffman hesitated as he formed the words in his head. "Tell him that him finding me is a much better situation than me finding him. You understand that?"

The woman took the number reluctantly, like she was touching an object of shame, something filthy beyond description. She put it on the table without looking at it.

"Yeah," she said. "I understand that."

When Hoffman got back to the park, Yuri was no longer by the basketball court with his little circle of pothead friends. Hoffman did a walk-around and didn't see him anywhere. He was getting worried and then saw the black pickup, parked along a side street off South Pearl. It appeared at first that there was nobody in the truck, but as he drew near he could see the soles of a pair of cowboy boots above the passenger window.

Yuri was stretched out across the front seat, his hat pulled low over his eyes. The truck windows were down — it would have been sweltering in there otherwise — and Hoffman stood quietly by the passenger door for a moment, looking at the Russian, whom he assumed was sound asleep. Even with that, though, he aggravated Hoffman; there was something arrogant about the fact that he was taking a nap in the midst of their search for Soup. And the cocaine.

"What are you staring at, copper?" Yuri said.

Hoffman started. He waited for Yuri to remove the hat from his eyes, but he didn't. He did smile, though, that same insinuating grin that infuriated Hoffman, although he wasn't sure why.

"I could smell you standing there," Yuri said. The smile grew wider. "See? You even smell like copper."

"Having a little snooze after dealing grass to the homeboys?" Hoffman asked.

Yuri sat up, thumbing the hat back. "I do not snooze. And I do not sell grass to those boys. Is free of charge. What — you are going to arrest me?"

"Let's just stick to the job at hand," Hoffman said.

"Remind me — what job is that?"

"Funny man. Were you a comedian back in Russia?"

"Hey, I am funny man," Yuri said. "I could have been stand-up comedian."

Hoffman was sweating bullets in the jacket. He took it off, opened the truck door, and threw it on the seat.

"You need to relax," Yuri told him.

"I'm relaxed."

"You have not been relaxed since first we meet. I think you need vacation. You need to go to camp."

"Yeah, right."

"No, I am serious. I know of a camp where you should go. I will go with you."

"What the fuck are you talking about?"

"A camp that I have just heard of."

"What camp?"

"Is called Pop's."

TWENTY-TWO

Dusty's sister lived outside the town of Cairo, about forty miles southwest of the city, and Virgil took Route 32 south. Dusty rode silently, still angry with Virgil for disabling her truck. For Virgil, it was an indication of how worried she was that she'd even gotten in with him. It seemed she was going to get her son out of harm's way, first and foremost, and if that meant putting up with Virgil for a while, she'd do it. After that, Virgil wasn't sure. But he doubted she was done with it, as she'd claimed back at the apartment.

Travis seemed unaware of the drama surrounding him. He'd brought his glove and ball with him, and he sat between Virgil and Dusty, popping the ball in and out of the glove.

"Do you play baseball?" he asked Virgil once they were out of the city.

"I used to."

"Hardball or softball?"

"Hardball."

"That's what I want to play," the boy said. "What position were you?"

"Catcher."

"Awesome." He thumped the ball into the glove again. "I want to be a shortstop. Like Derek Jeter. Some day we're going to Yankee Stadium to see a game. Right, Mom?"

"That's right."

"You should come with us," Travis said to Virgil.

Dusty made a noise at that, something between a snort and a scoff. Travis glanced at her and then at Virgil, as if he was trying to figure out what was going on between them. After a time he put the glove and ball on the seat beside him. He kept watching Virgil as he drove.

"What happened to your arm?" he finally asked.

Virgil started to tell him the hay mow story but he stopped. Kids get lied to enough in this world.

"I got beat up," he said.

"Wow," the boy said. "By bad guys?"

"Yeah."

"You going to get them back?"

"I'm not sure. You think I should?"

"I would," the boy said. "I'd zap them

with a laser rocket."

"I'll keep that in mind."

Virgil felt Dusty's eyes on him. When he glanced over, she looked away. They were well out of the city now, passing through farm country. In fact, when they reached Cairo, they would be fifteen minutes or so from Virgil's farm.

"My uncle Dave's got a race car," Travis told Virgil.

Dusty turned to her son. "Travis, are you never quiet?"

"I'm just telling Virgil," the boy said.

"What kind of car?" Virgil asked.

"Um, I'm not sure," the boy admitted. "It's got mag wheels, though. I help polish them sometimes. Did you ever drive a race car?"

"Never," Virgil said.

They rode in silence for a time. Presently they came to the turnoff for Kimball's Point. There was a large sign with an arrow on it, and the name of the town. Virgil watched as Travis straightened up, his lips moving as he sounded out the lettering.

"Hey, Mom, it's Kimball's Point," he said.

"Yeah," she said.

Travis turned to Virgil. "My mom used to work there. She helped build boats."

Virgil could practically feel Dusty stiffen,

even though she was on the other side of the cab. After a moment she glanced over at him. She was not happy, her expression warning him to leave it alone. Then she looked at her son.

"And to think I was so proud when you first learned to talk," she said.

Nobody said much else for the rest of the trip. Dusty's sister had a house on a paved country road a few miles east of town. It was a brick ranch-style wedged between a patch of pine forest and a field of alfalfa. The place had a huge yard and a separate garage that sat off to the side behind the house. When Virgil pulled in, he could see the dragster Travis had mentioned, parked inside the garage. Virgil drove up to the house and when he shut the engine off, a woman walked out the front door, as if she'd been watching for them. She looked like a slightly older, slightly heavier version of Dusty. She gave Virgil a wary look; she'd obviously been expecting just Dusty and the boy.

Dusty grabbed Travis' backpack and they both got out. Virgil hesitated, not knowing how long they might be there, and then he got out too and stood by the truck. Dusty somewhat reluctantly introduced him to her sister.

"My sister Julie," she said. "This is Virgil."

Julie didn't seem particularly enthusiastic about meeting Virgil. When he said hello, she gave him another critical once-over, no doubt taking note of his battered appearance this time, and turned back to Dusty without saying a word. It seemed she wanted to ask her sister something but wouldn't in front of the boy.

"Virgil got his arm broke by some bad guys," Travis announced.

That didn't help matters.

"What's going on?" Julie asked, still looking at Dusty.

"Nothing," Dusty said. "Travis, take your backpack inside."

Julie watched as the boy trudged through the front door and into the house before turning to Dusty. "You in trouble?"

"No."

"Don't lie to me." She indicated Virgil. "What's this guy's story?"

"Well, he's not deaf," Dusty said. "If that's what you're thinking."

"I really don't care," Julie said.

"My truck broke down. He's just giving us a lift." Dusty glanced at Virgil, then back to her sister. "There's something I got to do. Can you just keep him for the weekend, Jules?"

Julie glared at Virgil once more but seemed to resign herself to the fact that that was all the information she was going to get. Maybe she was used to it, but being used to it and being happy about it were two different things. "All right," she said. "You know I'll take him anytime. But I don't like the looks of this. Why don't you both stay here for the weekend and let the train wreck here take care of whatever it is."

"Because it's not his to take care of," Dusty told her.

"Next time I just might stay in the truck," Virgil said.

Dusty almost smiled at that, but her sister didn't come close. Travis came out of the house again, carrying his ball glove. "Aunt Julie, do you have any neats oil?"

"What?"

"Neatsfoot. I'll buy you some," Dusty said to the boy. She glanced at the house, then turned to Julie. "Where's Dave?"

"Took the boys to town."

Dusty nodded. "I have to use the bathroom."

She went inside, leaving Julie and Virgil standing awkwardly in the yard. When Dusty came out a few minutes later, her expression was tight, and she was moving quickly. She wouldn't look at her sister. She leaned over to kiss Travis and when she did Virgil saw the hard bulge beneath her shirt at the back.

"Okay, dude," she said. "See you in a couple of days. You be good."

The little boy pulled away from her kiss. "Okay," he said. "Bye, Virgil."

They drove away in silence, Dusty staring morosely out the passenger window as they headed back to the main road. It was obvious that she was upset about dropping the boy off or, more accurately, about the circumstances that had led her to do it.

"Don't be mad about the boy mentioning your connection to Kimball's Point," Virgil said finally. "I know about the boat. And about Parson, and the cocaine."

"And you're still hanging around? Man, you really are stupid."

"Beginning to look that way," he said. "Although I had decided earlier today that cut-and-run was the smart move. So what about it? I will if you will."

"No."

"Why not?" Virgil asked. "Is it about the money?"

"Got nothing to do with money," she said without hesitation. She was quiet for some time, shaking her head, as if having a conversation with herself, considering what more to tell him. "All right," she said at length, "I'll tell you my sad little story, farm boy. Or at least as much as you need to know. And when I'm done, we'll find an auto parts place so you can buy me a new rotor for my truck, and then you can drop me off and head on back to the country. You good with that?"

"Depends on the story."

"Depends on the story," she mimicked. "Well, I only have the one, so like it or not, that's what you get." She exhaled, running her fingers through her short hair. "Shit, if I'm going to spill my guts, I need a drink. Let's find a bar or a roadhouse or something."

They came upon a place a few miles farther on, a stucco building with faux palm trees out front and a smiling Mexican wearing a sombrero on a sign on the roof. The bar was called Pistolero Pete's. Virgil drove around back of the place and parked against a freshly painted plank fence.

"I can lock the truck," he said. "If you want to leave that gun in the glove box. Unless you're figuring on robbing the joint."

She gave him a sharp look, and she held it for a few moments, as if challenging him. Then she leaned forward to pull the revolver from the back of her jeans.

"No, I'm not figuring on robbing the joint," she said. She opened the glove compartment and put the gun inside.

It was Friday evening and the roadhouse was a busy place. The Mexican atmosphere inside was every bit as genuine as the fake palm trees out front. The drink specials were listed on a blackboard above the bar and featured, among other choices, a thirty-two-ounce margarita. Virgil and Dusty got a couple of Buds and found a corner that was somewhat out of the earshot of the loud camaraderie of the drinkers up front.

"What's your brother-in-law going to say when he finds out you stole his gun?" Virgil asked.

"I'm hoping to put it back before he does."

"Why do you think you need a gun?"

Dusty shrugged. "Better to have it and not need it than the other way around." She tipped the bottle back. "Would have been good advice for Brownie. Right?"

"You saying that whoever killed Brownie might come looking for you?"

"How can I answer that when I don't know who killed Brownie?"

"Maybe you don't know," Virgil said, "but I'm guessing you have a theory."

"Theories are for mathematicians."

"Talking to you is frustrating." Virgil

glanced at the drinkers at the bar. Many looked to be farmers, or construction workers who hadn't gone home after getting off work, still wearing dirty jeans and work boots. "So you know how to use a gun?"

Dusty laughed. "A little. I belonged to a . . . I guess you could call it a social club. Jefferson Park, back in the day. We were firearm enthusiasts."

As she talked, she was taking in the room around them. She was looser now than she'd been earlier. Virgil wondered if it was because of the gun, if she felt more at ease now that she could protect herself. Thinking about it, though, he realized it wasn't that at all. It was because she'd dropped the boy off. Whatever else happened, her son was safe. She took a long pull on the beer, then set her bottle down and glanced over to see him watching her.

"All right," she said, as if resigning herself to an unsavory task. "Remind me again what you want to know."

"Why you can't leave this alone."

"Oh yeah, that." She looked around again. "Fuck, I could use a smoke."

"You smoke?"

"No. I quit when I was pregnant with Travis. I miss it sometimes. Days like this, I miss it a lot. But I can't go back to it." She smiled. "Kids ruin everything, you know that?"

"Tell me the story," Virgil said.

"All right, you asked for it." First she tipped the Bud back again, as if gearing herself for the telling. "I grew up in the city. Typical story, my old man left when I was a kid, there was no money, I hung out with the wrong people, all that shit. I was in a half-ass gang, did some time in juvie, probation, blah, blah, blah . . . I'm just going to fast-forward through all that, okay? Summer I was twenty-one I got busted for dealing hash. I had an uncle in Kimball's Point — well, technically a guy living with my aunt, name of Big Jim Cunningham — who told the courts he'd take me in, put me to work in his boatyard. I wasn't into it but it kept me out of jail. Turned out I loved it. That's what started me with the carpentry."

"I wondered about that," Virgil said.

Dusty nodded. "Big Jim restored older boats sometimes and once in a while he'd buy one down in Florida or the islands and we'd sail it up through the intercoastal, from the Gulf or the Caribbean all the way to Kimball's Point. I got to know that trip pretty well, could run it on my own if I needed to."

She hesitated then, smiled as if to herself.

335

"Okay," she said. "One weekend I met Parson at a regatta, up near the city. We, um . . . hit it off, lack of a better term. Fast-forward again. Ended up moving in to-gether. All I knew about him was that he owned some buildings in the city. And he had money. He gave me the twenty-carat treatment. You know? All that stuff a girl dreams about." She gave Virgil a look. "Well, maybe you don't know about that."

"I'll use my imagination."

"So, seven years ago — we'd been together a little over a year — we took a vacation to the Bahamas. One day we're in some little marina and Parson finds this forty-four-foot Chris-Craft called *Down Along Coast*. Just stumbled on it, or that's what I believed at the time. Beautiful boat — completely restored, all polished mahogany and brass. He wants to buy it. He was going through a divorce, though, or so he claimed, and he didn't want his wife to claim half of the boat. He convinces me to put it in my name, temporarily. And we sail it home. Apparently you know what happened next."

Virgil nodded. "Story I got — the cops raided you out in the river, Parson threw the cylinder overboard and then followed it."

"That's it," Dusty said. "Somebody ratted

us out and the cops were waiting. Parson went over the side. Fucker could swim like an otter. I never learned."

"So you're left holding the bag?"

Dusty finished her beer. "Parson had it all planned from the start. There was no ex-wife, no pending divorce. He just didn't want the boat in his name, in case things went sour. When the shit hit the fan, he went for a swim and I went to jail for three years."

"For what?"

"They found a few ounces of coke on the boat. They decided I was trafficking, which I wasn't. But they convinced the DA."

"Was it Parson's dope? The stuff they found?"

"It was our dope," she said. "Purely recreational. It's a long trip from the Bahamas to Kimball's Point. A girl could get bored." She half smiled. "What — you think you're drinking with an angel here?"

"I never thought that for a minute."

"You don't have to sound so convinced," she said. She stood up. "I need another beer. You ready?"

Virgil nodded and watched as she walked across the room. He thought she looked good in her jeans and the man's shirt, and the locals drinking at the bar thought so too. The guys were all watching as she walked by, but nobody got too close, and nobody spoke to her. She had a hands-off quality about her, a sort of built-in defense that made her unapproachable. She paid for the beers and carried them back to the table.

"So there you go," she said, sitting down. "Satisfy your curiosity?"

"Nope."

"Why not?"

"You never answered my question," Virgil said. "I didn't ask how you were involved. I asked why you're *still* involved."

"Oh, that," she said, and smiled, as if she thought she might have gotten away with something. "It's simple. I'm on parole. If the cops find that cylinder and decide to connect it to me, I'm going back to jail. And for a lot longer than three years this time."

"How can they do that?" Virgil asked. "The thing was at the bottom of the river."

"Listen, you're driving down a road, cops chasing you. You toss a bag of grass out the window. The cops find it, it's *your* grass. It might not be in your possession, but it's your grass. They might use the same argument here. They might not get a conviction but I can't take that chance. I need to know what Hoffman plans to do with the shit."

Virgil sat back and looked around the

room, pulling on the Budweiser. When he glanced back at her, she was watching him quietly with intelligent green eyes, waiting for the next question, which she had probably already anticipated.

"Who's the guy in the Mercedes?" he asked.

"Cherry."

"Who's Cherry?"

"Cherry is Parson's good buddy," Dusty said. "He owns a gym in the city." She paused for effect. "He's also the guy who ratted Parson out to the cops. That's why they raided the boat."

"Shit," Virgil said. "And Parson doesn't know?"

"Cherry would be as dead as disco if Parson knew. I just found out myself."

"How?"

"Brownie told me," she said. "Once I got that fat fucker talking, he couldn't stop. He was still on the force back then so he knew all about it. Apparently the cops suspected that Cherry was dealing steroids at his gym, to high school athletes looking to get noticed by the college scouts. But when they raided the place, they came up empty. So they hit him at home, and they got a big surprise. Cherry's computer was loaded with pictures of naked little boys. He was selling more than 'roids. I got a feeling that Cherry could have handled the bad publicity over a steroid bust. Kiddie porn is another thing altogether. Especially for a conceited ladies' man like Cherry. So he rolled over on Parson to keep things quiet."

"And now he found out that Brownie talked," Virgil said.

"That was my fault," Dusty said. "I said something stupid at Parson's the other day when Cherry was standing there listening. Looks like he figured things out." She paused for a long moment. "He knows that I know. And he's panicking, if he killed Brownie."

"So why not tell Parson?"

"I almost did. I came real close. But if Parson didn't believe me, I was in deeper than ever. Cherry is a fucking nut, and he's always strapped. Always."

"Which is why you borrowed the gun."

She half smiled. "Just trying to level the playing field."

"Sounds like you're enjoying this."

She shook her head. "No, I'm not. I go back to jail and I lose my son, I lose the most important thing in the world to me. There's nothing even remotely enjoyable about that. You understand?"

Virgil watched her for a moment, how

earnest she was in this, then nodded. "So what next?"

"I told you. You drop me off and go back to your chickens."

"I don't have any chickens."

"You know what I mean. Go home. I'm going to try and find Hoffman, and this Russian cowboy and Scoop, or whatever his name was. If I can set something up between them and Parson, maybe they'll leave me alone. And it would eliminate any police involvement. All I want to be is clear of it."

"What about Cherry?"

"I don't know about Cherry," she said after a moment. "If he killed Brownie . . ." She hesitated again. "I'm hoping he's smart enough to realize I haven't told Parson. But I don't have a lot of faith in Cherry's intelligence."

"All right," Virgil said. He finished his beer and stood up. "Let's find Hoffman."

"You're not coming along. Why would you get involved in this?"

"Sonofabitch stole my boat."

"That line worked the first time I met you. Not anymore. This isn't your business, Virgil Cain."

Virgil displayed his cast. "They made it my business. So I'm involved. You might as well get used to it."

"Go home, farm boy," she said. "This isn't your thing at all. I got no choice but to do this. For fucksakes, go home."

"I don't take orders from you."

Dusty got to her feet. "Anybody ever tell you you're a stubborn bastard?"

"Look who's talking."

They went outside and got into the truck. As Virgil was backing up, he had a sudden thought and he stopped. "Soup," he said.

"What?"

"It wasn't Scoop. It was Soup."

Dusty looked over. "Tall skinny dude. Missing a front tooth?"

"Tall and skinny as a rake. He could have been missing a tooth. Things were moving pretty fast."

"Soup Campbell," Dusty said. "From the park. Used to be a basketball star until the pipe got him." She sat thinking. "What would he be doing with Hoffman?"

"He knows you then?"

"Yeah."

"Remember I told you he hid the paper with your number on it?" Virgil asked. "That explains it."

"Still doesn't explain what a guy like Soup would be doing with Hoffman."

"He really didn't look like he was having much fun." Virgil laughed. "Come to think of it, I haven't had much fun with Hoffman myself."

She looked at him a moment before smiling. "Now who's the one enjoying himself?"

Virgil hit the gas. "See if we're still laughing when it's over."

TWENTY-THREE

It was nine o'clock by the time they got back to the city. Dusty gave directions and they headed straight for Jefferson Park, driving through the heavy Friday-evening traffic. They left the truck on a side street off Grand and walked the two blocks to the park.

"Why do you think he'll be here?" Virgil asked.

"I don't," Dusty said. "But I got no idea where else to look."

The park was emptying out of joggers and walkers and people tossing Frisbees. Obviously it was a different place after dark, and one element was departing just as another, different, one appeared. Several people spoke to Dusty, mainly down-and-out types, sitting on benches or just shuffling along on the grass. She asked after Soup, but it seemed as if nobody had seen him for a few days.

"Let's take a walk down South Pearl," Dusty said. "There's some diners and bars we could check out."

As they started to leave, they saw a woman moving along the sidewalk that angled through the park, pushing a peanut cart slowly, as if weary after a long day. The woman was huge, with reddish dreads and a scarred face.

"Shell," Dusty called but the woman didn't hear, or chose not to.

They caught up to her as she pushed the cart onto the walkway that led out of the west end of the park. This time she turned when Dusty called to her.

"Dusty," she said. "You here again?"

"Hey, Shell," Dusty said.

The big woman looked past her to Virgil, suspicious. "What's up?" she asked.

"You seen Soup Campbell around?"

"Why the fuck everybody looking for Soup today?" Shell asked. "He America's Most Wanted or something?"

"Who else is looking for him?"

"Piece of shit not worth talking about."

Dusty shot Virgil a look before turning back to Shell. "What's going on? What's Soup been up to?"

"Same thing he always been up to, I expect. But I ain't seen him in a week or

345

more. That boy's been in a bad way for some time. And now it look like he's running with the worst."

"Who was looking for him?"

"Scumbag cop name of Hoffman."

"Today? Hoffman was here today?"

"A few hours ago. And he's hot to find Soup. Not your regular shit neither, you ask me. Something else going on with that fucking Hoffman. Threatened my ass, said he would get me thrown out the country."

"What did you tell him?"

Shell's hands on the cart handles were clenched, the muscles in her large forearms twitching. "Told him what I had to, to get shed of the man. Told him that Janelle might know." There were tears forming in her eyes. "I must be getting weak. But I told the motherfucker what he wanted to know. I ain't proud of it, girl."

And she walked away, pushing the heavy cart before her.

For a moment Virgil thought the woman, Janelle, was going to tell him to wait in the hallway. She didn't seem overjoyed to see Dusty either, but after some deliberation she let them both in. She was thin and attractive, with long straight hair. Maybe thirty-five. There were toys scattered about

346

the small apartment, and finger paintings pinned to the fridge, but there was no child in sight. The woman had been stirring a pot of macaroni when they arrived, and she turned it off to talk to them.

"I'm starting to get nervous now," she said when Dusty asked about Soup. They were sitting across from each other at the kitchen table. Virgil hung just inside the door.

"You seen him?" Dusty asked.

Janelle nodded. "He was here last night. High as a pine. And running scared, though the dope took the edge off that. But I could tell. Never seen him like that before, about to jump out of his skin."

"Who's he scared of?"

"He didn't say. You know Soup, he isn't much for sharing his load. But all he talked about was getting out of the city. That boy never leaves the city. But he was carrying a backpack, like he was fit to travel. Where would he get a backpack?"

"Was Hoffman here?"

Janelle took a long moment and she nodded again. This time she didn't elaborate. Virgil, leaning against the door, could see the contempt in her eyes, just hearing the name.

"What did you tell him?"

"I didn't tell that prick nothing."

347

"What did he want?"

"Claiming Soup ripped him off."

"Oh shit," Dusty said. She glanced at Virgil.

Janelle followed her eyes, staring at Virgil for a long moment before looking back at Dusty. "What's going on here, Dusty? You haven't been around here for years and now you're back asking into this. Where have you been?"

"On the straight and narrow, Janelle."

"Doesn't look to me like you're not walking any straight and narrow today. What's Soup got himself into?"

"A lot of trouble, if he ripped Hoffman off," Dusty said. "We're not talking a couple of grams here, Janelle. This is bigtime."

"Soup doesn't do big-time. Never has."

"Well, he may have moved up," Dusty said. "And that's why he's scared. Where would he go, Janelle?"

"I don't know. And that's the truth. You know how he is, and it's a big enough city. If he's flush, no telling what he might do."

"You said he wanted to leave though."

"Crack talk. He's got nowhere to go. Like I say, he's never been out of the city. The only time —"

She stopped herself from talking then, pulled back within herself, shooting Virgil that look again.

"What were you going to say?" Dusty asked.

Janelle got to her feet and walked across the room to the stove. Even though the burner was off, she removed the lid from the pot and give the macaroni a stir. When she turned back, she fixed her stare on Dusty. "How do I know what you're up to, Dusty? You haven't been around here all this time and now you show up with some dude, got a broke arm and a bashed-in face, and I'm supposed to tell you everything I know? Seems like Soup's a hot commodity these days. Well, I can remember you puffing on that same pipe, and we both know where it took you. So how am I supposed to know you're not going to do him harm?"

Dusty sat back in the chair. "I don't know how to answer that," she admitted. "But I wouldn't hurt him, Janelle."

"How about this?" Virgil said. Janelle turned to him. "I got this arm and this face from Hoffman and his buddy. Now they're looking for your brother, and so are we. So I guess you have to pick your poison. Who would you rather have find him?"

"How about neither?" Janelle asked.

"I can't see that working for Soup," Virgil said.

Janelle didn't look at either of them then, just dropped her eyes to the floor as she considered it. "Only place I can guess is Pop's Camp," she said. "And that's nothing but a wild guess. He never said anything to me about any place."

"What's Pop's Camp?" Dusty asked.

"Place up in the Adirondacks," Janelle said. "You remember — old dude named Pop Chamberlain worked at the Y here, lot of years. He had a camp up north, used to take kids from the neighborhood there every summer. It was a basketball camp, but they had swimming and fishing, all that stuff. Soup loved it there. He even worked there a couple summers when he got older, helping out with the younger kids. He kept in touch with Pop all the years. One time Soup was a teenager, maybe fifteen, sixteen, he ran away from home twice. That's where he went both times."

Dusty looked at Virgil.

"I'm saying it's a long shot," Janelle said. "But I don't know where else he would go, not outside the city."

"Where in the Adirondacks?" Dusty asked.

Janelle thought. "I can't remember. One of those little lakes up there. I was never there though. It was just for the boys."

"Would Pop take him in?" Dusty asked.

"Would he take him in if he's using?"

"Pop's been dead for years. For all I know, the place isn't even there anymore."

"You ever been up in those mountains?" Dusty asked. "There's like a thousand lakes up there. How the fuck are we supposed to find a place called Pop's Camp that might not even exist anymore?"

They were walking back to Virgil's truck. It was full dark now and the street had taken on a different atmosphere. Dusty was glad that Virgil was along. She had never been concerned walking the neighborhood back when she was living there, but things had changed so much in the past few years. The faces were different; the vibe was different. She didn't feel part of it anymore. Lately, she didn't feel part of anything.

"Like the guy lost out in the country who asks the old-timer for directions," Virgil said as they walked, "and the old-timer says, 'Drive along this road here and turn left where the old maple tree used to be.' "

"Is that supposed to be helpful?" she asked.

"I can do better."

"Yeah?" she asked doubtfully.

They were at the truck now. Virgil smiled at her over the roof as he unlocked the door.

When she got in, she was still waiting.

"I said *yeah?*" she repeated.

"I can tell you where Pop's Camp is."

"Where?"

"Place called Crow's Landing."

"And how would you know that?" she asked. Still skeptical.

"You recall me mentioning a boat?" Virgil asked.

"Only about fifty times."

"That's what was written across the back of it. I remember because it took me most of a day to sand it off. So, unless there's more than one Pop's Camp in the Adirondacks, I'd say that's the place."

"Then let's go."

"It'll have to wait until morning now. I've got chores to do."

"Shit," Dusty said. She sat staring out the windshield as Virgil checked the rearview mirror for traffic. "Soup's probably not even there."

"His sister said that's where he used to go when he was on the run. Besides, you got any other ideas?"

"No," she admitted.

"Then we might just as well chase this one down," Virgil said. "You want me to drop you at home?"

She hesitated and he knew she was thinking about Cherry.

"Might be better if you slept at the farm," Virgil said. "That way we can get an early start. I got room."

She still wouldn't look at him, and he could tell she was a little pissed that he was trying to save her again. But she also seemed a little grateful at the same time. "How do I know this isn't part of a master plan to get me alone out there?"

"Yeah, that's it," Virgil said. "So far I've got a stolen boat, a broken arm, and a knot on my head about the size of Vermont." He put the truck in gear and pulled away from the curb. "I'm one smooth operator."

TWENTY-FOUR

When Virgil came in from doing the chores, he found Dusty at the stove in the kitchen, heating spaghetti sauce from a jar on one burner while some pasta boiled in a pot on another. They'd stopped at her place for a change of clothes before leaving the city and he saw that she'd changed into khaki pants and a faded cotton shirt. Her hair was damp. The sink had been half full of dirty dishes when he'd left earlier; now they were washed and sitting in the strainer.

"I used your shower," she said.

"No problem."

"Any idea how old this spaghetti is?" she asked, holding up the box.

"I would say . . . less than a year," he estimated.

"Christ," she said.

"Spaghetti doesn't go bad."

"You can eat first then," she said. "And you don't believe in washing dishes?"

"I got one arm," Virgil said.

"Right," she said. "I forgot about that. You wouldn't be able to do the dishes. You can bale hay, and feed cows and combine wheat. You can steal the rotor from my truck and throw it in a fucking storm sewer, but there's no way you could wash dishes."

"That spaghetti about done?" Virgil asked.

After they ate, Virgil made a pot of coffee — another thing he could do with one arm, Dusty pointed out — and they sat on the side porch. There was a half-moon rising and the barns and outbuildings were clearly visible across the yard. A couple of barn cats came out into the moonlight and sat cleaning themselves on the concrete pad outside the milk house. Maybe ten feet apart, typical cats, each pretending the other didn't exist.

"What's that smell?" Dusty asked.

"Probably the horses in that field yonder."

"I like it."

"Yeah?" Virgil said. "I always assumed your average city person didn't care for the smell of manure."

"I'm an average city person?"

"I guess not," Virgil said after thinking about it. He removed his Mud Hens cap, hung it on the arm of the chair, and pushed back his hair with his fingers.

"What's with the bird, anyway?" Dusty asked.

"It's a mud hen."

"And what's that?"

"It's a bird."

Dusty sighed. "We've established that. How come you're wearing a hat with a mud hen on it?"

"I used to play for the Toledo Mud Hens," he told her. "This is the cap I wore."

"And you're not allowed to wash it?"

Virgil gave the cap a look as if seeing it for the first time. "I never gave it much thought."

"That's obvious." She settled back in the chair, getting comfortable. "You're lucky living out here," she said. "Just listen to that."

"Listen to what?"

"Silence." She took a drink of coffee. "There's no such thing where I live. Night or day, it's never quiet." She didn't say anything for a time. "I have to get out of there. I have to get my son out of there. Before it's too late."

"Too late for what?"

"For everything."

"Well, it looks like your sister managed it," Virgil said.

Dusty, her head tilted back against the

chair, nodded.

"She's a tough nut, isn't she?" Virgil said. "She looked at me like I was running a Ponzi scheme."

"Big sisters are protective."

"She was protecting you from me?"

"From everybody. You just landed in her sights." Dusty glanced over. "She's a little judgmental at times but I owe her . . . everything. She's been a second mother to Travis. Actually, she was his first mother. I had him when I was in stir. Julie took him home and raised him until I got out, two years later. You want to talk about fucked-up meetings. Try walking up to a two-year-old and saying, 'Hi, I'm your mother. I just got out of prison.' He's already walking and talking. He's already his own little person. And you have to try to fit yourself into his life without freaking him out."

"He seems okay," Virgil said. "I mean, the kid could use a jar of neatsfoot oil, but I wouldn't say that makes you a bad mother."

Dusty smiled, looking across the yard to the barn and the cats lolling in the light. She sipped at her coffee.

"I looked for your computer while I was waiting for the water to boil," she said after a while. "I wanted to Google Crow's Landing."

"I don't have a computer," Virgil said.

"I figured that when I didn't find one."

"What would I do with a computer?"

"You could Google Crow's Landing."

Virgil shrugged and drank his coffee. The cattle in the back pasture, out of sight of the house, began to moan and the lowing floated across the air. Dusty turned her head toward the sound; it seemed to take a moment before she recognized it.

"Place might not be easy to find," Dusty said, glancing back to Virgil. "It's probably not even the name of a town. Shit, it might just be a spot where a guy named Crow landed a boat a hundred years ago. How we going to find it?"

"We will."

"So you know where to find it?"

"Nope," Virgil said. "But I know where to find a guy who does. I don't need to gurgle anything."

"Google."

"That either."

"Okay." She shook her head, as if Virgil was being obstinate and she wasn't going to give him the satisfaction of an argument.

"What's your real name?" Virgil asked. "Even your sister calls you Dusty."

"It is my real name," Dusty replied, again watching across the yard. "My mother was a singer, a professional actually, for a while anyway. Sang under the name Irma Lachance. Her real name was Betty Saunders. Anyway, she was a blues singer, pretty good too, I guess, sang in a couple of clubs in Jersey. Atlantic City once, some blues festival. And she worshipped Dusty Springfield. So that's how I got the name."

" 'Son of a Preacher Man.' "

"You're not going to sing to me, are you?" she asked.

"You've been through enough," Virgil said.

Dusty, smiling, sipped her coffee.

"What happened to your mother?"

"She was a drunk and she died."

Virgil glanced over at her. She was still staring straight ahead, holding the cup with both hands, up near her face. After a moment she exhaled and turned to him, looking to shift topics. "So where's your wife, Mr. Cain? What's she going to say when she gets home and sees me?"

"I don't have a wife."

"No?" Dusty feigned surprise. "I guess that Lady Schick on the edge of the tub is yours then. Along with a few other feminine touches I noticed. How often do you shave your legs anyway?"

"For Chrissakes."

"Well?"

"I have a friend . . ." Virgil began awkwardly.

"A friend?" Dusty repeated. "What, she comes over to use your bathtub? Where is she now?"

"France. Why do you need to know this?"

"Hey, you wanted to know everything about me. Turnabout is fair play, dude." She was smiling now. "What's she doing in France?"

"Visiting long-lost relatives."

"She didn't invite you along?"

"No." Virgil realized for the first time that Claire hadn't asked him to go with her. Not that he could have gone, with the harvest and everything else. Still, she could have asked.

"Too bad," Dusty said, looking out over the yard again. "If you were in Europe, you wouldn't have been on the river that day. And none of this would be happening. What does she do, your friend?"

"She's a cop."

Dusty turned to him. "You're kidding me. Does she know about all this? Have you talked to her?"

"I talked to her. She doesn't know."

Dusty fell quiet while she deliberated. "Okay. You didn't tell her. And the reason you didn't tell her is because she would have given you good advice. Like, forget about your goddamn boat and tell the cops about the cylinder. Why do I get the feeling you're not real good at taking advice?"

"I had no idea you were such an expert on me."

Dusty laughed. "I'm getting there."

Virgil stood and tossed his remaining coffee onto the grass, then turned and went into the house. When he came back he was carrying a bottle of Jameson and a couple of glasses. He poured for them both.

Dusty was still smiling. "Giving me liquor so I'll quit asking about your love life?"

"Worth a try," Virgil said, sitting down. "So you want to leave the city. What's keeping you?"

Dusty tried a little of the Irish whisky. "Money," she said. "I want to buy a house and I don't have enough for a down payment. I could swing the mortgage payments. I'm already paying rent, wouldn't be much different. But I need money down."

"No boyfriend?"

"No."

Virgil took a sip and savored the whisky on his tongue before swallowing. In the pasture field by the barn, the horses were walking toward the water trough. They always came in a bunch, never in ones or twos. It was the herd mentality, Virgil assumed, from the days when horses ran wild and were wary of predators. Nowadays it wasn't really necessary but apparently the instinct remained. Horses were safe in the modern world. Safer than people in some respects. He had another drink and then asked, "Does Parson know that Travis is his son?"

Dusty had her glass halfway to her mouth. Her eyes narrowed, then she took a healthy slug. "There you go, being smart again."

The moon crossing the sky dropped just enough to shine fully on her face beneath the eave of the porch. She looked like a kid sitting there. A kid with a lot of weight on her shoulders.

"No, he doesn't know," she said slowly. "And I don't want him to know. If he finds out, I'm fucked. He'll take Travis away from me. There is no doubt in my mind about that." She stared straight ahead, her eyes defiant. "He can't find out."

"The courts would never give him custody."

"The courts won't be involved," Dusty said flatly.

"And you're sure he doesn't know."

She took another drink, needing it now to address the situation. "No, I'm not. I think he might suspect something."

"That's why you want to leave the city."

"I was looking for a house before all this," she said. "This ups the ante. Through the roof."

Virgil looked at the liquor in his glass, thinking. "So he's been out of your life since that night on the boat?"

"Yeah."

"And then I find the cylinder and suddenly he's back in your life."

"Yeah. Way to go."

"And you don't want him getting too close," Virgil said. "Because if he does, he's going to find a little boy who looks like him. And the math works too."

"You're right on the money."

Virgil saw that her glass was nearly empty and reached for the bottle. "So if you track down the coke, and hand it over, then he's out of your life again. That the way it is?"

"I'm hoping that's the way it is."

It was midmorning when Hoffman walked into Yuri's office behind the pool hall the next day. He found the Russian at his desk, talking on the phone while rolling a cigarette. There was a rotund black man on the couch, with an acne-scarred face and a wispy goatee. His bare belly showed where his tight T-shirt didn't meet his sweatpants, and he had a dreamy, spaced-out look on his face that was all too familiar to Hoffman. The office smelled strongly of pot.

"Mr. Hoffman," Yuri said when he hung up. "I wish you to meet my new friend Jay Dee."

"Yo," Jay Dee said and Hoffman didn't reply.

"I am deputizing Jay Dee," Yuri said. "Because Jay Dee knows how to find the camp owned by the man Pop. Jay Dee used to go there with Mr. Soup, when they are teenagers and playing the basketball."

Hoffman regarded the man on the couch doubtfully. "Where is it?"

"Adirondacks," Jay Dee said.

"We know that," Hoffman said. "But where?"

"Man, I don't know the name of this road, that road. I'm gonna know when we get there. I been there a lot of times. I got like a map in my head. We get there, I'm gonna know."

Hoffman looked at Yuri, eyebrows raised. The big Russian just smiled as he stood up and walked to a cupboard in the corner. He pulled out an Adidas sports bag and tossed it on the desk, then went back into the cupboard for a bottle of vodka, a handful of energy bars, and a large bag of peanuts in the shell. He put everything in the bag, then opened the top drawer to the desk and brought out a Colt .44 revolver, checking that it was loaded before tucking it in his belt. Finally he reached into the same drawer and produced an Uzi automatic pistol and a couple of clips. Both the Uzi and the ammunition went into the bag and he zipped it shut.

"Okay, now we are prepared," he said, and smiled again. "Is like we are going on little picnic. You agree, Mr. Hoffman?"

"It's no fucking picnic," Hoffman said.

Yuri wanted to take his truck but Hoffman vetoed the idea. The new deputy, Jay Dee, reeked of pot and body odor and the Russian himself wasn't exactly a fanatic when it came to personal hygiene. Hoffman had no intention of being crammed in the cab of a pickup for hours with the pair of them. They took his sedan.

They left the city just after eleven o'clock, driving north on 87, Hoffman behind the wheel with Yuri on the passenger side and Jay Dee sprawled in the center of the backseat, legs splayed, his hands resting on his big belly. With the long drive ahead of him, Hoffman once again considered the bizarre predicament he found himself in. Since the day he had seized the cylinder from the hick at the marina it was as if he'd been caught up in a ridiculous movie. A very long and ridiculous movie. If Soup wasn't hiding out in the camp up north, and Hoffman had little faith that he was, the movie would just get longer, although he doubted it could get any more ridiculous. Of course, Hoffman could end it at any time, just walk away from it all, take his pension and live with it, but he'd invested too much time and effort now for that to be a consideration, and the promise of a payoff was too big. He had come this far; he would play it out.

He wished he had scored a GPS system from the force before he'd retired. Now he was stuck with a state road map and the vague recollections of the pothead in the backseat. For a guide he had the lunatic in the front. At this moment the lunatic was looking at the map, charting their route. He had his seat back all the way and one big black cowboy boot was resting on the dash. His Stetson was pushed up onto his forehead.

"So what is first exit we take?" he asked. "There is U.S. 9, which takes us to Lake Placid. Is where they have the Olympics one time."

"Yeah," Jay Dee said brightly. "I remember

going through there."

Yuri glanced over at Hoffman, smiled, and looked at Jay Dee in the backseat. "This is where we go. You can stand easy for now, Deputy Jay Dee. We will not need your expertise until we reach the mountains of the Adirondacks. This is learning experience for me. I did not know they are having mountains in the New York State. But they cannot be big, like the Rocky Mountains?"

"They're not the fucking Rockies," Hoffman said irritably.

"They're big enough," Jay Dee said. "You wouldn't want to climb one, dog."

"There will be no mountain climbing on this trip," Yuri said. "This is strictly hunting expedition. Our quarry is Mr. Soup. He is a small quarry, I will admit, but so far a formidable one." He paused to look out the side window, off into the distance. "However, is not like the old days on the Great Plains, when the men hunt the buffalo. Foolish men — they were indiscriminate with their shooting and almost they make the buffalo . . . what is the word when an animal is no more on the earth?"

"Extinct," Hoffman said.

"Extinct," Yuri agreed. He sighed. "How I wish I could have participated in the buffalo hunt. I would have had Sharps fifty-caliber rifle. Can shoot one-half mile, this rifle. Who knows — maybe they would call me Buffalo Yuri, like the great Buffalo Bill."

"The dude that started the football team?" Jay Dee asked.

"You're a moron," Hoffman said.

Yuri gave Hoffman a look. "Come on, Mr. Hoffman. Jay Dee is making joke, I think. You must join in. This is great adventure we are on. Why is it you cannot enjoy yourself?"

Hoffman said nothing as he swung into the left lane to pass a tractor trailer. Yuri watched him for a moment longer, then turned back to Jay Dee, who, Hoffman suspected, had not been making a joke.

"Tell us about Pop's Camp," he said. "How is it that you go there?"

"Shit, most everybody I knew went there, one time or another," Jay Dee said. "This old white dude, Pop Chamberlain, used to run the b-ball program at the Y, and then like once a year he'd take a whole busload of kids up to the camp. Didn't cost us shit neither. I don't know where the money come from, but we never had to ante up a dime. I went three, maybe four times."

Yuri glanced at Hoffman. "Mr. Soup — he is going with Jay Dee to this camp."

"Yeah — I remember him being there. Him and me weren't never too tight. He

368

was a big fucking star on the court, and I was this little fat kid, you know? Everybody said he was going to college, he was gonna play in the NBA, all like that. Shit, one pull on the pipe and that motherfucker wasn't going nowhere."

In the front seat, Yuri shook his head. "Unfulfilled potential. Is a sad thing."

"Whatever," Jay Dee said. "The camp was cool, though. Played ball every morning but in the afternoon we got to swim and fish and drive around in boats and shit. They had this big mess hall, and the old guy's wife would cook for us. If we caught us some fish, old Pop would clean them up and she'd cook that."

"I would have liked to attend a camp like this," Yuri said. "I am working from the time I am nine years old."

"It was cool, man," Jay. Dee said, and something came to mind. "Well, it wasn't all cool. They had this stage at one end of the gym and once a week they would bring in this band, fucking guys with like fiddles and banjos and shit, and they'd try to teach us to square-dance. Ever see a black man square-dance?"

"Never," Yuri said.

"Well, you ain't about to neither. A nigger don't square-dance. Even Stepin-fucking-

Fetchit never did that shit."

Yuri smiled. "What about wild animals? Some buffalo would be too much to ask, I am presuming."

"I never seen no buffalo," Jay Dee said. "But there's bears. Black bears. They hang out at the dump."

"At the dump," Yuri said. "That is undignified. If I was a bear, I would be a noble bear. I would not eat garbage."

"You get hungry enough, you might," Jay Dee said. "As long as they wasn't thinking about eating me, I didn't fucking care what they ate."

"Is good point," Yuri said. "So when is the last time you see Mr. Soup?"

"I see him around all the time," Jay Dee said. "But we don't run in the same circles. I don't smoke that shit and I don't snort it. I might do a little hydro from time to time but I got it all under control, you hear? I got to think about my career."

"What's your career?" Hoffman asked, glancing back. He was sick of the man's voice already and they hadn't driven thirty miles. Maybe this would shut him up.

"I'm in the music business, dog." Jay Dee's voice held an element of incredulity, as if he expected Hoffman to be aware of this. "I mean, all the way in — producing, performing, deejaying. Jay Dee the Deejay, you dig?"

"Right," Hoffman said. "Where do you work out of?"

"Happen to be between gigs at this very moment," Jay Dee said. "Working on my own shit. Just getting it together, making it tight. Gonna do a CD of my own material. I'm gonna be a force, you watch."

"Yeah, we'll be watching for that," Hoffman said. He shot Yuri a glance and the big Russian shrugged.

"Is good to dream," he said.

"Like Soup?" Hoffman asked. "He was going to be a basketball star. Look where it got him."

"I am sad for Mr. Soup," Yuri said, agreeing. "He made a bad decision. I am afraid he is like the buffalo on the Great Plains. He is in danger of becoming extinct."

By the time they reached the exit for U.S. 9, the future rap star Jay Dee was sound asleep in the backseat, head back, mouth open. Hoffman stopped for gas outside of Elizabethtown and the man never as much as stirred.

They drove west, where the road began to rise, running between rock cuts and pine forest. The traffic was steady; it was Saturday afternoon and people would be heading for their cottages and lake houses. Yuri had removed his boots and his dirty socks were now planted on Hoffman's dashboard. He had dozed off for a while as well, and when he woke up he reached into the athletic bag at his feet and retrieved a couple of the energy bars, which he ate, washing them down with slugs of vodka. When he offered the bottle over, Hoffman refused. He could see bits of food floating inside.

A few miles along, Yuri turned the radio on and began searching for stations. There was hip-hop and new country and golden oldie rock-and-roll, but evidently none of that was to his liking and after a few minutes he turned it off. He read the road map for a time, tracing their route to Lake Placid with his large forefinger.

After he tossed the map aside, he looked out the window for a while, and presently drew the Colt revolver from inside his coat and began to point it at the passing trees, making shooting noises, like a child playing cowboys and Indians, then grew tired of that and laid the gun in his lap. He glanced into the backseat at the slumbering Jay Dee, and turned to Hoffman.

"I am bored," he said. "Tell me your sad story, copper."

"I don't have a sad story."

"Oh, but everyone has sad story. If I tell you mine, it will break your fucking heart."

"That case, I'd rather not hear it."

"Don't worry," Yuri said. "Is not for you to know. But what about you? You are respected policeman, protecting citizens of the community, and now you are involved in this dirty business. Surely you have story."

Hoffman drove in silence for a while and then jerked his thumb in the direction of Jay Dee. "There's my story right there. Guys like him. I spent thirty years out on the streets. And I've seen the scum and the garbage out there, dealers and addicts and thieves and pimps. I've thrown them in jail and watched them walk because our court system is run by Mickey-fucking-Mouse. After a while a man gets sick of it. After a while a man just throws his hands up. You can only beat your head against the wall so many times."

Yuri began to laugh. "You sound like bad novel!" he said. "You are man of great integrity but system fails you. You have no choice but to go bad."

"You have no idea what I'm talking about," Hoffman said. "I don't give a shit what you think anyway."

"Is good. Because I am not buying this

story. I think it is about the money with you. Same as everybody."

"Okay, so it's about the money. Who the fuck are you — Mother Teresa?"

"I am mother to nobody," Yuri said. "I am merely businessman." He sighed and glanced out the window. "But I am sad because I am born too late. In my heart I am cowboy."

"You're a fucking cowboy, all right," Hoffman said. "That's the one thing we agree on."

"I am cowboy," Yuri said. "Do you know how I know this?"

"I don't need to know how you know this."

"I have a code. That is how I know. A man must have a code. What about you, Mr. Hoffman — do you have a code?"

Hoffman shook his head, wishing the Russian had stayed asleep. "Yeah. Sure."

"No," Yuri said slowly. "I don't think so. You do not strike me as a man who has a code. Tell me — what is your favorite Western movie?"

"I don't watch movies."

"This is your problem," Yuri said. "I have all the movies. The Clint Eastwood, the John Wayne, the Randolph Scott." He paused. "Alan Ladd in *Shane.* This is great character. At first you think this is wimpy little guy, but later you see he is made of iron. But a man with his time running out. Is very sad to watch. Is symbolic thing. Like the Rooster Cogburn. You know the Rooster Cogburn?"

"Gee, I don't think I know anybody named Rooster."

"John Wayne is the Rooster. I speak now of the original *True Grit.* In the end is Lucky Ned Pepper and three others, and Rooster is alone. On the prairie. With Winchester rifle in one hand and Colt .45 in other." Yuri took the revolver from his lap and raised it in the air, the barrel pointing straight at the windshield. "Fill your hand, you sonofabitch!"

The loud exclamation awakened Jay Dee in the backseat. His eyes flew open and he looked frantically around, as if not quite knowing where he was. Yuri laughed again, glancing over at Hoffman, who stared at the road ahead where it continued to rise into the green mountains in the distance.

It was beginning to wear on Hoffman. The grinning Russian, the thieving Soup, the idiot in the backseat. He couldn't wait to be shed of them all.

TWENTY-FIVE

Montgomery Woodbine drew the map on the back of a flyer advertising replacement windows. He and Virgil were sitting at his kitchen table while Dusty stood a few feet away, just inside the back door. When they had arrived twenty minutes earlier she had refused the old man's offer of a chair. She had been antsy and nervous since they'd gotten up that morning at the farm. She had slept the night before on the couch in the living room, declining the use of one of the bedrooms upstairs, and after Virgil had gone up to bed, he'd heard her go out to his truck and return. He knew she had gone to retrieve the gun from the glove box. She was sleeping when he came down in the morning and the revolver was on the coffee table, within reach.

She had been quiet on the drive out to Woodbine's farm and Virgil was certain she was thinking about the boy. He tried to get her talking — about her work, her search for a house, anything — but she wasn't in the mood to converse. Maybe she thought she'd said too much the night before. Especially about Travis and the fact that Parson was the boy's father. She was good at keeping things inside. Virgil suspected that she didn't trust too many people, and why would she after what had happened? Besides, nothing she might say would change anything at this point. It was obvious she had made her mind up as to what she needed to do, and what she needed to do was keep Parson from the boy. It occurred to Virgil that that was another reason she'd wanted the gun, not simply for self-preservation.

But if it came down to using the gun, she might lose her son either way. And surely she'd taken that into consideration too. But still she was keeping it inside. Virgil suspected it was a lonely time for her, taking it all on by herself.

At the kitchen table Woodbine was being very precise with the directions to Crow's Landing, and although Virgil knew by now that he was a thorough man by nature, he also suspected, as before, that the old man simply enjoyed having company. He'd offered them coffee when they arrived but they had both had their fill earlier. Still, the old man was taking his time and Virgil again wondered just how often his children visited him. Meanwhile, Dusty's impatience was filling the room.

"Once you get to Bass Lake," Woodbine was saying, "you follow the south shore road running west, and about five miles along you'll come to a road that takes you to Carter's Bay. They'll be a sign says Carter's Bay. Turn there, it only goes the one way off the main road, and right away you have to go left. Should be another sign that says Crow's Landing. Used to be anyway. But you have to go left and it'll take you right there. It's a dead-end road. The cottage we used to rent is the second-last one and then you go a little piece and Pop's Camp is at the end. You can't miss it. There's a bunch of cabins and a big gymnasium where the boys played sports."

Woodbine studied the map for a moment longer, then added a couple of details before finally handing it to Virgil. "This got something to do with your boat?"

"Not exactly," Virgil said.

"Well, I hope you're not looking for Pop. I heard he passed away."

"No," Virgil said, standing up now.

"Just going on a holiday?" Woodbine

persisted. He stood up as well and nodded in Dusty's direction. "Is this the wife?"

"I'm not the wife," Dusty said quickly.

"No, that's not the wife," Virgil said, smiling.

"We're going on a little fishing expedition," she told the old man.

"You'll catch fish there," Woodbine said. "At least we always did, my boys and me. Perch and pike, maybe some crappie. Nothing real big though. A lot of them lakes was fished out years ago."

"Maybe there's a big one left," Virgil said.

Dusty indicated the map in Virgil's hand. "Well?"

"Yeah, we should go." As soon as he said it, Dusty turned and went out the door.

"That young woman's in a hurry," Woodbine said.

"Yeah."

"Women don't usually get that excited about fishing."

"Depends on the fish," Virgil told him.

Woodbine looked out the kitchen window, where Dusty was walking toward Virgil's truck, parked in the driveway. When she got there, she leaned against the front fender and looked expectantly back toward the house.

"Pretty girl," the old man said. "Why'd

you let her mark herself up with them tattoos?"

"I didn't have any say in it," Virgil told him.

"Oh, I know what you mean," Woodbine said, still watching out the window. "Women don't listen." He turned toward Virgil. "I still like 'em though."

"Me too," Virgil said. "Thanks for the map."

The old man could have been a map maker if he hadn't gone into farming. Four hours later they stopped by the entrance to a macadam road that ran north into the bush off the main highway south of Bass Lake, looking at a sign with an arrow on it indicating Carter's Bay. They had driven straight through, stopping once for gas and some fried chicken and fries for lunch. Dusty, in the passenger seat, kept the map in her hand throughout and now she held it up and pointed ahead a few hundred yards down the paved road, to where a gravel lane angled away into the trees.

"That's it," she said.

As Virgil turned the truck onto the paved road, Dusty's cell phone rang. When she answered, Virgil stopped the truck, concerned she might lose the signal in the trees.

"Hey honey," she said, and she listened for a moment. "Oh, we're outside the city, just taking care of a couple things."

She glanced at Virgil while she listened again.

"That's Aunt Julie's call, dude," she said. "Her house, her rules. You know better than to ask me that." She waited again. "Virgil's busy driving the truck right now." She paused. "Okay." She handed the phone to Virgil, rolling her eyes slightly as she did.

"Hi," he said.

"Do you know how to throw a curveball?" Travis asked.

Virgil smiled. "Yeah."

"Will you show me sometime?"

"Sure."

"Cool. Okay, bye."

Virgil was still smiling as he handed the phone back to Dusty.

"What was that about?" she asked.

"Guy stuff."

She gave him a look, and Virgil put the truck in gear. They drove through the heavy brush that lined both sides of the narrow roadway. The lane was just wide enough for one vehicle and when they met an SUV coming toward them, both pulled over into the tree branches to squeeze past. Within five minutes the lake came into view and from there the lane snaked along roughly parallel to the shoreline. There were cabins spotted here and there along the shore, and a few boat launches.

After a quarter hour, they arrived at the end of the road, where they came upon a ramshackle two-story lake house, with several cabins behind. A large field separated the main house and the cabins, with a baseball backstop at one end. A white building, obviously the gymnasium Woodbine had mentioned, stood at the opposite end of the field from the ball diamond. The property sloped downward from the gym to the lakeshore, where a half dozen sagging docks jutted out into the water.

The place appeared to be deserted. The wooden shutters on the main house were closed, plywood was nailed over the windows of the cabins. The paint on the buildings was faded and peeling, the grass of the ball field overgrown.

Access to the property was denied by a chain across the entrance, secured by padlocks to wooden posts at either end. There was a sign nailed to a large spruce tree just to the left of the entrance, made from a slab of rough lumber, painted red at one time, and on it in white letters they saw:

POP'S CAMP

TWENTY-SIX

They were sitting alongside a road that ran east from Route 3, looking down into a little valley where a crossroads featured a gas station and an establishment advertised as Dot's General Store.

They were lost.

They had been lost for nearly two hours, and Hoffman felt as if any moment he was going to lose his mind as well. It was apparent that Jay Dee no longer had any idea where Pop's Camp was located, if he ever did. He kept telling Hoffman to turn here, or turn there, and he would lean forward to look out the windshield for several moments before saying, "That didn't used to be here."

As Hoffman's blood pressure was climbing, Yuri had remained as cool as a clam. At one point he had opened the bag of peanuts and eaten the entire contents, tossing the shells onto the floor at his feet. He was still nipping at the vodka from time to time and sharing it now with Jay Dee. Yuri seemed to be of the opinion that they would find the place, sooner or later. They had stopped at a dozen gas stations and stores and bait shops, asking directions, all to no avail. Not only did nobody know where Pop's Camp was, they hadn't talked to a single person who had even heard of the place. But Yuri remained unfazed.

"Now that store looks familiar," Jay Dee said now, gazing down into the ravine.

"Every fucking thing you see looks familiar," Hoffman snapped.

"All this shit up here is the same," Jay Dee said. "Fucking outdoors."

"Enough," Yuri said. "Go down. We will go and ask Dot of the general store."

"Right," Hoffman said. "I'm sure Dot and Jay Dee are old friends."

They drove down to the sprawling general store and parked in the gravel lot alongside. The place had a coffee shop built onto the store, and it sold live bait out back as well. But then, everybody sold live bait.

"I'll go scope the joint," Jay Dee said.

"*I'll* check it out," Hoffman told him. "I think these people up here are nervous of your kind."

"What you mean — my kind?" Jay Dee demanded.

Hoffman opened the door. "You're a bright boy. Figure it out."

He went into the store. There was a girl, maybe sixteen, behind the counter. Just Hoffman's luck; he would have preferred someone older, someone who'd been around the area for more than ten minutes. Of course the girl had never heard of Pop's Camp.

"Anybody else around here might know?" Hoffman asked.

"My girlfriend works in the coffee shop."

Hoffman walked to the shop entrance to have a look, thinking he might find an old-timer sitting there having coffee, somebody with some knowledge that extended back a few years. The place was empty except for another teenager, standing behind the counter, looking at her cell phone.

"Never mind," he said to the first girl, and left.

Hoffman walked out onto the store's wraparound veranda and stood there, looking at the intersection before him. There were signs, maybe a dozen in all, mounted on posts all around the crossroads, signs with arrows pointed in every direction, indicating the way to this lake or that town or somebody's hunting camp.

Not only did Hoffman not know which

sign might help him out, he hadn't even the slightest notion of which direction to take. The only person more ignorant than himself in this regard was the fucking wannabe rap star in the backseat. The man they'd brought along as a guide. Hoffman wondered if he was cursed. Would it have been too much to ask for Yuri to turn up a guy who actually *knew* where the camp was? Apparently hundreds of inner-city kids had been there, but Yuri managed to choose the muddled mess that was Jay Dee. Just once, Hoffman would have liked something to go exactly as it should. One time, just to see what it felt like.

When he got back in the car, he regarded his two traveling partners before starting the engine and driving over to the intersection. He stopped and indicated the array of signs, turning toward the backseat.

"Okay, dimwit," he said wearily. "Anything there strike a chord?"

"Watch the name-calling, dog," Jay Dee said, but he leaned forward and had a look. "Bass Lake!" he exclaimed at once. "That's it! How come I couldn't remember that?"

"An hour ago, you thought it was Stoney Lake," Hoffman reminded him. "Before that you swore it was Lake Samuel."

"It's Bass Lake, motherfucker, and I'll

even tell you why. All the time we fished there, we never caught no bass. Perches, and pikes and sunfishes but no bass. And we were all the time wondering how that fucking lake got its name. I'm telling you it's Bass Lake."

The sign for Bass Lake had an arrow pointing west, and beneath the arrow it said twenty-one miles. Hoffman glanced at Yuri and Yuri returned the look before turning to Jay Dee in the back seat. He smiled.

"This is why I bring you along," he said. "I knew you would remember. Is hard to remember things sometimes from long ago. But always I have faith in you. Now we go to Bass Lake, and you will take us to Pop's Camp. Yes?"

"No problem," Jay Dee said. "Just get me in the area, dog."

When they arrived at Bass Lake a half hour later, Jay Dee was just as lost as before. They were parked by a gravel road that ran a couple hundred yards down to the water's edge and as Jay Dee complained again about how everything had changed since he'd last been there, Hoffman spotted an old man launching an aluminum boat into a shallow creek that emptied into the lake a short distance away.

They drove over and stopped the man as

he was getting into the boat. The old guy wore a red-checked shirt and suspenders and a briar pipe was tucked in the shirt pocket. He looked like a fisherman on a TV show. Whatever he was, he was considerably less confused than Jay Dee. He didn't hesitate when asked about Pop's Camp.

"That's Bill Chamberlain's old place," he said.

As it turned out, the camp was less than three miles away. After the old man gave them directions, they returned to the main road and headed west along the lakeshore road. From time to time they could see the water through the trees to their right.

"I told you," Jay Dee said triumphantly. "I'll take you straight there now. I know this area, now that I see it. My mind is tight like a fucking snare drum. I don't forget shit."

"Is good job," Yuri agreed. "You have been good deputy, Jay Dee." As he spoke he was watching up ahead, where they were approaching a side road that led south into the dense bush, away from the lake. "Pull in here, Mr. Hoffman. I need to make piss."

Hoffman looked over irritably. "We're going to be there in a few minutes."

"But I need to make piss now," Yuri said pleasantly. "Pull in."

Hoffman made the turn onto what appeared to be an old logging road, narrow and deeply rutted in places, likely from locals on four-wheelers. The going was so rough that Hoffman grew worried about his car's undercarriage and he rolled to a stop a hundred yards or so along the lane. Yuri glanced behind them, to the main road they had just left. "Drive a little farther. I am private person in such matters."

Shaking his head, Hoffman took his foot from the brake and idled along the bumpy road, while Yuri kept motioning with his hand for him to go further. When they were deep in the bush, about a mile from the main road, Yuri told him to stop.

"Jay Dee, you must come with me and watch for bears," Yuri said as he opened the door. "I am not familiar with this animal." He laughed. "I do not want to get eaten now that we are so close to Pop's Camp."

Hoffman looked in the mirror and saw the uncertainty in Jay Dee's eyes, and then a shrug of the rounded shoulders. It was an odd request, but since there was nothing ordinary about the Russian, there was nothing out of the ordinary either. Jay Dee got out and Yuri instructed him to walk before him into the thick brush. They were out of Hoffman's sight for less than a minute when he heard the gunshot. It took twice that long for Yuri to reappear and when he did he was pulling up his zipper. Apparently he really had needed to piss.

When he climbed back into the passenger seat, he opened the cylinder on the Colt and retrieved the spent casing, slipping it into his shirt pocket. He reached into the Adidas bag and found a fresh .44 cartridge, which he loaded into the revolver. He gave the cylinder a spin and placed the gun on the seat between himself and Hoffman.

"Jay Dee will not be joining us for the rest of the trip," he said.

They parked the truck alongside the lake road, a few feet from the entrance that was chained off, and walked in. The closest cottage to Pop's Camp was a quarter mile farther back and had appeared to be deserted when they drove past. They saw no vehicles in the drive, although there were towels on a clothesline, and a small punt pulled up to a wooden dock along the shore.

Approaching the main house, Virgil was inclined to believe that they'd made a wasted trip. There was no evidence of anyone on the premises and nothing to suggest that anybody had been there for a long time. Grass and weeds grew up through the gravel of the drive; there were shingles missing from the roof of the house. Virgil spotted the electric meter on the wall, walked over, and saw that it wasn't turning.

"Power's off," he said.

"Which means —" Dusty started to say, but then they both heard a sound and she stopped.

It was a soft thumping noise, coming from the gymnasium beyond the baseball field. The sound got louder as they angled across the overgrown field to the front of the building. There would be a series of thumps and a pause and then it would begin again. The noise grew more familiar the closer they got.

The windows to the gym, like those to the cabins, were boarded up, but someone had removed the plywood from a couple of them, likely to let in some light. It was easy to assume that the same someone was responsible for the thumping noises from inside.

Keeping close to the side wall of the building, Virgil approached one of the uncovered windows and looked in. After a moment he gestured for Dusty to come forward.

Soup was shooting hoops. He was wearing only sneakers and a pair of baggy shorts, and he was using half the court, circling around from the center to either drive the basket for a lay-up, or shooting from three-

point range before running in for the re-
bound. The sweat was rolling off his thin
frame and he appeared to be completely
focused on his game. For a man on the run,
he seemed oblivious to the notion that
somebody might be watching him.

After a moment, Virgil ducked down
below the sill and moved to the other side
of the window, looking for an entrance. He
saw one to the far right, a door that was
partly ajar. He pointed it out to Dusty and
then she put her hand on his arm, gesturing
inside.

Soup had stopped. Wiping his face with a
dirty towel, he walked over to a sagging blue
couch along the wall. There was a duffel
bag on the floor beside the couch and he
knelt down by the bag and dipped his little
finger inside, brought it up twice, once to
each nostril. Then he flopped onto the
couch on his back.

Dusty leaned close to Virgil. "That must
be some high-quality dope, if Soup's snorting it," she said softly. "He always liked the
pipe."

On the couch, Soup exhaled heavily a
couple of times and his eyes closed, his
expression nearing rapture.

At least near enough that he didn't hear
them enter and didn't hear them cross the

hardwood, they were nearly on top of him before he knew they were there. Even then, Dusty had to announce it.

"Soup, you got any idea how bad you're fucking up?" she asked.

Soup's eyes flew open and he jerked himself to a sitting position and stared at her, his palms out front in a defensive position.

"Who the fuck are you?"

"It's Dusty, Soup. Get your head out of your ass."

It took him a moment to finally recognize her. "Dusty! What you doing here?"

"Looking for you, dude," she said. "What are you doing — reliving your glory days?"

Virgil was hanging back, thinking that Soup might make a run for it and he would have to try to stop him. Soup's eyes went from Dusty to him, his breath coming in gasps, and then back to Dusty.

"What's going on?" he asked. Then something registered in his brain and he looked back at Virgil. "Hey, you the guy, you got your boat stole."

"Yeah," Virgil said.

"And your arm broke too. That crazy fucking Russian."

Dusty knelt down and had a look at the contents of the duffel. Soup was apparently still working on the first packet of coke, which was maybe three-quarters gone. He couldn't have used all that in a couple of days, she knew. He must have sold some off to finance his trip north. The other packages were still tightly wrapped, untouched. It would take him a hundred years to snort all that blow. Of course, he would never last even if he tried. His heart wouldn't handle snorting it and his head wouldn't handle owning it.

"How'd you guys find me?" Soup demanded.

"Wasn't all that hard," Dusty said, standing up. "And if we could do it, so could anybody else that might be looking for you. Somebody like that crazy fucking Russian. You know?"

Soup was too wired to appreciate the not so subtle message Dusty was trying to convey. He turned and found a shirt that had gotten stuffed down in the couch cushions and took a moment to put it on, having trouble first with the collar and then with the buttons. His nose was running and he wiped it on the sleeve.

Virgil had a look around the gym. It appeared to be a regulation court, although right now there was only one basket, the one Soup had been using. There was a stage at the other end, beside the door where they'd just entered, and the backboard and basket there were swung up toward the ceiling on a pivot, clearing the view for an audience. There was a denim jacket on the stage, which Virgil assumed belonged to Soup.

Also suspended from the ceiling, in front of the stage, was a large section of netting and inside the netting were stored dozens of basketballs, still inflated. The netting was held in place by ropes in a pulley system, tied off at the side wall to the left, opposite the door.

The gym air was musty and dank, and it retained the faint odors of sweat and athletic gear. Cobwebs gathered in the corners and high on the walls where they met the ceiling. The floor itself was covered in a thin layer of dust, except where Soup had been playing one-on-one with himself. The only ventilation came from the open door by the stage.

There was a table a few feet from the old couch, with chrome legs and a red top; on the table was a dirty backpack, along with some two-liter bottles of soda and bags of chips and pretzels and licorice. There was a carton of Camels there too, and a disposable lighter alongside a small glass pipe.

Soup had now managed to button the

shirt. "What's up, Dusty? Why you following me?"

Dusty indicated the duffel. "We're following that," she said. "And we're taking it with us."

"Fuck you are."

"It doesn't belong to you, Soup."

"I say it does. I got possession."

Virgil glanced at Dusty.

"You think you're going to have possession when Hoffman finds you?" she asked. "Because he's looking hard, Soup. Doesn't that concern you a little bit?"

Soup shrugged. "He ain't gonna find me. Not here."

"Are you that fucking high?" Dusty asked. "We just found you."

Soup considered this for a moment. "Yeah, but you always been smart, Dusty."

"If I was smart, I'd be a hundred miles away," Dusty said. "Just what were you planning to do?"

Soup was still twitching inside the shirt, craning his neck and working his shoulders as if it didn't fit right. "Lay up here a few days, get my shit together. Then I been thinking I might get on down to Philadelphia. I got a bro there, help me move some of this product."

Virgil came closer now. It didn't seem as

if Soup was about to make a run for it, and even if he did, it wouldn't matter, so long as he left the duffel behind. "You call this getting your shit together?" he asked.

"What the fuck you know?" Soup said. "You best remember I tried to help you, homes. When Hoffman and the cowboy was beating your ass."

"I remember," Virgil said.

"Who's the cowboy, Soup?" Dusty asked.

"Some Russian badass, showed up in the city a couple years ago," Soup said. "Moves a lot of hydro, some meth, he was hot for this deal. Crazy motherfucker. He more dangerous than fucking Hoffman ever be."

"Then do you really want him to find you?" Dusty asked. "Don't you think you'd be better off coming with us?"

"I don't know," Soup said slowly. It seemed that the gravity of the situation was just now getting through to him. The fact that he had in all likelihood been whacked out of his mind since stealing the coke had probably led to a certain level of denial on his part. He took a deep breath. "Shit. What the fuck am I gonna do?"

"I wouldn't advise you to head back to the city," Dusty said. "You got any money?"

"Got a few dollars," he said. "I sold a few grams before I split."

Dusty turned to Virgil, as if seeking his opinion. "Probably get a bus in Lake Placid," he said. He looked at Soup. "You say you got a friend waiting in Philadelphia?"

"Yeah."

"All right then," Dusty said. "You'd better stay gone a long time." She indicated the backpack. "Get your stuff together. Let's get out of here."

"You not gonna take all that blow, Dusty," Soup said. Not asking really, but pleading.

"I am."

Soup winced. "I'm gonna need something. Keep me going. I can't do no bus ride cold turkey."

"We'll buy you a coffee at the station," Virgil said.

"That's fucking cold, man," Soup said. "I tried to help you."

"And we're trying to help you, Soup," Dusty said. "Believe it or not."

Virgil watched as Soup began to rub his knuckles. The thought of losing all that dope wasn't sitting well with him.

"Let's go," Dusty said.

"I only need, like, a pinch to travel on," Soup whimpered. "That shit pure as snow."

Dusty glanced at Virgil, and he knew what she was thinking. If it came down to a choice of Soup traveling with a bad need, or Soup traveling mellowed out, it might be best to go with the second option. He was going to have to get straight when he got to Philadelphia, but first he had to get there. Virgil nodded to Dusty and she turned back to Soup.

"Take the rest of that," she said, indicating what was left in the open packet in the duffel. "You'll be jumping out of the bus window otherwise."

Soup knelt down on the floor and gently lifted the packet from the bag, cupping it in both hands like it was a baby bird and placing it on the table, where he went to work carefully folding the cellophane up so it wouldn't spill. For the moment, it was all in the world he cared about, all that he was even aware of.

Virgil was anxious to get out of there now. There was no telling who had seen them arrive and anybody who did would quite likely assume that they were breaking and entering. Virgil wasn't looking forward to trying to explain away a couple million dollars in cocaine to any local cops who might show up. When Soup began to pack his clothes and his soda and his snacks into the backpack, Virgil walked over to the stage to retrieve the jacket lying there.

Dusty bent down to zip the duffel shut and when she did her T-shirt rode up at the back. From across the room Virgil saw the butt of the .38 at the same instant Soup did, but before he could open his mouth, Soup had the gun in his hand.

"Don't nobody move!" he shouted. "Nobody move! Get back, y'all!"

His eyes were wild and his hands shaking as he jerked the barrel of the gun back and forth, from Dusty to Virgil. Dusty, still kneeling, straightened slowly, shaking her head, as if more disappointed than angry.

"You idiot," she said.

"Get back!" he yelled again, and Dusty put her hands out to the side. Virgil remained where he stood, twenty feet away. Soup came forward and grabbed the duffel by the handles.

"Soup," Dusty implored him.

"You be quiet now," he told her. "I heard enough already. You trying to rip me off for my good shit. I didn't invite you all here. I don't want to shoot nobody, Dusty. Please don't make me shoot nobody. I'm a dangerous man."

"Soup, let's talk about this," she said.

"No! No more talk. I got the gun now. I'm in charge now." He pointed the revolver at Virgil. "Step aside, mister."

401

Virgil moved to his right, and Soup began a wide circle around them both, the duffel in one hand and the revolver in the other. He was halfway to the door when he stopped, thought for a moment, and came back toward them. He pointed the gun at them again, the barrel shaking.

"What you driving?" he said. "Gimme the keys."

Dusty involuntarily glanced toward Virgil, and Soup noticed. He pointed the muzzle of the revolver at Virgil's head.

"Gimme the fucking keys!"

Virgil still didn't move.

"Okay, tough guy," Soup said. "You wanna play it like that? That's cool. But how about this? How about I shoot Dusty?" He swung the barrel toward her.

"All right," Virgil said at once. He took the keys from his pocket and tossed them over. They slid across the floor and Soup had to scramble to pick them up. When he straightened, he gave Dusty a look.

"I wouldn't never shoot you, Dusty," he said. "I had to say it though. Man wouldn't listen to me."

Keeping the gun on them, he backed across the gym floor to the open door and went out. Virgil looked over at Dusty.

"I knew that gun was a bad idea," he said.

She opened her mouth to reply and the shooting started.

TWENTY-SEVEN

Soup was hurled back through the doorway as if yanked by an invisible cable, his body moving faster than his feet, his torso jerking back and forth as the slugs tore into him. The shots came from just outside and there were a lot of them, seven or eight in all, and they didn't stop until Soup collapsed on the floor in front of the stage. He lay there on his back, his right leg twisted awkwardly beneath him. When he went down the revolver slipped from his right hand and clattered across the hardwood, stopping a few feet away. But his left hand still held tightly to the duffel that had cost him his life.

Hoffman walked in then, slowly, still nervously holding the Glock on Soup. Hoffman's face was contorted, and he was sweating heavily. The big Russian in the black cowboy hat followed. In contrast to Hoffman, he was practically sauntering, his expression jovial. Hoffman walked over to Soup and kicked him in the ribs, apparently making certain he was dead. He put the Glock in the holster on his belt and knelt down to pry Soup's fingers from the duffel. So intent was he on the task that he hadn't noticed Virgil and Dusty, standing across the gym.

But Yuri had.

"What do we have here?" the Russian asked. He pointed a large forefinger at Virgil. "You I know. You are fisherman who lose his boat."

Since the eruption of gunfire taking Soup out, Virgil had been looking for a way to escape. It seemed there was only the one exit, and with Hoffman and the Russian standing there, it wasn't an option. That left the windows, but there were just two that were uncovered and they were high and solid-looking in spite of their age. It would be an iffy proposition to take a chance on going through one of them. But staying put was hardly an alternative; Virgil only had to look at Soup lying dead on the floor to know that. Beside him, Dusty appeared remarkably calm.

Hoffman had been about to open the duffel when Yuri spoke, and now he stood up slowly. He was clearly surprised to see them and immediately put his hand on his gun.

"And you," Yuri said, aiming his finger at Dusty now. "You must be girl who cut the ear of the fat man. Now this I enjoyed. Man was big crybaby. Boo hoo . . . my ear is cut. And he spills his beans to you." Yuri let out a guffaw, then grew serious. "But it is never explained to me why are you involved in this matter?"

"She's working for Parson," Hoffman said.

"Parson again," Yuri said. "Who is this Parson?"

A look passed over Hoffman's face. Virgil, watching, was sure that Hoffman was instantly regretting bringing up the name. It had been an impulse, and now he couldn't bring it back.

"He's nobody," Hoffman said quickly. "Lowlife dealer trying to horn in on this."

"Parson owns what's in the bag," Dusty said.

"But Mr. Hoffman is owner," Yuri said.

"He stole it," Dusty said.

"He stole it from me," Virgil said. There was something off about the Russian, something he couldn't name, but it seemed that it might be a good thing to keep him engaged. Maybe he wasn't as tight with Hoffman as Virgil had imagined.

"That's bullshit," Hoffman was saying.

"The cocaine was seized as a result of a police investigation." He indicated Virgil. "This man had no right to it. He's lucky I didn't lock him up."

Yuri regarded Hoffman, his mind working, then he turned and crooked a large forefinger, gesturing for Virgil and Dusty to come closer. "We must get to bottom of this," he said.

As they walked over, Virgil moved around to Dusty's left, putting her closer to the door, hoping she might get a chance to make a run for it. Yuri noticed the move.

"Far enough," he said. He then walked to Hoffman and took the duffel from his hand. He heaved it up onto the stage and patted it affectionately, like it was a favored pet, before turning back to Hoffman. "This fisherman. Where is his boat?"

"In my garage, under confiscation," Hoffman said defiantly. "It was deemed an integral part of a drug smuggling operation and as such it was seized to be held for evidence."

Yuri held up his hand. "Hold on," he said. "You are confusing me. One minute you talk like cop, the next you are attempting to sell to me cocaine. You cannot be both, Mr. Hoffman. We need to make clear who is the owner of this merchandise. If I am intending to buy it, I need to know this."

"It belongs to me," Hoffman said. "It's that fucking simple."

"But this fisherman, he says you took it from him," Yuri said. "And I believe that this girl concurs with this story."

"She's an ex-con, working for a dealer," Hoffman said. "You can't believe her."

Virgil watched as Yuri turned his attention to Soup's body and it came to him what the Russian was doing. He was making a show of it, posing as a man of principle, seeking the facts of the matter. But in truth he was a man who had recognized an opportunity.

The opportunity to get the cocaine for free.

"Why do you shoot Mr. Soup?" Yuri asked the cop.

"Because he stole my property," Hoffman said. "He's a common thief."

"I can forgive Mr. Soup," Yuri said. "He was addict. But you, Mr. Hoffman, you do not impress me. You steal this man's boat and also you take from him the cocaine. However, when Mr. Soup does the same thing, you call him thief and shoot him down like mad dog in the street. You have come to me under false pretenses, Mr. Hoffman."

"It belongs to whoever controls it," Hoffman said. He was whining now, very aware that things were going sideways in a hurry. "I'm the one who did the groundwork. I'm the one who brought it to you. I put my ass on the line with the fucking department!"

Yuri considered this, tilting his head back and forth in an animated way, like a man deciding which item to order from a menu, then he removed his coat, folded it, and placed it carefully on the edge of the stage. When he turned back toward Hoffman, Virgil saw the heavy revolver tucked in his belt. The Russian held his hands out slightly from his sides, like a gunfighter. Apparently he had decided on his order.

"You have no code," he said to Hoffman. "You are Ned Pepper."

"Jesus Christ!" Hoffman said. He began to back away.

"Fill your hand, sonofabitch," Yuri said softly.

It appeared at first that Hoffman had no intention of pulling his gun, but unfortunately he was in the same predicament as Virgil and Dusty — the big Russian was between him and the door. He continued to back away but suddenly he stopped. Maybe he saw something in the Russian's eyes, something that suggested the inevitability of the situation. He reached clumsily for the

Glock and Yuri pulled the Colt and shot him in the chest four times.

The sound of the gunshots rocketed through the building like rolling thunder. Virgil heard Dusty gasp as Hoffman took several faltering steps backward and then, his back to the wall, slid down the concrete surface to rest in a sitting position. After a few seconds, he rolled over onto his side and was still.

"You know, I could never cotton this man," Yuri said, still speaking softly.

Virgil, watching the Russian carefully, was wishing that he'd emptied the gun. He knew there were two shots left. But two was better than six. Maybe there was a way for them to make a break. If Virgil could create a diversion, there was a chance Dusty could make it to the door. And if Virgil could somehow make the Russian fire two shots without hitting him, he could rush him. He was aware, though, that the man had just fired four times at Hoffman, never missing once.

It was an iffy proposition all around and in any event it didn't last very long. It almost seemed as if the Russian was reading his mind. He carefully wiped his prints from the revolver and dropped it beside Soup, a couple of feet from his outstretched hand. Then, before Virgil could move, he reached behind his shirt to produce an Uzi automatic pistol. He gestured with the barrel in the direction of the two dead bodies.

"This tells whole story, yes?" he said. "Shootout at OK Corral. Dirty cop and crackhead desperado. The ballistic evidence will match nicely. Tragic thing."

As he talked he made certain to keep himself between Virgil and Dusty and the door. Virgil glanced behind him, once more considering the side windows, maybe forty feet away. Covering that much ground would take too long. Turning back toward the Russian, his eyes fell on the rope tied off to the wall beside the stage, holding the netting overhead in place. He glanced up quickly, to the basketballs in the netting, and then Yuri began to talk.

"Now this is part which bothers me," he said. "I mean this sincerely. I know nothing about you two. Maybe you are good people. Maybe not. Maybe you even have code, like me. On other hand — maybe you are no better than Mr. Hoffman. I will never know."

"Take the drugs," Virgil said. "We don't even know your name."

"But you know my face," Yuri said. "And you are very persistent in the pursuit of this bag of goodies. This makes me nervous, and I do not wish to leave here feeling nervous. I trust you can understand that."

Virgil took a couple of steps to his left, toward the wall.

"Where are you going?" Yuri asked. "You are going to run through a concrete wall?"

Virgil held his arms out, as if in surrender. Dusty turned to look at him and for a split second he shifted his eyes to the rope. Her eyes narrowed, as if she was trying to understand, but at least she had caught the look.

Yuri saw something too. "You be still. I am sorry for this but there is no other way. However, I think we must take a walk in the woods, the three of us." He gestured at Soup and Hoffman. "This is nice picture I make here. Two more bodies will just confuse things."

Virgil was still looking at Dusty and this time he glanced at the door, and back to her again. She nodded, not even trying to hide it from the Russian at this point. Virgil didn't know if she caught on to everything, but he had to be satisfied that she would break for the door if the chance presented itself.

"No more with the looks," Yuri said. "Is no good for you to dream of escape. I am very proficient in the use of this weapon. Come, we must go."

"We don't get a chance?" Virgil said. "You gave Hoffman a chance. Shit, I thought you were a cowboy."

"I am cowboy."

"Drugstore cowboy maybe," Virgil said. "A real cowboy would give me a chance."

Yuri smiled. It was obviously the type of thing he liked. "You want a chance? What chance?"

Virgil reached slowly into his pocket and produced his buck knife. Opening the blade, he held the knife forward toward the big Russian.

Yuri laughed. "You have never heard the joke about the foolish man who brings a knife to a gunfight?"

"I've heard it," Virgil said. "I guess you've never seen a movie called *The Magnificent Seven.*"

"I have!" Yuri shouted. "Is a movie I love. With the great Steve McQueen. I know what you refer to. Is James Coburn — the man with the knife. Is a character I admire very much, I must say. Unfortunately for you, you are not James Coburn."

"You ain't Steve McQueen."

Yuri actually appeared hurt by the remark. Virgil crouched slightly, flicking the blade back and forth, like a hoodlum in the movies. But he moved once again to his left, within five feet of the rope where it was tied off to the wall.

"You got grit, fisherman," Yuri said. "I will give you that." He dropped the Uzi to his side and squared up to face Virgil. "I will count to three. If you can throw the knife quicker than I can draw, then maybe you will win. But I do not think so."

"Start counting," Virgil said.

"One —"

Virgil leapt to the side and cut the rope, heard it whipping like lightning through the pulleys as the netting fell away. Yuri was standing directly under the middle of the load, and as the basketballs cascaded onto him he began firing wildly with the machine gun. The instant he cut the rope, Virgil hit the floor and began to scramble across the hardwood. He glanced up quickly, hoping to see Dusty disappearing out the door.

But Dusty had no such intention. When Virgil looked up she was sprinting toward Soup's body, sliding on her hip across the floor for the last few feet. She grabbed the .38 in both hands and from her knees she let loose on the Russian, who was firing at Virgil scurrying across the floor, random shots hitting the bouncing basketballs, the balls popping like firecrackers, the air whooshing out of them. Dusty's first shot hit Yuri in the shoulder, jerking him back against the stage, and her second took him just beneath his left eye. His head went back, and his black cowboy hat flipped off. Both elbows caught the edge of the stage for a moment and then he pitched forward onto the floor.

The balls were still bouncing, slower and slower, the hissing of escaping air fading away to nothing. When the noise stopped, Virgil stood and walked over to Dusty. She was still on her knees, the revolver in her hands pointed even yet at the dead Russian. She was trembling. Virgil reached down to help her to her feet. She glanced up at him, as if she wasn't quite sure who he was, then looked at the revolver in her hand.

"I knew that gun was a good idea," he told her.

Twenty-Eight

"We have to move," Virgil said. "No telling how far those gunshots might travel. This might be hunting country, but that sounded like a war."

"Shouldn't we call somebody?" Dusty said. She stood looking at the bodies scattered across the gymnasium floor.

"Who we going to call?" Virgil asked. "This was self-defense. Self-preservation. But you're on parole. You want to try to explain to the cops what happened here?"

"Someone would have to explain to *me* first," she said.

"Let's go."

After they'd wiped down everything they had touched, Dusty gathered the duffel once more and they headed out. Moving toward the door, Dusty looked at Soup's body, bent and crumpled on the floor, his eyes wide open, and went back for his jacket, which she placed over him, covering his face. Walking past the dead Russian, Virgil saw her hesitate before leaning down to pick up the Uzi. She glanced at him, and once again he knew she was thinking about Cherry. She probably never stopped thinking about Cherry.

They got into the truck and drove away along the narrow gravel road. Virgil kept expecting that they would meet the police but they saw no one. Maybe random gunfire wasn't all that rare in the area. And Pop's Camp was pretty secluded. They saw a number of people at the cabins they passed on their way out, but nobody seemed to pay them any mind.

By the time they were back on the main highway, heading east, it was early evening. It was a long drive back to the city and Virgil was still concerned that someone had noticed something and taken down his plate number. If there was nothing on the news by morning, it meant that the carnage at the camp hadn't been discovered. He decided that the smart move would be to lie low overnight.

"Okay," Dusty said without hesitation when he suggested it. "Christ, I'm tired to the bone."

A short time later, they saw a sign advertising Ronnie's Rustic Cottages, with an arrow pointing north. It was dusk when they took the road down to a small lake, about a mile long and half that distance across, surrounded by evergreens. Ronnie's was a humble operation, with a main house attached to a registration office and several imitation log cabins behind, stretched along the lakeshore. A tall thin woman with frizzy red hair checked them in, and they asked for the cabin farthest from the office. By the time they parked and went inside, it was nine o'clock.

The cottage featured a combination kitchen–living room, a bathroom, and two bedrooms, rough-hewn pine furniture, and pictures of mountains and streams and Indians on horseback. The place smelled of cleaning fluids.

Virgil brought in the box containing the remaining pieces of chicken and fries they'd bought earlier. Dusty carried the heavy duffel from the truck and placed it on the floor in the living room. She turned to look at Virgil, then sat down on the couch and put her hands over her face. He thought for a moment that she was crying, but when she took her hands away her eyes were dry. He had no idea what was going through her head. The last couple of days would have broken most people.

Virgil went back out to the truck. When they left the farm that morning he'd thrown some cheese and crackers in a Budweiser cooler bag and stashed it behind the seat. Along with the food, he'd brought along the bottle of Jameson they opened the night before. Back inside, he placed the bag on the kitchen table and took out the whisky. While he went through the cupboards, looking for glasses, Dusty walked over and had a drink from the bottle. She looked at him, then drank again before putting it down.

She looked tired and distracted as she sat down at the table. Virgil poured some whisky into plastic cups and put one in front of her. After taking a drink, she reached for her purse. She found her phone and began to search for something else, finally dumping the contents onto the table in frustration. After a moment she came up with a business card, which she placed flat in front of her. From where Virgil stood, he could see a caricature of a hot rod on the card. Dusty opened her phone to punch in the number, and stopped.

"Shit," she said. "My battery died." She turned to Virgil. "You wouldn't — no, of course you wouldn't."

She glanced around and saw a phone on the kitchen counter beside the fridge, brought it over to the table, punched in the number on the card.

"I got your dope," she said when someone answered.

Virgil could clearly hear the man's voice in reply, asking if she really did have it, his voice rising with doubt.

"Why would I say it if it wasn't true?" she replied. Dusty, absently studying the scattered articles from her purse as she talked, now reached for a torn page from a real estate flyer, featuring pictures of a dozen or so houses. One, tagged *Cobleskill 3-Bedroom,* had been circled in pen. Dusty placed the ad on the table, smoothing the creases in the paper with her fingers.

The man said something else that Virgil missed.

"How I found it is none of your business," Dusty said. "You want it, it's for sale."

Saying it, she wouldn't look at Virgil. In fact, she seemed a little surprised herself at the statement. Virgil thought he heard the man on the phone chuckle, then he asked how much.

Dusty looked a moment longer at the real estate ad, then reached for the plastic glass and took a slug. "Sixty-eight thousand dollars."

For a time there was nothing from the

other end of the line, and then Virgil heard the man say something that sounded like "All right."

"I'll see you tomorrow," Dusty said and hung up.

She sat quietly for a moment, taking another drink before gathering her possessions and putting them back in the purse. She still wouldn't look at Virgil, leaning against the counter.

"At least you talk a good game," he said.

"Fuck you," she said. "You don't get to judge me."

"I'm not judging you," he said. "You're the same as the rest of them. It was always about the money." He poured more whisky for himself. "Hey, maybe I am judging you."

"It wasn't about the money," she snapped. "It was about me staying out of jail." She tossed the real estate ad carelessly toward him. "And now it's about getting my kid out of the city. Why should I give it to Parson for nothing?"

Virgil indicated the duffel bag on the floor. "Let's dump it in the lake."

"I just made a deal."

"I heard you," Virgil said. "So you get your money and that shit hits the streets."

"You going to moralize now?" she asked. "Little late in the game for that, isn't it?"

She reached for the cup but stopped. "Don't think I haven't thought about that. Guess what — I'm not in charge of all the bad shit that goes down in this world. All I can do is keep my own little corner clean."

"Keep your corner clean and Parson happy," Virgil said.

"You want me to admit that's part of it?" she asked. "Well, it is. There's no way he's getting any part of my son. So tomorrow I hand him his cocaine and I hope I never see him again. I have to trust him just this once. Is that too much to ask?"

"I don't know the answer to that."

"Well, neither do I." She indicated the bag on the floor. "I do know that I did three years inside for that shit. And I did something today that's going to be in my head forever. So I'm going to pretend that this bag owes me. Fuck the moral considerations. And fuck Parson too, once it's over."

Virgil didn't want to argue with her anymore. He wasn't at all sure that she was wrong. It was just that he wished it had turned out differently. On every level since he had encountered Dusty in his wheat field that day, he wished it had turned out differently. Not so much for himself, but for her. He watched now as she got wearily to her feet.

"I have to sleep," she said. She indicated the first of the two bedrooms. "Can I sleep there?"

"Yeah."

When she was gone Virgil sat down at the table. He drank more of the Jameson and picked at the cold chicken in the cardboard box. He should have been tired but he wasn't. Back at the farm, his calves would be hungry, and he hoped the horses had water enough to last them until morning. He sat there for maybe an hour, listening to the faint sounds of the lake outside, and to the breeze in the trees, and finally he got up and walked into the other bedroom. There were French doors that opened onto a deck overlooking the water and Virgil pulled the blinds to look outside. The moon was on the rise, crossing the sky just above the horizon, casting a shimmering light on the surface of the lake.

He stripped to his shorts and lay down on the mattress. There was a wool blanket at the foot of the bed and he pulled it over him, trying to put from his mind everything that had gone on. Just as he was slipping off, he heard a noise and looked up to see Dusty standing in the doorway, barefoot, but still in her jeans and shirt.

"Can I sleep here?" she asked, and he said yes.

She got into bed and curled up beside him, her body touching his but just barely. She seemed to relax within seconds and pretty soon he could tell she was asleep. Virgil lay there in the quiet, listening to her steady breathing and watching the moon outside.

Parson was in the garage, aimlessly surfing the Internet, when the phone rang. He stood and walked around the shop while he listened to Dusty on the other end. He couldn't say what he'd been expecting but it wasn't this. Enough time had passed that he was beginning to believe the cocaine was gone forever, though he had no problem believing she'd found it. There was no reason for her to lie about that, and it wasn't like her to lie anyway. Besides, he was the one who had sent her after it in the first place. He was a little surprised that she was asking him to buy it from her. Maybe she was getting jaded and greedy, like everybody else in the world.

Not that Parson had any intention of paying her. It was his dope. He'd paid for it in the Caribbean seven years ago and just because it had been at the bottom of the

Hudson ever since didn't mean he was about to pay for it again.

After Dusty hung up he stood looking at the call display for a moment. Ronnie's Rustic Cottages. With the number and area code. He went back to his computer and while he typed the information into Google, he called Cherry's cell.

"She's got it," he said when Cherry answered.

There was a long pause. "Tell me where I'm going," Cherry said.

"Have it in a minute," Parson said, looking at the laptop. "Shit. She's halfway across the state. I'm sending you the link. I need you to go there tonight."

"Sure thing."

"And Cherry . . . don't hurt her," Parson said. "I mean that. Just get the coke. Leave her alone — there's something I need to ask her."

There was no reply from Cherry.

"You hear me?" Parson said.

"I hear you."

Twenty-Nine

Virgil lay awake a long time and just when it seemed he wouldn't sleep at all, he must have nodded off. When he woke, the moon was high in the sky and brighter than ever. The wind had come up and the surface of the lake was choppy, with little whitecaps farther out. The wind whistled through the trees surrounding the cottage, emitting a loud moaning sound. He saw by the clock on the table beside the bed that it was twenty past three. Dusty's body against his back was warm, her breathing rhythmic and even. Virgil stayed quiet for a few minutes, but he had a nagging feeling that something had caused him to wake up.

He slipped out of bed, pulled his pants on, and walked out into the main room of the cottage and immediately saw that the lights were on in the office up front. The building had been dark when Virgil had gone to bed. Why would the owners be up now? Daylight was still a couple of hours off. He walked to the front door and stepped outside. A car was idling in the driveway just past the office, beyond the glow of a light mounted on the gable of the building.

He crossed the lawn in his bare feet, angling to his left, where a number of large spruce trees provided cover. He went up the slope that led to the office until he got close enough for a good look at the car parked in the drive. It was a blue Mercedes roadster.

So much for trusting Parson.

Virgil moved behind one of the spruce trees and waited. After a few moments the office door opened and a man walked out. He had dark hair and he was dressed entirely in black. The redheaded woman who had signed Virgil and Dusty in earlier stood in the doorway, wearing pajama bottoms and a long pink T-shirt. She was talking amiably, pointing in the direction of Virgil's truck, and he replied in a like tone, saying that they were expecting him.

When the woman went inside the man walked back to the Mercedes and a few seconds later the lights in the office went out, then the lights in the adjoining house. When the man shut the roadster off, Virgil turned and headed back toward the cabin,

keeping to the row of trees along the narrow lane. Stopping there in the shadows, he
waited.

The moonlight was so bright that he could
clearly see the man making his way toward
Virgil's truck, parked in front of the cabin.
Virgil decided not to go back inside, but
instead retreated beyond the corner of the
building. Again in shadow, he waited for the
man, who approached cautiously, stopping
to take a look in the big front window before
continuing around to the rear of the cabin.
Virgil retreated once more, finally concealing himself behind a stand of rough cedar
shrubs that marked the property's rear
boundary.

The man moved quietly along the side
wall of the building, and when he emerged
from the shadow into the moonlight Virgil
could see his features, his pumped-up arms,
the gold jewelry around his neck. He
stepped up onto the deck and approached
the French doors that opened to the bedroom where Virgil had slept. The bedroom
where Dusty was sleeping yet. From where
he crouched Virgil could clearly see Dusty's
form inside, curled on the bed beneath the
wool blanket. When the man was a few feet
away he stopped and looked through the
glass doors for a long moment, as if trying

to make out who it was on the bed. He was no more than a dozen feet from Dusty.

He pulled a long-barreled gun from his coat.

Virgil was lucky for the wind. If it wasn't for the waves slapping the shore and the leaves whipping in the trees, he never would have reached the cabin without the man hearing him. He leapt from his hiding spot and sprinted barefoot across the rough lawn, his heart pumping wildly. The man was drawing a bead on Dusty when Virgil jumped onto the deck behind him. The man half turned at the sound, and Virgil stepped in close to him, turning his shoulders to the right, like a hitter in the batter's box, and then taking a home-run swing with the cast on his left arm, striding into it with all his weight. The hard plaster took the man flush across the face; Virgil could both hear and feel the nose cartilage being crushed beneath the blow. The man grunted loudly; he was unconscious before he hit the wooden deck.

Virgil sat on the couch, looking at the man called Cherry, now sprawled on the living room floor where Virgil had dragged him after knocking him out. The man called Cherry was still unconscious. In fact, Virgil had never seen anybody *that* unconscious, and he was beginning to wonder if he was going to wake up.

Cherry's nose was a mess, spread across his face like a toad mashed on the highway. Blood was congealing around it, and down both sides of his mouth. Virgil's cast was broken where it had hit the man, but he felt no pain in his arm and he was reasonably sure he hadn't done further damage to the bone. He sat on the couch, with the bottle of Jameson and a cup on the table beside him. He held Cherry's semiautomatic in his hand, a Browning .45, fitted with a silencer, which is why the barrel had looked so long when Virgil first saw it in the moonlight. If there was any question that Cherry had come to kill Dusty, the silencer answered it.

Virgil took a drink and waited for Dusty to return. He thought back a couple of weeks, to the day he'd taken the two steers to the abattoir, and his decision afterward to stop at Slim's for a beer and some wings. That was the day Mudcat McCluskey had come in with the stripers in the cooler, and that was the day that Virgil had decided to go fishing off Kimball's Point, resulting in his hooking the cylinder.

The next time he took steers to the abattoir, he'd head straight for home afterward.

Dusty came back, carrying the keys to Cherry's Mercedes in her hand. She nodded to Virgil, saying it was done, crossed over, and put the keys back in Cherry's pants pocket where she had found them. Virgil stood up and handed her the Browning, then filled the plastic cup with Irish and, kneeling down beside Cherry, tossed half the contents in the man's face. Cherry made a slight noise and Virgil splashed the rest of the whisky down the front of his shirt, soaking him. Then he slapped Cherry several times until finally he began to come around.

Still, it took the better part of five minutes for the man's head to clear and when he finally realized his predicament, he was noticeably surly. He got unsteadily to his feet, the back of his hand against his battered and bleeding nose, and once he had his wits about him, he began to utter dark threats to both of them. They allowed him to go on for a bit, then Virgil grabbed him by the scruff of the neck, propelled him to the door, and shoved him outside, where Cherry tripped on the steps and went sprawling to the ground.

"You're a dead man," he told Virgil as he got to his feet again.

"You'd be a lot more convincing if you

weren't so stupid and beat up," Virgil said.

Dusty had walked out onto the small porch and now she stood beside Virgil, the .45 at her side. Cherry eyed them both and then, realizing he was finished for the night, turned and walked toward his car. He was still wobbly on his feet; anybody who encountered him would have no trouble believing he was blind drunk.

They waited until he got into the Mercedes and drove off. Back inside the cabin, Virgil watched as Dusty picked up the phone and dialed 911.

"I've just been sideswiped by a drunk driver," she said when a dispatcher answered. "A Mercedes convertible." She listened as the dispatcher questioned her. "U.S. 3, about two miles south of Obertville." Glancing over at Virgil, she smiled. "As a matter of fact, I did get the license number."

THIRTY

The cabin cruiser called *Down Along Coast* had an open back deck, where there were canvas-backed chairs and a table made of teak. Parson was sitting on the deck, drinking coffee and staring out at the river. It was shortly past eleven o'clock and he looked as if he'd been up for hours. His eyes were red, his cheeks unshaven.

Virgil and Dusty stood on the lawn maybe fifty feet away, watching him. They had pulled up to the mammoth garage housing Parson's vintage cars a few minutes earlier, out of Parson's sight and, with the sound of the river, out of earshot too. When they didn't see him inside, they'd walked around the building, to the expanse of lawn leading to the boat slip.

Dusty put her hand out to stop Virgil from advancing farther, walked another ten or twelve feet, raised the Uzi in both hands, and without a word of warning strafed the side of the boat, emptying the clip, ripping the cedar planking to shreds, clanging bullets off hardware, breaking windows.

Parson practically burst out of his skin, leaping to his feet and diving below the railing, where he scrambled on his hands and knees for the cabin. Only when the shooting stopped did he dare to have a look. His eyes widened when he saw Dusty.

"What the hell is this?"

"You sent Cherry to kill me!" she screamed.

"Hell I did."

"You're a liar."

They heard shouting from the house next door, a large white Victorian a couple of hundred yards away. "What the hell's going on over there?"

Parson was fast on his feet. "Just scaring these damn Canada geese off," he shouted back. "They're shitting all over my dock." He stood up, his hands in front of him, as if they would deflect any further gunfire. "Put the gun down, Dusty."

"It's empty anyway," she said and tossed it carelessly on the lawn.

Parson climbed out and walked over to pick the gun up before turning to survey the damage it had inflicted. "Look what you did to my boat."

"You sent him to kill me," Dusty said.

When Parson turned to look at her, it seemed to Virgil that he was genuinely puzzled at the accusation. After a moment his eyes went past Dusty to Virgil.

"I heard about you," he said darkly. He glanced toward his neighbor's house. "Let's go in the shop."

They followed Parson inside, where he walked over and slumped into a chair behind a desk. He now seemed more weary than scared or pissed off. Virgil glanced around the huge building, at the dozen or so cars parked there. His eyes went past the Corvettes and Mustangs and Jags, to an old coupe in the far corner, partly covered with clear plastic.

"I've been up all goddamn night," Parson said. "What did you do to Cherry?"

"Not what I should have," Dusty replied.

Parson put both palms to his temples and sat like that for a moment, as if trying to arrange his thoughts. "I got a phone call a couple hours ago," he said. "Cherry's been arrested up north. Suspicion of drunk driving. The cops found about a hundred pounds of cocaine in the trunk of his car." He paused for effect. "Cherry wasn't aware there was cocaine in the trunk of his car."

"What a drag for Cherry," Dusty said.

"Him being such a stand-up guy and all."

"I told him not to hurt you, Dusty. He wouldn't go against me."

"He was going to kill her," Virgil said. "I was there."

"Who the fuck are you again?" Parson demanded.

"I'm the guy who cold-cocked your buddy Cherry before he could shoot Dusty. That's who I am."

Parson stared at Virgil a moment but turned back to Dusty. "Cherry wouldn't go against me."

"He might," Dusty said. "If he found out I knew it was him who set you up seven years ago."

Parson opened his mouth but nothing came out. He sat back in the chair, blinking. "Cherry?" he asked.

"Yeah, Cherry," Dusty said. "Think about it. How many people even knew you were bringing the coke up from the islands? It was Cherry. The cops busted him for kiddie porn, and Cherry gave them *you*."

"Cherry," Parson repeated, confused.

Virgil left them to their conversation, went walking along the row of cars toward the coupe in the corner. Parson saw him, but his mind was too wrapped up in what he was hearing to care.

"And so," Parson said to Dusty, "you planted the coke in Cherry's car."

"I don't know what you're talking about," Dusty said.

"You're full of shit." Parson shook his head, and the businessman slowly returned. "Why didn't you just shoot him and bring me the coke?"

"You are unbelievable," Dusty told him.

When Virgil reached the coupe in the corner, he pulled back the plastic for a better look. A few inches behind the passenger-side window there was a bullet hole. Virgil put his finger in the hole, as he'd done roughly a year earlier. It looked as if the car hadn't been touched since he'd seen it then. He left the plastic pulled back and walked back to the front of the shop.

"If the cops have the coke, then I guess that's the end of it," Dusty said. "I'm going to have to believe you when you say you didn't send Cherry to kill me. But now we're finished, Parson. You and I are square. I need to hear you say that."

"I'm not so sure we're finished, Dusty," he said. He watched Virgil returning before turning his eyes on her. "Tell me about your son."

She was ready for him. "What about him?"

"You do have a son?"

"Yeah."

"Tell me about him."

Virgil stopped a few feet away now, watching her. She had to be a jangle of nerves inside, but she was cool as could be where it mattered.

"I don't know what to tell you," Dusty said. "He's a kid. He likes Superman and Iron Man. And baseball. If I let him, he'd brush his teeth once a month." She paused before dropping the lie. "He turns four next Saturday. I'm taking him to Six Flags."

"He's four?" Parson asked.

"Almost."

Parson nodded slowly, shifting his gaze to Virgil. "You're his father?"

"That's right," Virgil said. "I don't know what business that is of yours."

"You want to get on my bad side, asshole?" Parson asked.

"I couldn't care less what side of you I'm on," Virgil said, seeing the chance to shift the topic from the boy. "Look at you. I've got one arm and you still won't get out of that chair. A minute ago you were asking Dusty why she didn't kill your pal Cherry for you. You always need somebody else to do your dirty work for you."

"For you, I might make an exception," Parson said, glaring at Virgil, the veins in his neck bulging.

"Fine," Virgil said. "Right this minute works for me. When we're done, you're going to pay that old farmer the money you owe him for that coupe over there."

"I got no idea what you're babbling about," Parson said.

"No?" Virgil said. "The old boy he told me that it was a big colored guy who stole his car. That might not be politically correct, but a thief is a thief. The only reason you were able to steal the car is that he took you for a straight shooter, same as him. So you're either going to pay him his ten grand or give him the car back. I'm going to make sure you do. I've never called the cops on anybody in my life." Virgil smiled. "But for you, I might make an exception."

Now Parson's mouth was open, but he seemed unable to make a sound. He glanced from Virgil to Dusty, and finally looked away from both, choosing instead to focus on his row of beloved cars. "Get the fuck out of here, both of you," he said. "I never want to see either of you again. Just . . . go."

Virgil drove Dusty across town, back to her apartment. When he pulled up out front he reached under his seat and brought up the rotor from her truck.

"You asshole," she said.

"Yup."

She took the rotor and put it in her pocket, then sat quietly for a time, looking out the windshield. "I have no idea what to say, Virgil."

"Go get your son."

"I will."

"Is it really his birthday next week?"

"Yes."

"And you're going to Six Flags?"

"Yeah. You want to come along?"

Virgil thought for a brief moment and he nodded. "Maybe I'll get him some neats-foot oil."

"He would like that." She opened the door to go. "Where are you going now?"

"Home. I got animals to tend to." He looked at her. "Then I have to find out where Hoffman lived."

"Why?"

"Apparently my boat is in his garage."

ACKNOWLEDGMENTS

Thanks to the usual suspects at Simon & Schuster Canada and at Scribner in the United States. To Jen Barclay — thank you for your early read and your enduring friendship.

And *gracias* to my agent, Victoria Skurnick. With a *k*.

ABOUT THE AUTHOR

Brad Smith was born and raised in southern Ontario. He has worked as a farmer, signalman, insulator, truck driver, bartender, schoolteacher, maintenance mechanic, roofer, and carpenter. He lives in an eighty-year-old farmhouse near the north shore of Lake Erie. His novel, *One-Eyed Jacks,* was nominated for the Dashiell Hammett Prize.